D0663681

A MOON

They had reached the yew arch which led to another portion of the garden, but Bucksted did not draw her through. Instead, he turned to her and whispered, "Lady Tiverton is standing in the shadows of the draperies and believes we cannot see her. No, no. Pray do not glance in her direction. I think she may be spying on us, trying to determine for herself whether or not we are a love match. This would be an excellent opportunity to exhibit our *fondness* for one another that she might make a good report to the gabblemongers on our behalf."

He touched her chin with his gloved finger, and a shiver went down Eleanor's neck. She looked into his eyes, which were shadowed but glittering in the faint moonlight.

"I suppose we shouldn't forgo the moment since who knows when another shall come our way," she said.

"I was thinking the very same thing."

She tilted her head slightly. "Do you know how very handsome you are?"

He seemed surprised. "Thank you. That was a lovely compliment."

She smiled. "You are used to hearing as much, aren't you?"

"Not from my unbetrothed, I'm not."

She giggled. Her heart felt light, and she found she was enjoying his gentle banter very much.

"I don't think it will be necessary that I kiss you again. I daresay that were I just to lean toward you thus"—his lips brushed the side of her mouth—"it would appear that I was kissing you indeed."

Eleanor felt frozen by the pleasure his lips were giving her, for they were ever so lightly making a path up her cheek and his breath was warm against her skin. Suddenly she was tingling all over . . .

Books by Valerie King

A DARING WAGER
A ROGUE'S MASQUERADE
RELUCTANT BRIDE
THE FANCIFUL HEIRESS
THE WILLFUL WIDOW
LOVE MATCH
CUPID'S TOUCH
A LADY'S GAMBIT
CAPTIVATED HEARTS
MY LADY VIXEN
THE ELUSIVE BRIDE
MERRY, MERRY MISCHIEF
VANQUISHED
BEWITCHING HEARTS
A SUMMER COURTSHIP
VIGNETTE
A POET'S KISS
A POET'S TOUCH
A COUNTRY FLIRTATION
MY LADY MISCHIEF

Published by Zebra Books

MY LADY MISCHIEF

Valerie King

Zebra Books
Kensington Publishing Corp.
http://www.zebrabooks.com

ZEBRA BOOKS are published by

Kensington Publishing Corp.
850 Third Avenue
New York, NY 10022

First Printing: May, 1999
10 9 8 7 6 5 4 3 2 1

Printed in the United States of America

One

Kent, England
1811

Eleanor Marigate searched the distant hill carefully, her heart beating strongly in her breast. She was situated in the west tower of Hartslip Manor, staring at the precise point at which a carriage would appear at the peak of Juniperhill before beginning a careful descent. She could only guess at the hour at which Lord Bucksted would arrive since he was traveling to Kent in easy stages from his town house in London. His letter had indicated that, though he could not say precisely how long the journey would require, he was certain he would arrive in time to partake of his nuncheon at the manor.

She had, therefore, been stationed in the tower since ten o'clock, waiting restlessly for his good lordship to arrive, yet two hours had already passed. Where was the wretched man?

She fidgeted in the small window seat of the tower, the hard gray blocks cushioned with worn red velvet pillows. She was ready to cast her dice, to change abruptly the course of her immediate future, yet she could do nothing until her betrothed, the august Earl of Bucksted, made his appearance.

Ordinarily, she wouldn't have minded his tardiness since she thought him a pompous fool. Today, however, she had to intercept him before her mother discovered what she was about. Of late,

Lady Marigate had become horridly suspicious of her every gesture, step, word, and at times even her unspoken thoughts!

Eleanor had tried to conceal the true state of her feelings, but somehow her feather-headed mama had divined her sentiments. This alone amazed her, because her mother was not precisely a woman of great intellect. Yet, for all her extravagant habits, her addiction to trumpery and the superficialities of *tonish* life, Lady Marigate had more than once proved extraordinarily perceptive.

The truth was, if her mother suspicioned even in the slightest why it was she meant to waylay Bucksted's traveling chariot before it reached the gates of the manor, Lady Marigate would undoubtedly lock up her eldest daughter in one of the twin manor towers and let the flesh rot off her bones. Regardless of Eleanor's feelings, Lady Marigate intended for the betrothal festivities to proceed as planned.

Eleanor had other intentions entirely!

She surveyed the countryside, her heart still beating strongly against her ribs. The Kentish hills rolled gently on and on, the green grass of each knoll sparkling in the June sunlight, still no carriage appeared.

Another minute passed, then another. She sighed and clasped her hands together tightly in front of her. She must speak with him before he greeted Lady Marigate. She must.

Lord Bucksted was the new owner of Hartslip Manor, a fact which Eleanor had always known would one day ensue. Her father and the beautiful Marchioness of Chalvington were distant cousins. Somehow, in a truly wretched debacle of Fate, that woman's son, the Earl of Bucksted, as heir to all the rights, privileges, and titles of the Marquess of Chalvington, had proved to be the next male heir of Hartslip.

She had not known Bucksted growing up, even though his father's estate, Whitehaven, was situated less than nine miles distant. Bucksted was ten years her senior, and his interests had always been entirely separate from the young daughter of a lesser baronet and distant relation.

Yet how unkindly Fate had dealt with her, since from the time she could remember her heart had belonged to every chamber, every receiving room, every tree-lined avenue, every formal and informal garden, every beehive in the home garden, every mulchy piece of land that belonged to Hartslip. Her beloved papa had given her this profound affection for the manor, for he had taken her about the estate from the time she could remember. But he had passed away nearly a year ago. During the intervening time Bucksted had graciously permitted Lady Marigate and her three daughters to remain at Hartslip that they might recover from the devastation of their loss.

She blinked. Did she see movement on Juniperhill? Yes! Two pair of horses topped the rise. Two postillions managed the lively teams, drawing the equipage to a halt at the crest. One of the postillions dismounted to place a skid in front of the rear wheels of the vehicle.

Her heart began hammering in her chest.

Bucksted had arrived at last!

She did not wait to watch the carriage begin its descent even though it had always been a favorite pastime of hers to see various equipages manage the fairly steep hill. She turned, instead, toward the door and fled the small round chamber. She had scarcely three minutes in which to intercept his vehicle.

She began tripping lightly but carefully down the spiraling staircase of the tower. Over the centuries, the stone stairs had become worn and uneven from so much use. But she knew each step by heart which permitted her to make her descent more rapidly than otherwise. She kept one hand braced against the cool gray stones of the wall as a familiar dizziness from the hasty, circular path teased her brain. She couldn't help but smile. She felt very childlike suddenly, a sensation she hadn't experienced in a long time. Her heart was light, her legs and ankles felt strong beneath her, and she thrilled to be doing something about her future instead of waiting for Fate to club her over the head yet again. She would reach Bucksted in time, she would speak to him, she would settle her future before her mother could intervene.

When she reached the bottom step, she slowly pushed open the thick, heavy wood door and saw what she had hoped to see, that the wide, stone-flagged entrance hall was deserted. Relief flooded her, for if any of the servants or, worse yet, her mother had discovered her presence, her schemes would have faltered then and there. But the manor was wondrously quiet, and without hesitating, she closed the cumbersome door behind her, picked up her skirts of lavender-sprigged muslin, and began to run.

She raced lightly through the entrance hall, her silver slippers making only the faintest of thuds on the stone, then ran into the vestibule lined with long doors of small-paned windows. An instant later, she was outside.

The air was cool which served to soothe the excited prickle of heat flushing her skin. If she had escaped unobserved, all would be well.

If only she could reach the lane in time!

If only Lord Bucksted would prove reasonable!

Too many unknowns in this daring scheme of hers. Yet she had to try. She knew very well that her entire happiness depended upon at least *trying,* and should Olympus smile on her, she would succeed.

She skirted the charming dower house called Squirrel Cottage, fled past the low crescent of carefully pruned hornbeam shrubs, and darted down the gray, stone-flagged path of the nuttery. She was breathing hard, the hand-sewn seams of her delicate silk slippers threatening to give way with each step she took. Numerous hairpins began to slip from the riot of black curls bouncing at the back of her head.

In late spring, the hazelnut trees were fully leafed and formed a lacy canopy over the walkway. The scent of ferns, the sweet haylike smell of woodruff, and the orange, red, and gold primroses called to her as she hurried by. She drew the damp earth into her lungs, her mind fixed on intercepting Bucksted's traveling chariot. She could hear the rhythmic crunch of gravel as the vehicle approached briskly from the northern end of the estate and knew that the equipage was moving far more rapidly than she had planned for. Two pair of horses could easily carry the coach along at a brisk ten miles per hour! Would she reach the earl in time?

She turned to her right, carefully sidestepping bright red primroses and gently pushing aside switches of hazelwood in order to reach the break in the neatly trimmed hedge of yew. She squeezed through, feeling the damp leaves from a recent shower clinging to the delicate muslin of her Empire gown. A few feet of unscythed grasses stretched for several hundred yards lengthwise between the estate walls of both stone and yew and the densely planted hedge of predominantly blackthorn, bramble, elm, and holly. She jerked quickly to the left. From over the hedge she could see the carriage not twenty feet away. The turnstile was another ten or eleven. She began to wave her arms and shout for the postboys to draw in their teams.

All the while, she ran. She found the turnstile and, with some difficulty, pushed through, but to her dismay, at the same moment the carriage shot past her at a spanking pace.

"Whoa!" she called out, taking a billow of rock-dust full in the face. The hedges facing the highway were covered in what looked like white powder from the continuous grinding away of the rock-laid road by the wheels of the carriages, carts, and wagons which utilized the highway. She whirled around and coughed, walking slowly back toward the hedge. She couldn't believe her careful plan had dissolved so quickly.

The next moment, however, she heard a voice call out, and the town chariot began slowing down. She peeked to her left, squinting her eyes against the still billowing dust, and was thrilled to see that somehow Bucksted had seen her and had ordered his carriage to a halt.

Lord Bucksted felt a sting of shock surge over him.

Could it be? Was it possible? Had Eleanor Marigate actually waved down his coach in what he could only determine was an extremely hoydenish manner? What on earth was his bride-to-be thinking in exposing herself to the ridicule of the neighborhood in doing so?

He opened the door and in a quick movement leaped to the rough macadamized stones of the highway. He looked in the direction of the hill and saw Eleanor, hunched over slightly, coughing, and still enduring the hapless roiling of dust from his coach's wheels. Fortunately, the dust was settling quickly onto the grassy edges of the highway.

He couldn't credit his eyes. She was breathing hard, which could only mean she had been *running!* Was she so enamored of him, then, that she must hurry to meet him?

How truly singular! How very surprising! How utterly inappropriate!

He had never thought of Eleanor as a particularly romantic sort of female. But then, he had to admit he scarcely knew her. In the past several months, since having offered for her, he had been in her company only twice on visits to her home as a matter of ceremony. She had been rather shy with him each time, something he had not quite expected, for she had been described to him as a lively young woman. Yet, her shyness had not displeased him, for he felt she showed the exact sort of nature he wished for in a wife—a gentle submissiveness which he valued above all else. From the time he could remember, he had determined on wedding a female who was conformable to his notions of what the future Marchioness of Chalvington should be like.

What, then, was the meaning of her present conduct in waylaying his coach? Surely she must know that such manners would hardly please him? Surely he had made his expectations clear to her in the many letters he had sent to her on the subject? Good God! Her hair was sitting in a lopsided lump on the side of her head!

As the dust settled completely, his bride-to-be turned toward him and smiled, albeit faintly. His booted feet began marking a quick path up the highway. He stepped from the rocks onto the narrow border of ankle-high grass. He silently practiced words of admonishment about not making a spectacle of herself or exerting herself in a manner unseemly for a young woman or a young bride, and certainly not in a manner wholly unacceptable for the next Countess of Bucksted.

The closer he drew to her, however, the more his speech got lost in her beauty. Faith, but he had forgotten how exquisite she was. His heart began to pound. Her eyes were as blue as he remembered, deep, clear pools which invited poetry and adoration. Her black hair was the color of a raven's wing and her complexion was a beautiful cream blended with summery rose petals. If he hadn't been such a sensible man, his head might have been turned by such a lovely country maiden. Fortunately, however, he had had every reason to offer for her since in doing so he could fulfill his promise to her father to be of assistance to the family in whatever way seemed proper. Sir Henry Marigate had been a distant relation on his mother's side. He held familial duty high in importance.

Almost as high as proper manners!

Having long since given up on Cupid's arrows to select a wife for him, he had chosen what he believed was a malleable young woman of some ability and intellect, *and beauty,* whom he intended to mold into a very fine countess, indeed. He had trusted his many letters to have made his wishes clear. Apparently, he had not been specific enough. Or perhaps some reason he could not fathom had brought her racing to the King's Highway.

When he finally reached her, she bit her lip and he understood that something untoward must have, indeed, happened.

"Good God, Miss Marigate, whatever is the matter? You are overset. I can see it in your eyes." She pulled at the tangle of her hair distractedly and brought part of the pretty mass dangling to her shoulders. The sight of her hair so loosened caused his chest to tighten. He had forgotten entirely how her beauty made him feel, as though he were in the midst of an exotic dream.

"My lord," she said, still slightly breathless from running. "You cannot imagine how grateful I am that you heard me and stopped your postillions from going an inch farther toward the house."

Thoughts of the pox or the plague streamed abruptly through his mind. "Is there some illness among the servants? Dear God, not your mama! Your sisters?"

She chuckled—yes, it was most definitely a chuckle—and a quick smile replaced her somber expression. "Mama is quite well, as are my sisters. Even the servants. It is just that I was certain once you crossed the portals of our home, you and I would not be spared these minutes, so necessary to your happiness as well as to mine, in which to speak."

He took a deep breath, relieved that the health of the inmates of Hartslip Manor was in tolerable order. "You wished to speak with me? But I don't understand. Surely we will have ample opportunity to converse privately, especially given our relationship." He looked into her face and withheld a deep sigh. He had waited a long time to take a wife, and his patience had been rewarded. He found, oddly enough, that he wanted to kiss her.

In a quiet voice, he added, "The gardens alone will afford us immeasurable opportunity for as much conversation as either of us could wish for. I understand they are quite extensive."

Her brow grew furrowed. She blinked twice at him as though not precisely comprehending the nature of his suggestion. "Yes, but not until it is too late. My lord—" She paused suddenly and swallowed hard. "The fact is, I cannot marry you after all, and I simply had to tell you before you arrived at the manor. Once Mama had sunk her talons into you, and the whole round of events was set in motion, I knew I would never be granted an opportunity to say as much."

Lord Bucksted felt the warmth drain from his face, and a strange, unfamiliar dizziness drifted through his brain. Good God, if he didn't think it impossible, he would swear she was jilting him? But that was unthinkable! What female in her right mind would not want to become a countess? And when, precisely, had the chit found her tongue, for in the past two visits she had spoken scarcely a dozen words to him. She had been all nods and murmurs of agreement. Now, it would seem, she could not stop speaking!

"You are breaking off our engagement with scarcely less than a fortnight before the wedding?" he asked, incredulous.

"Yes," she responded quite boldly. She then cocked her head and frowned. "My lord, you do not look at all well!"

He turned away from her and was presently forcing his stomach to unknot itself that he might draw in a deep, full breath. The acrid taste of rock-dust, still clinging to the air, traveled the length of his tongue.

How could this be? Eleanor Marigate was ending their betrothal? She was nearly two and twenty, a spinster by all rights. How was this possible? She had no dowry and her mother was deeply in debt and, once he took possession of Hartslip Manor, they would have no place to live. She was being nonsensical, unreasonable.

Another wretched thought assailed him. He had been harshly criticized for choosing a provincial bride. He could not begin to imagine the sneers, the snide remarks, the gabblemongering he would be forced to endure once the *beau monde* learned he had been rejected by his countrified bride-to-be. But there it was—the impoverished ape-leader from Kent was jilting him.

He was disgusted.

He was enraged.

He looked east, his gaze taking in the lovely Kentish landscape rising in bloom as the season moved inexorably toward summer, at the oasthouses on the east side of the lane, as well as the cherry and apple orchards striving energetically to fulfill their promise of bountiful summer harvests, at the scattering of tiled farmhouses along the southwestern end of the Medway Valley. He let out a deep sigh of dismay. Why couldn't she have informed him of her decision before he had quit his cozy London town house, before he had permitted two of London's most powerful hostesses to plan *fêtes* in honor of their betrothal, before he had accepted the hearty congratulations of hundreds of well-wishers? But most especially, why couldn't she have ended their engagement before Miss Daphne Westwell had confessed her longstanding affection for him?

"But I love you, Aubrey," she had said in her warm, deep-throated voice. "I have always loved you. Didn't you know as much?" He had not been entirely surprised, for she had sought his company assiduously over the years. She had teased him a little, "And you must remember that true connubial happiness can only come about when two people know each other extremely well, as you and I do, and when at least one of them is willing to endure every manner of peccadillo in the other."

"And you are willing to endure such from me?" he had asked teasingly.

She had nodded. Her brave smile had faltered. She had clung to him, settling her blond curls on his shoulder, she had wept a little. "I love you ever so much."

A feeling very much like regret had rippled through him even then. Now he was sick at the thought that he had chosen Nellie Marigate over lovely Daphne. Daphne would never have mortified him in such a manner. Never.

He took another deep breath and felt Miss Marigate's hand on his sleeve. "I have caused you great distress," she whispered. "But I promise you, I didn't mean to. I thought you would be appreciative since ours is not a love match. Are you not, even in the smallest degree, grateful to have the wedding called off?"

"Why would I be grateful?" he queried stiffly, looking back at her. He could not believe her naïveté. "Why would you think for one moment I would be content with such a pronouncement?"

Her brows flew sharply together. He could see the chagrin in her eyes and on her dove's complexion. But he could not be sympathetic. Her hand fell from his arm, and she took a step backward. "Because you are not in love with me and because you offered for me out of a sense of duty."

There was much truth to what she said, but he didn't comprehend in the least what that had to do with her belief that he would be happy to be out of the bargain. "You are being too romantic," he countered. "I had not thought you were of such a turn of mind."

"Then . . . then you are not hoping one day to fall in love?"

He smiled a half-smile. His face felt strangely stiff. "I don't consider it a necessity to a prosperous marriage."

She appeared horrified, and he was once again surprised.

"Come, come," he responded. "Surely you are not so innocent as to believe all the unpredictable, incomprehensible yearnings of love are far better suited to creating a happy union than respect and admiration?"

Her shoulders seemed to settle more deeply over her back. "I have always thought that respect and admiration were a precursor to love as much as to a good marriage. Do you respect me then, Lord Bucksted? Do you admire me? Is that what you are saying?"

Again, he was taken aback, for he hadn't considered her in this light. His decision had been about duty and about the belief that she would make a conformable wife.

"I see," she murmured. "Then I am at a loss as to understand why you have offered for me."

He could hardly tell her that he believed she would behave herself according to his strictures once they were married. "I am not presenting my case with even the smallest amount of precision or decorum," he said. "Please trust that I would never have offered for you if I did not believe we suited one another quite well."

"How would you know?" she asked solemnly, her gloved hands spread wide. "When you know nothing about me! For all you know, I might be an outlaw of some sort, involved with highwaymen, or . . . or perhaps even smugglers."

"You are speaking pure nonsense now," he stated as though he was closing the matter once and for all.

"My lord, whether it is nonsense or not, you have no way of knowing, given the fact that you've spent so little time with me. I say again, I cannot marry you. Sir, the truth of the matter is, whatever you might think of me, *I* do not in the least esteem *you*."

He started. He blinked. He opened his mouth to speak, but fell into something akin to a trance. When he could order his vocal cords to function, he sounded hoarse even to his own ears. "What do you mean? Pray, tell me precisely what you mean."

She took a deep breath and plunged in. "You are high-handed, you think far too much of your own consequence, you consider your needs as paramount, you haven't a particle of compassion for the poor, you are vain, you value only your own opinions, and . . . and in all these months you've made not the smallest effort to discover how I might think on even the mildest of topics. From the moment you came to us this past January, you pontificated on every subject imaginable. I had hoped the defect could be set down to a mere fit of nerves associated with making an offer of marriage, but your letters merely confirmed my opinions. And your last one enumerating the degree of silence you felt would be required by your bride in the presence of an entire list of personages and servants, well! Need I say more?"

He was not in the midst of a dream but a nightmare! Time lost all meaning. A buzzing sounded in his ears. He wanted to move his feet or his hands, he wanted to speak, but he found he was completely immobile.

When at last he could speak, he turned to her and said, "Then why, in God's name, did you wait until now to tell me?"

He saw that tears brimmed her lashes, and some of his anger dissipated.

She said, "Because of Mama and my sisters. But I have since decided that I shall find some other means of providing for them, for all of us. Somehow."

"I see," he responded. His head was still reeling.

"Lord Bucksted, you cannot be in the least overset by this. If you search your heart, I am convinced you will find nothing but relief residing there."

"You forget, Miss Marigate, all those who have taken weeks to make the proper preparations for this sennight of our betrothal celebrations. I am not, in this instance, thinking only of myself, as you have suggested . . ."

"Yes," she replied solemnly. "There is that . . ."

How could she think so poorly of him? He would have tried to answer her, to make her see the horrendous nature of her decision, but the onset of a shrill, feminine voice prevented him.

"Eleanor!" Lady Marigate cried out from the direction of a narrow, orderly woodland just beyond the hedge.

"Mama," Eleanor breathed, anguished. "Oh, I knew she would try to cast a spoke in the wheel!"

Bucksted glanced at her and suddenly had a much larger understanding of his betrothed's *circumstances.* Her complexion paled, and she touched the puffed sleeve of her gown as though wishing she could draw it protectively over her neck.

Lady Marigate's bonnet appeared some ten feet away. "Nellie, my darling! Are you there?" A poke bonnet of dark blue silk, covered with an expanse of gold fabric, could be seen bobbing along the top of the hedge.

Bucksted laid a hand on Eleanor's shoulder and whispered, "Say nothing to her of this, I beg you. I would like a little time to think, to ponder what ought to be done next. Will you allow me this much?"

Eleanor looked up at him, a frown still marring her pretty forehead. She searched his eyes and responded quietly, "Of course."

"Nellie, I know you're there!" Lady Marigate cried out. "Speak to me."

"Here, Mama," she called to her parent. "I am just chatting with Lord Bucksted."

Lady Marigate arrived at the turnstile and squeezed herself through with some difficulty, for she was very high in the flesh. "There you are, my pet, and dear, dear Lord Bucksted." Her voice was a charitable falsetto that could either charm or grate, depending on her predisposition to the object of her discourse.

She would have been my mother-in-law, Bucksted thought with what he recognized as a distinct sigh of relief. Her face was white with a liberal use of powder, her lips darkened from a generous portion of rouge. Her gold shawl hung from the brim of her poke bonnet, nearly covering her eyes, and a heavy emerald ring glared at him from over white silk gloves. Her gown was of a matching dark blue silk, with several rows of ruffles about the hem. Her dark blue slippers were covered with mud.

"My dear Lord Bucksted, you must wonder at this singular greeting we have bestowed on you. But dear Eleanor and I thought it would be such fun to, to attack your coach in a really highwaymanlike manner. Do you not think it has been a great lark?"

He drew in a breath to answer her, but he needn't have bothered.

"Of course you do," she trilled in her falsetto, responding for him. She then called out to the postillion. "You there! Postboy! Take Lord Bucksted's coach to the stables." She then took up his arm and drew him toward the turnstile. "But do come along, this way. I shall take you through my dear, departed husband's nuttery.

The hazelwood trees are so lovely this time of year, but of course they belong to you now.

"It's all so very sad and all because of a wretched entail"—she clucked her tongue—"leaving us destitute except for your great generosity in offering for one of my poor daughters. Nellie will make you an excellent wife—even though none of the local lads would look sideways at her, for if you must know her tongue is a bit too ascerbic for most—and you may depend upon her dutifulness, for I have trained her since she was a babe."

She rambled on, "You can see for yourself she has a pleasing eye with regard to fashion, though this particular shade of lavender does not set off her eyes to such advantage as her rose sarsenet or her yellow silk."

She released his arm to squeeze her way back through the turnstile, and as soon as he was on the other side as well, she quickly took possession of his arm once more. "Oh, my, you will be so pleased at the bloom of the primroses this spring—such brilliant colors. They make almost a carpet among the ferns and geraniums." She paused for a moment to bark at her daughter. "Come! Nellie!" She flung this last order over her shoulder as though commanding an army.

Eleanor watched her mother's bobbing bonnet and heard the endless flow of chatter, which she now believed would have driven Lord Bucksted from Hartslip anyway, regardless of her own actions. When her father had been alive, he had been daily equal to the task of keeping Lady Marigate's volubility in strong check. But since his demise, the widow's tendency to talk incessantly had become a storm-swollen stream that couldn't seem to find a place to drain effectively. Eleanor had long since given up feeling mortified by her mother's peculiarities, so it was only with a certain sense of long-standing resignation that she followed behind.

Her less exalted place in the train gave her a welcome moment to review her conversation with Bucksted. She was glad it was over, that the truth was out, yet she was still quite surprised at how distressed he had seemed. She knew he did not love her, so she had convinced herself that he would be in some manner grateful she had ended the betrothal. He didn't seem in the least content, however. Although she supposed much of his irritation could be set down to the fact that she had not broached the subject until the eleventh hour. What man would not be furious, especially *my Lord Bucksted?*

She felt her lip curl in a strong measure of disdain.

She could not like *his lordship* for precisely that reason; he would forever be, to anyone who chanced upon him, *his lordship*—not a man of flesh and blood by half, not a man with whom she could converse with ease, not a man she could even *grow* to love, of that she was convinced.

She considered him and the truly odd circumstance of his ever having offered for her in the first place. She had accepted out of a sense of desperation, for she didn't know what would become of her sisters or her mother if she did not. Yet at the very same moment, her acceptance had been the worst sort of betrayal, not because she knew she would one day jilt him, but because of the secret life she lived.

No one knew her terrible, yet oh-so-exciting, secret that for nearly a twelvemonth she had been engaging in the smuggling trade, just as she had suggested to Bucksted earlier. She had come to the business partly out of a pure sense of adventure, which she shared with her dearest friend from childhood, Martin Fieldstone, and also because the sale of French contraband to local Kentish merchants was highly lucrative.

The funds she received from her weekly nocturnal visits to Broomhill on the coast had been applied not to her family's distress but to continuing her father's philanthropic endeavors. His death had ended a multitude of contributions he had made regularly to the relief of the poor, and those who had relied on his efforts were left without the subsistence necessary for survival. When the opportunity presented itself to raise much-needed monies through smuggling, Eleanor did not hesitate. She saw no harm in the sale of smuggled goods because the profits went to a good purpose.

Yet, now, as her gaze followed after Bucksted, she realized that it was the worst sort of sham to have accepted of his hand when all the while she lived a secret life as a smuggler. How relieved she felt to have put an end to the betrothal.

Besides, she truly detested the man.

She watched him walk in his oh-so-gentlemanly fashion beside her mama. She would give him that, he was very much *the gentleman.* He was tall, and his broad shoulders were well laid back—stuffed with his pride, no doubt. His waist was narrow and fit. Her good friend, Martin Fieldstone, had told her of his athletic ability. Apparently, he was a Corinthian of no mean order, a Nonesuch in matters of driving and use of the pistols. He was a member of the Four-in-Hand Club and had a great reputation among the bloods of the *ton.* Martin said he had once tried to emulate Bucksted's manner of flicking the whip over the leader's ear, but had failed miserably to accomplish even a semblance of the man's considerable style.

She would give Bucksted that, then. He had the demeanor of a gentleman and a great deal of sporting ability.

He was also quite wretchedly handsome which was what, for a very brief time, had persuaded her to accept the offer of his hand in marriage in the first place—foolish female that she was. His hair was a dark brown, worn today beneath a stylish, beaver hat, and his eyes were an unusual hazel in color. His face was all masculine lines and angles. He took one's breath away. Both her sisters had sighed more than once over his elegant features. His nose, which should have warned her of terrible things to come, was completely and utterly patrician perfection.

She was struck suddenly, as she watched him, by the careful cut of his clothes. There might be many things she found less than admirable about Lord Bucksted, but elegance of person was not one of them. He was dressed in a brown coat that fitted his broad, athletic shoulders to a nicety, yet veered attractively to a narrow waist. Buff pantaloons clung to muscular thighs, and glossy black hessians completed a portrait of a man more comfortable in the saddle than in sitting about a drawing room for hours on end.

She felt a sudden twisting and turning in her stomach as she watched the easy athletic grace of his steps. She might not wish to marry him, but she could not deny that he was an exceedingly handsome man in every respect.

At that moment, he chanced to look back at her, almost as though he had been reading her thoughts. As a blush crept up her cheeks, a strange smile entered his eyes, then moved quite abruptly to his lips. Her stomach took another hard twist; only this time the sensation moved up to her heart and gave a quick squeeze. How very peculiar! She could hardly breathe!

Lady Marigate tweaked his arm and his attention reverted back to her.

Eleanor swallowed hard. She didn't understand the nature of his teasing, knowing smile nor did she comprehend the butterflies presently running riot in her stomach. She had so little experience of men after all. All these years she had been fully occupied, alongside her beloved father, in philanthropic endeavors, so much so that a deep, intimate knowledge of the male gender was completely lost to her.

How then could she account for the oddly nauseous sensations she was feeling?

She clasped her hands behind her back as she strolled through the nuttery. Perhaps she was merely feeling ill from having run through the gardens earlier, or perhaps the rock-dust was making her feel poorly. Yet, even now, as his deep resonant voice finally broke through one of her mother's sentences, she felt her stomach knot up all over again.

How *very* peculiar!

So, she would give him all these: he bore himself like a nobleman, he outranked most gentlemen in sporting abilities, he looked like a Greek god, he dressed in a manner to please the fastidiousness of Beau Brummell, he was well educated, had the finest connections in the land, was wealthy beyond imagining as the heir to the Marquess of Chalvington, and he made her stomach feel as though butterflies had taken up residence there!

There, however, his finer points ended, she decided with a brisk nod of her head, all of which were, in her opinion, entirely superficial and useless. She had rather wed a goat than *my Lord Bucksted!*

Two

When the trio reached the end of the shaded canopy of hazelnut trees and were halfway through the quizzical, miniature, elfish garden of Squirrel Cottage, Bucksted stopped quite suddenly and addressed Lady Marigate.

"Madame," he began solemnly, effecting a courtly bow, "I do beg you will permit me to take your daughter for a turn about the gardens before we retire within."

Lady Marigate began hurriedly, "But my lord—"

"Thank you," he gushed uncharacteristically. "For you must know I have a great deal to say to her." Here he winked.

Eleanor opened her eyes very wide. Bucksted winking? How very odd!

"Oh—well!" Lady Marigate cried. She fluttered her hands, she glanced askance at Eleanor, she opened her mouth like a little bird. "I—I suppose, a few minutes would be perfectly acceptable since you are betrothed. Of course—"

"Thank you, madame, or dare I say, *Mother?*"

This was nearly too much for Eleanor. She pursed her lips together to keep from laughing outright. Surely her parent would know that she was being humbugged. How surprised she was when Lady Marigate fell into a puddle at his feet. Her expression grew strangely young and simpering. "Oh, my dear Bucksted. What a delight you are! Your manners are of the very finest, and to be addressed with such affection! I am moved beyond words."

She turned to Eleanor who saw writ in her mother's features

a certain triumph. Lady Marigate said, "Mind, only a few minutes, for I daresay Cook has nearly completed the preparation of our nuncheon."

"Of course, Mama."

In a flurry of movement, Lady Marigate and her blue silk skirts disappeared around the bend of Squirrel Cottage. Lord Bucksted turned toward Eleanor, and again she felt a strange twisting of her stomach that was not at all unpleasant. Now that she had told him she would not marry him, he seemed *different* to her somehow.

He advanced on her, his eyes aglow with an unfamiliar light. She did not know what he was about and was dumbfounded when he took her arm. Feeling quite nervous of a sudden, she queried, "Then it is all settled?"

He did not answer her, but glanced around cautiously for a moment, then drew her backward toward a tall yew hedge shaped in the form of an elegantly trimmed, tall crescent and housing a statue of Zeus. Whatever was he doing?

Finally, he spoke in a soft voice, "In between your mother's numerous words, I have been considering our, er, circumstances, and I have a proposal to lay before you. Will you hear me out?"

She nodded, feeling utterly bewildered. His behavior of the moment was wholly unlike him, or was it, perhaps, that she had never known him before? She confessed to herself that she was intrigued.

"Yes, of course I will," she agreed readily.

He nodded briskly and launched into his speech. "By ending the betrothal, you make your personal circumstances a thousandfold worse, since in recent days I have settled nearly four hundred pounds of new bills submitted to me by local tradesmen, debts most recently contracted by your mother."

Eleanor's hand flew to her mouth. "Oh, no!" she cried. "Why did you not write to me and tell me? This is abominable. I am utterly mortified. Were they from . . . from the milliner's?"

"And the dressmakers."

She groaned. "You were very right to upbraid me for waiting until this eleventh hour to dissolve our betrothal. Mama said I must have proper bridesclothes, and I told her that what I had was sufficient, but I think by now you must know what she is."

He frowned slightly. "Have you not seen these articles, then?"

"No, my lord. Undoubtedly she was intent on surprising me—probably this afternoon."

He shook his head. "Pray, will you please call me anything other than 'my lord.' I can hardly bear it."

"How shall I address you?" she asked ingenuously. He was such a stranger to her that anything other than "my lord" seemed like an improper familiarity.

"Bucksted, if you please."

With a little practice, she thought she might manage that, especially since for the barest moment she feared he would insist she address him by his Christian name and that she could never do. "As you wish," she responded quietly.

He held her gaze, and she saw his mind begin to work anew as his eyes moved from feature to feature. He was still frowning. She realized she wasn't half as afraid of him in this moment as when she had confronted him in the lane. He seemed much more human to her, even likable to a degree, for much of his stiffness of manner was gone.

She realized she had not been in his company apart from her mother or sisters, and wondered if this circumstance might have altered his normal behavior. Regardless, she addressed the subject at hand. "I promise I shall pay you back—every tuppence," she reiterated. "Mama was not always so, so irresponsible—never when Papa was with us." Sir Henry had been able to keep his wife in strong check. Since his death, however, Lady Marigate had given herself free rein to purchase whatever bit of trumpery chanced to fall beneath her eye. She was, as it turned out, a hopeless spendthrift.

"There is no need for you to do so!" he cried. "Damme, I wish— I mean, I do beg your pardon, if you will but hear me out I believe both our dilemmas can be solved."

"Yes, my lor— I mean, yes, Bucksted, pray continue."

"Your earlier pronouncement has put me in a severe quandry since it is primarily my friends and acquaintances who have graciously arranged several intricate entertainments in honor of our betrothal. My mother, as you know, has planned an enormous ball for tomorrow night, as well as all the festivities for the island celebration. Lady Tiverton, one of our most exclusive London hostesses, has been orchestrating the final ball of this week for months on end, and Lady Penryn has contracted the famous Catalani to sing in our honor on Thursday."

"Catalani?" she inquired, utterly astonished. The songstress was renowned for her velvet voice and incredible range. She felt dizzy. "I—I had no idea!"

"I meant to surprise . . . my bride-to-be." He let the words weigh heavily in the air between them.

"Oh, Bucksted," she murmured, chagrined.

He drew close to her. "And . . . I had thought to take you to the fair just outside of Headcorn, on Tuesday."

"To the fair?" she queried, stunned. Her low opinion of him did not allow that he would take anyone to a fair nonetheless condescend to attend one himself!

He smiled crookedly. "I have, on occasion, been known to enjoy the simplicity and liveliness of such events."

"I must admit, Bucksted, I never thought you would."

It was his turn to appear chagrined. "Good God! You must think me a dull dog indeed!"

"Yes," she responded succinctly.

"Well, it is no wonder you wish yourself well out of our marriage contract. However, might I persuade you to agree to play out our betrothal week for the sake of so many who have labored on our behalf?"

Her heart sank. She had wanted an end to the whole business, now, today.

"Please?" he begged softly, drawing very close to her. He still had hold of her arm.

She felt dizzy in the nicest way as she looked up at him. "I don't know what to say. I hate a sham which is what I feel I created these many months and more when I accepted your offer of your hand in marriage. For if you must know I only did so for Mama's, and for my sisters' sakes."

"I am beginning to comprehend as much," he said. He squeezed her arm gently. "I have always been sorry that the entail was left as it was. The property ought to have gone to you. If you will set aside your own disinclination for my sake, at the end of the sennight, after all the *fêtes* have been attended and hopefully enjoyed, I promise to release you entirely from our betrothal. In addition, I offer this—the settling of your mother's debts as numbered in our contracts, the right to live at Squirrel Cottage so long as the need remains, and an annuity for your mother for the remainder of her life."

Her mouth fell agape. She was completely astounded by his generosity. "Bucksted, I can't agree to this!" she cried. "It is wholly unacceptable to me."

"I can comprehend your feelings. I only ask that you extend yourself a trifle to understand mine. I wish to avoid the scandal which would ensue were I suddenly to announce to the *beau monde* that my bride to be has no wish to become my wife and that everyone who has journeyed to the Medway Valley to take part in a week of celebrations can now return to their respective homes and laugh themselves silly at my expense. Beyond that," he grew very serious, "I shudder to think of the pain such an act would inflict on my mother. You know what the gabblemongers will do to her. She would be the brunt of a dozen cruel jokes."

Eleanor felt herself pale. What he was speaking was true. She was not so far removed from regular society that she did not know how torturous a barbed tongue could be.

"I have only been thinking of myself," she stated solemnly.

"I would have to agree with you, though I daresay I cause you pain in saying so." He drew in a deep breath and asked softly, "Will you not consider my offer, if not for my sake, then for my mother's? At some point following the end of our sennight together, we may effect a violent quarrel, you shall call our betrothal off, and that shall be the last of it."

She saw the pleading look in his eyes and weighed the matter for several minutes. She had spoken boldly before, when she'd promised to repay Bucksted for settling her mother's debts, but how could she ever do so unless of course she took up smuggling as a trade and not just as an addendum to her father's philanthropies. The very idea of doing so, however, made her shudder.

"You seem distressed, of a sudden," he said.

She could hardly tell him the nature of her thoughts, that she was considering becoming a professional smuggler! What would he think of her then?

The idea, however, struck a quirky chord of amusement within her, and she began to smile. She wondered what Bucksted's face would look like were she ever to tell him the truth.

"Now you are smiling!"

"I am sorry, Bucksted, and I do apologize for my quixotic behavior. I, I am merely stunned by your offer and somehow I can't seem to find my equilibrium." Oh, the whiskers she was telling when all she was really thinking about was her smuggling activities. Of course she would never, *never*, resort to the acquisition of contraband in order to support her family; such a horrendous notion was decidedly beyond the pale. And yet, what was she to do?

She brought her thoughts to order and considered her present dilemma. The truth was, she had no idea what she could possibly do to repair her family's fortune other than by wedding a man of substance. Once she jilted Bucksted, where would she go, or her mother and sisters? She quaked at the very idea of it.

With these thoughts banging about in her head, along with the vision of the sufferings Lady Chalvington would endure were the betrothal to end so abruptly, she decided to agree to his present scheme. He could protect himself and his mother from scandal, and she would secure something of a future for her family.

"Very well," she acquiesced. "For your mother's sake and for mine, I will agree to it."

"Thank you," he said. He was visibly relieved and smiled down at her.

Oh, what a smile that was, full of sunbeams and blue skies. She felt dizzy, as she had before, and swallowed hard. She became acutely aware that his arm was still wrapped tightly about hers. "Is there anything else?" she whispered.

His expression seemed caught as he held her gaze steadily. "Faith, but you are so beautiful," he whispered.

"I—I don't know how you can say so when I must present a truly wretched appearance with my hair unloosed from its pins as it is."

He shook his head. "Quite the contrary." He gathered up a handful of her long, black locks. "Your hair dancing about your shoulders is very comely, to say the least."

Her heart was racing. Her breath came in little wisps. She had no idea whatsoever what was happening to her. "So," she whispered softly, "are you done with me, then?"

"No," he murmured, "for it has occurred to me that in order to carry off our deception properly, you will need to pretend you are at least a little in love with me."

The deep resonance of each syllable was making her limbs tremble. "And how would I do that?" she murmured almost insensibly. He had mesmerized her somehow, with his words and the deep tones of his voice.

He slid an arm about her waist as though it were the most natural occurrence in the world. "You could begin by accepting a kiss from me now and then without running away." He smiled faintly, and she felt caught as she had never been before.

She lifted her face to his by way of agreement. "I believe that would be wise, not to run away, I mean. It would look very odd in me to be forever thwarting your advances yet proclaiming that I love you."

"Very odd indeed," he breathed, taking her chin in his gloved fingers as he drew her against him.

He leaned down and placed his lips upon hers. They were warm and moist. She trembled. Her lips parted beneath his. She leaned more daringly against him, for what reason she knew not. His kiss became more roving and free. She felt his tongue touch her lips. In her surprise, she parted her lips a little more, and his tongue instantly rimmed the inside of her own.

At that moment, though her mind was filled with something near fright, Eleanor found herself drifting out of the garden and into a world about which, until this moment, she had been utterly unaware. A prickling of desire flowed through her as he kissed her. Her feet no longer touched the ground. She knew he was supporting her about the waist, indeed both his arms were hugging her tightly, but her entire attention had become fixed on the feel of his tongue and his lips, and nothing else seemed to exist.

She had never known such pure delight before. The sensation was akin to dancing with angels, she thought distractedly. Every nerve in her body was suddenly alive, and she thought, quite wickedly, that she could go on kissing Bucksted forever.

Her spirit flitted about the beautiful gardens of Hartslip Manor, her heart swelled to twice its size; she should have felt full of shame but did not, she only wanted the kiss to go on and on and on.

After a long moment, however, he drew back, his own expression hazy and lost, at least so it appeared through her own misty vision. She blinked slowly a time or two. Her feet floated back to the grassy earth. She smiled and blinked a little more.

Then, as though a bucket of ice water had been thrown over her, she came to her senses. "Oh!" she cried, aghast. "Bucksted, that was very wicked!"

The smile began in his hazel eyes, slipped to his lips, and then he chuckled. In that moment, she almost began to like him.

"Good God!" he cried, apparently as stunned as she was by the kiss they had just shared. "What the devil was that?"

She bit her lip and felt a blush climbing up her neck and into her cheeks. "I don't know," she murmured, shaking her head and feeling utterly bewildered.

He touched her cheeks. "You will blush now?" he inquired facetiously. "When you have been kissing me as though you had been about the business your entire life?"

She could only giggle. "I have not been *about the business* my entire life. I've only been kissed once by John Markham when I was fourteen."

He knew Mr. Markham. His very soul became irritated at the thought that such a cow-handed whipster, his face still rampant with spots, had dared to take a liberty with his betrothed—and that when she was but a child of fourteen! "And what did you think of his, er, abilities?"

"I couldn't concentrate on the kiss very well, if you must know, for he had hold of my hand with his own and his palm was sweating profusely. I was never more disconcerted!"

At that he threw back his head and laughed. "What a baggage you are!" he exclaimed.

Eleanor smiled and chuckled with him. "I begin to think you are not such a bad fellow after all," she stated wonderingly.

His expression grew a trifle more serious. "My friends do not think me so very vile." He searched her eyes, and her stomach became knotted and excited once more. His words were full of blossoming hope.

She lowered her gaze, forcing herself to remember why she had rejected his hand in the first place, and once again her senses sobered. "We ought to be going in," she murmured at last. "Mama will be expecting us, and if Cook's carefully prepared viands are not consumed before they grow cold, she will be impossible to live with for the next fortnight. Cook is quite particular in that regard."

"Then we must not disappoint her." He offered her his arm.

Eleanor accepted his escort, but fell silent as they began walking back to the house.

Bucksted did not try to converse with her. He had seen the return of disapprobation to her eyes, as though she had been reminding herself of all his faults.

The sting of it burned him. He could not think what he had ever done to have earned such a low regard, but so he had. His bruised pride began to speak to him, encouraging him to find some manner in which to take a revenge of sorts upon his betrothed and her ill opinions of him.

He did not have far to search. The idea came to him in a quick, perfect vision. He knew what he must do. He must make her love him.

He breathed a very deep, satisfied sigh. He was, after all, a man of some ability. He believed himself completely equal to the task of turning Eleanor Marigate's disapproving heart toward him. Even if he had not been disposed to believe himself capable of it, the kiss they had just shared would have convinced him the task was not impossible.

But could he do it within the framework of their betrothal week? That was the rub. Seven days would not give him much time. On the other hand, because they were betrothed, he could take liberties which under ordinary circumstances would have been forbidden.

Yes, it could be done and by God, he would do it!

"These are my betrothal gowns?" Eleanor asked, dumbfounded.

Lady Marigate's heart swelled with pride. "You are to be a countess in less than a fortnight and one day the Marchioness of Chalvington. Would you expect me to do less when such an exalted future awaits you? Besides, you are my daughter and . . . and I love you. Oh, my dear! You . . . you have saved us all!"

Eleanor shifted her gaze from the dozens of exquisite gowns which presently swamped her bed and turned to regard her mother. Tears of joy and relief brimmed in her parent's eyes.

"Mama! Pray do not cry on my account." A terrible guilt assailed her. How disappointed her mother would be when she finally told her the truth. She added, "I'm sure we would have come about one way or the other. Good Mr. Barnett is quite fond of Margaret, and dear Kitty is so beautiful that I am convinced she is destined to make a brilliant marriage. My wedding Buckstead was not our only hope for the future."

"No, of course it was not," Lady Marigate responded brightly. "But only think of the advantages your match has brought to your sisters. You will present them at court, take them about the *beau monde* during the annual Season, and see each of them introduced to any number of acceptable young gentlemen."

"Mama," she breathed, her heart trembling. "What . . . I mean, what if these things should not transpire, would you be overly distressed or disappointed? You know I am not given to great society and . . ."

Lady Marigate cut her off immediately. "Stop talking flummery. No one expects you to be entirely accomplished at present, but in due time, as Bucksted's wife, you will most naturally be required to take your place in a variety of social events, and who better to guide you but Bucksted since he is nine or ten years your senior and quite full of Town Bronze. Pray, do not worry yourself over such trifles. What *I* wish to know, in particular, is your opinion of these gowns I had made up for you. I even took the liberty, and a very great one indeed, of allowing you at least two ball gowns that are not entirely white!"

An array of exquisite fashions was strewn not only on the bed but about the chamber so as to display each one fully. Muslin, silk, satin, tulle, calico, cambric, cashmere—all stared back at her, daring her not to love what she saw. "I have never seen a more lovely assortment of gowns in my entire existence. Not even Daphne Westwell possesses such exquisite costumes." Daphne was a near neighbor whose property bordered the Marquess of Chalvington's monstrous estate. The *on dits* had it that Daphne had for many years set her cap for my lord Bucksted and nearly fell into a decline when he offered for a provincial nobody instead of her own dear self.

"Then you are pleased?" her mother asked.

For all her faults, Eleanor mused, her mother did have a keen eye to fashion. Eleanor embraced her. "I couldn't be more pleased," she said. And that was the truth. She thought of the expense of the gowns and recalled unhappily that Lord Bucksted in fact had paid for them all from his purse.

Why had she waited so long to break off the engagement?

What a fool she had been not to have done so the last time Bucksted came to call, which was two months past. She had known even then that she could not wed such a horrible man.

She remembered his words—so discompassionate when she had spoken of her father's philanthropy. "Though his efforts will always do him great honor, I am convinced the poor do not strive hard enough to pull themselves out of their misery. Surely there is not one of us who has not had an ancestor somewhere in our past who simply decided, *This generation shall be the last to suffer penury.*"

"And do you suppose," she had responded dryly at the time, "that such a person would have employed the word, 'penury'?" She had stared at him with an innocent expression. He had taken her seriously and explained with great care that undoubtedly a person of low birth would not have, at that time, been capable of employing any such exalted turn of phrase, but his children, who would no doubt be educated at the finest schools, would certainly have done so.

"I am relieved to hear you say so, for I have no doubt had he spoken thusly, none of his hut mates would have been able to comprehend him in the least, and he would have been beaten from the village as a lunatic."

He had seemed a little baffled by her speech, but she had excused herself, saying that she had the headache, and had retired to her bedchamber until dinner, at which time she remained silent until he departed.

Only now, as she donned an elegant evening gown of a shimmering pink satin covered in a gossamer sheath of tulle, did she wonder precisely why, even when she disliked Bucksted so very much, she had enjoyed kissing him as she had. Really, it was quite incomprehensible!

An hour before dinner, Eleanor arrived at the drawing room and found Lord Bucksted, nattily attired in black full dress, awaiting her. She caught her breath when he rose to his feet, for she was struck as she had been earlier by his athletic figure. His broad shoulders angled to a narrow waist, his well-muscled thighs gave an elegant shape to his black satin breeches, and even his calves were nicely formed, which put her in mind of something mischievous her grandmother was used to say: *Marry a man with a fine leg, Nellie. You'll never go amiss.*

What a lively old woman her mother's mother had been, a favorite of Eleanor's. She had not quite understood the meaning of such an admonition until now, for something about Bucksted's "fine leg" appealed to her—mightily.

She couldn't help but laugh at herself a little, particularly since this man's "fine leg" was attached to such an indifferent, stuffy, old heart.

Earlier, after a very fine nuncheon had been enjoyed in his company, she had retired to her room to rest before dressing for dinner. Bucksted had been shown to a chamber especially prepared for him, where he was attended by his valet.

During her lie-down, she had had occasion to review the noontime's extraordinary events quite at length. The agreement to which she had acquiesced was almost as astonishing as the kiss she had shared with Bucksted. She still couldn't credit either had happened, especially the latter. She kept wondering, over and over, if she should attach any special meaning to the way she had felt while caught up in his arms. For though she kept reminding herself of the many disagreeable qualities he possessed—his pride and arrogance, his hard-heartedness where the poor were concerned, his ridiculous dictums on how his future wife should conduct herself—she still could not escape the strong impression that were he to try to kiss her again, she would let him!

How odd! How very incomprehensible!

She had often known females who had become distractedly attached to men whom they had professed to despise, but these females she had always set down as complete ninnyhammers, particularly when the attachment resulted in a marriage! Yet, here she was, behaving just like any one of these absurd young women. A few squeezes and a very nice kiss and she was already lusting to be kissed again!

How utterly mortifying!

As she looked at Bucksted now, and felt all those warm sensations again, she couldn't help but rail against a Fate that would have given her part of her ideal in the man, yet left the other part totally wanting in character!

Oh-h-h . . . *blast!*

She took a deep breath as she moved forward to greet the man who had kissed her so thoroughly.

"Good evening, *Eleanor*. Do you mind overly much if I address you by your Christian name?" He lowered his voice and continued, "Given our, er, circumstances, I thought that such an informality would serve to keep the gabblemongers from striking off in the wrong direction."

"I'm sure you are correct," she responded lightly. "I can certainly have no objection. You may call me Nellie, if you like. All my friends do."

He smiled faintly. "*Eleanor* will suffice."

If only her heart would not race so. "You do not like my pet name?"

He was silent apace. "I think it too familiar, even for a besotted bridegroom, at least in company. However"—here he lowered his voice—"when we are alone, I can see no harm in it."

There was excellent humor in his face, as well as a devilish light that threatened to undo her completely. She thought back to the two prosy visits she had had from him in the past few months when he'd spent nearly their whole time together lecturing her on how to be a proper countess. This was not the same man, she thought. Surely not! This man was charming and so very alive!

"There is just one thing," he continued. "I understand Lady Tiverton is coming to call this evening?"

"Yes, she completely overwhelmed Mama with her request to be present. She has never dined here before, you know, so I must conclude that the honor is an extension of your family's consequence."

"Do I detect a facetious note in your voice?" he queried. Again, his expression showed he was amused rather than offended or even disapproving.

"I shall speak plainly—" she began.

"I don't doubt that you shall."

"What do you mean?" she queried, a little stunned.

"Only that, having heard you speak quite plainly this afternoon, I wouldn't dream of expecting anything less from you."

She considered his speech. "No, I suppose not."

For some reason, this made him laugh.

She smiled in response. She realized he must find it amusing that somehow the meek little woman he had thought he was wedding was in truth a very outspoken female. She addressed his original question regarding Lady Tiverton. "I do not know her ladyship at all, except for what I have ascertained during two morning calls of recent weeks and the two which Mama, and my sisters and I, returned. Am I wide of the mark when I say that she is a very precise, calculating sort of woman who does nothing without a purpose?"

"You have hit the mark exactly," he said in just such a tone that caught her attention.

She could see that he seemed surprised. She realized that he had not expected her to be so perceptive, and she was struck by the humiliating realization that he did not consider her a very intelligent sort of female. She could only wonder yet again why the deuce he had offered for her if he had never had any real opinion of her. The whole of the betrothal had now become a complete mystery to her.

She queried, "What then is your interest in Lady Tiverton's appearance here tonight? Do you believe she means something by it?"

"She is one of London's most gifted and most prestigious hostesses. No one can enjoy the least success in Mayfair or the *entrée* into the most exclusive ballrooms without her approval. She is on intimate terms with Sally Jersey, Lady Cowper, and Princess Esterhazy. It is said that one must have her approval first before any of the Almack patronesses will provide the billets for entrance into that holiest of sanctums."

Eleanor was somewhat familiar with the rigors of tonish life because she had herself enjoyed two weeks in London during the spring the year before her father's death. Though Bucksted's circles had been far too exalted for her to enter, she had seen him once or twice but only as an unreachable star among a host of glittering luminaries. Her connections had not been fine enough to allow her to cross the portals of the famous Almack's Assembly Rooms.

However, the names which rolled off Bucksted's tongue so

easily were well known to her as a list of the most feared dragons of his ennobled society.

The truth dawned on her. "Goodness!" she cried. "Do you tell me that Lady Tiverton is here to *approve* of me?"

He nodded in mock solemnity.

"Why on earth did you say nothing before? You spoke not a word in your letters, though now that I recall the substance of them, I begin to see your true designs."

A faint color appeared on his jawline just above the snowy folds of his neckcloth. "As to that, I haven't the faintest notion what you are about. From the first, I have been confident that your elegance of manners, the way you comport yourself in society, and your careful tongue are sufficient to show you are well bred and to guide her ladyship to the proper assessment."

She saw something more. "What a rapper!" she cried.

Since he smiled a little sheepishly, she knew she had discovered the truth. She considered him for a moment, then spoke kindly. "Bucksted, I was raised by a wonderful gentleman and a gentlewoman, who, though lacking discretion at times, can hold her own in any drawing room. She has taught all of her daughters to do the same. I shall not discredit you before Lady Tiverton. However, I cannot help but laugh at the notion that you thought to train me. When did it enter your head that I was *conformable?*"

He smiled in response and shook his head. "I can see now that I was something of a fool in that regard only you were so quiet, so reserved."

"I was shamming it, and for that I do apologize. 'Twasn't fair to you."

She could hear her sisters approaching the drawing room.

He said quickly, "But do you think you can show a proper degree of affection when you dislike me so much?"

She wanted to shock him a little, so she quickly took hold of his arm and looked up at him with what she hoped was an adoring expression. "Is this what you want, *my dearest Bucksted,*" she gushed dramatically.

He laughed, then swept a sudden and unexpected kiss over her lips. "Precisely."

She could not credit he had kissed her again! "I believe you are a beast!" she cried.

And just as her sisters entered the drawing room, he whispered, "And you, miss, are a baggage."

Margaret and Katherine wore gowns of elegant white muslin, each with slightly different accents. Margaret had draped a paisley silk shawl over her elbows, and the high waistband of Kitty's gown bore a beautiful row of embroidered pink roses. They were attractive young women. Kitty shared Eleanor's black hair, but Margaret's was a shimmering dark brown, the same shade as their mother's. All of the ladies had blue eyes, yet Margaret's were round while Kitty's were a lovely almond shape.

Kitty had arrived at eighteen with a beauty and sweetness of character that had set all the young bucks in the Medway Valley to clamoring for her attention. Margaret, though protesting any hint that she had tumbled in love with James Barrett, was so thoroughly under the spell of Cupid that in recent weeks she was found to be daydreaming more often than attending to the practice of the harp or the use of her watercolors, the latter of which was her favorite pastime. Even reading had taken on a new challenge for Maggie. Eleanor had found more than one book open upon her lap, positioned upside down!

Margaret greeted Bucksted first, then Kitty, which was appropriate since so many rituals of social life followed precedence by age as much as by position of rank. He, in turn, spoke kindly to each which was something that did please Eleanor even while so many other things about him did not.

She found herself sighing as he led each lady to a comfortable chair or place on the sofa. He inquired after their afternoon activities with apparent pleasure. Kitty, however, with her youthful enthusiasm, quickly turned the subject. "Eleanor, your gown is exquisite and fits you to perfection. Mama showed us your wardrobe earlier. All of your new gowns are so beautiful!" She sighed.

Margaret beamed. "I hope one day that I might—" But here, with her thoughts and hopes so easily read, she broke off blushing.

To his credit, Lord Bucksted immediately filled the void.

"Though I have always admired the Greek trend of fashion, I have frequently felt that more young ladies ought to be permitted to wear the darker, more vivid shades. Undoubtedly, you, Miss Margaret, would appear to extreme advantage in a dark green or blue."

"I have always thought so, too!" she cried. "When I wear my spencer during the cooler spring months—it is just the shade of holly leaves—I always receive the nicest compliments." Again she blushed and Eleanor could not help but wonder what pleasant memory was assailing her.

Lady Marigate entered shortly after, flapping her arms in butterflylike movements. "Oh, my dears, I am glad you are all assembled for I heard a carriage on the drive." She drew in a deep, proud breath and announced, "Lady Tiverton is come."

A few minutes more and her ladyship entered the drawing room, comporting herself with elegance and civility.

She was a handsome widow who had lost her husband some five years past and who had not as yet been tempted back to the marital state. She was extremely wealthy, so that on the one hand she must be in constant danger of being pursued by fortune hunters and on the other hardly in need of a man to support her remaining steps through life. She had three children, who were not old enough to be presented to society, and so she went about quite alone, quite imperiously, and, to Eleanor's eye, quite contentedly.

Eleanor liked her, surprisingly enough. She was a bold woman, and presented her opinions succinctly. She dressed to perfection, as would be expected, and this evening wore a stylish white silk turban with a quite exotic feather draped over the top. Her gown was a brilliant and regal purple silk, rather décolleté yet not unattractive, and over her arms she wore a white silk shawl embroidered in a fanciful pattern of swirls with gold filament.

All the ladies felt obliged to curtsy slightly as they were presented in turn to her, and Lord Bucksted actually went so far as to possess himself of her hand and place a kiss upon her gloved fingers. Lady Tiverton smiled as she met his gaze.

Oh! They seemed to be sharing some joke.

Eleanor watched them and listened to them for a few minutes, finally ascertaining the nature of the joke. It would seem neither personage took themselves seriously, a circumstance which completely dumbfounded her.

What wonder was this! She had supposed and believed that at the core of Bucksted's character was the certainty that his consequence was everything. Apparently not!

Inwardly, she groaned. She began to sense that she was not yet acquainted with all there was to know about Bucksted. She squirmed a little. Had she misjudged him, then?

Because the party was so small, and both Lady Tiverton and Bucksted had a dozen anecdotes of London to tell, which each delivered with wit and humor, dinner became a lively affair. Eleanor responded with several amusing incidents from the surrounding neighborhood, as did Margaret. Even Kitty was able to share a little story of a kitten which she was able to rescue from a hayloft, but not without getting stuck up there herself since the ladder came away from the edge of the loft and fell to the opposite wall.

"How did you get down?" Bucksted asked gently, for already Kitty was blushing.

"I leaned out the window where the hay is dropped onto the wagons and called to old Mr. Wheeler. He was smoking the cherry trees and for a long time didn't hear me. But after a time, he took his ear horn from his pocket and listened intently to all four corners of the earth. When he finally positioned the pipe toward me, I called out as loudly as I could. He came at once, startled to see me leaning out the hayloft window. He helped me down, of course, but not without giving my head a severe washing about how young ladies should not be climbing ladders in the first place."

"And where is the kitten now?" Bucksted asked.

"He lives in the barn and keeps the mice population from overtaking the livestock."

Everyone chuckled, and Lady Marigate gave her youngest daughter an approving nod of her head.

When the second course had been removed, Bucksted refused

to remain with his glass of port, alone in the dining room. "For I had much rather be among a bevy of beautiful women than left to my own devices for even a few minutes. After all, what man has ever considered his sole company sufficient entertainment at any hour of the day?"

Eleanor just stared at him. He seemed so changed, so altered, so interested in pleasing, so different from his last visit. He was not this way before, surely he was not. She cannot have imagined the whole of it!

Later, she was absolutely astonished when Bucksted agreed to sing a duet with Margaret. Kitty, who had by far the cleverest fingers on the pianoforte, accompanied them with a stylish perfection which brought the three audience members to applauding with great enthusiasm when the song was finished.

"Bucksted!" Lady Tiverton called to him. "You must perform, with Miss Margaret and Miss Kitty, during the concert at Sophia's on Thursday. Everyone would be delighted."

Bucksted agreed at once, as did the sisters, both of whom were blushing with pleasure. What young lady, desirous of increasing her acquaintance, would not wish to be singled out in such a fashion.

Eleanor felt as though she'd been caught up in a dream. Bucksted was conducting himself just as she would have wished a husband-to-be to conduct himself. He was agreeable, enthusiastic in the plans of the ladies, and gentle with shy Kitty. Had she misjudged him?

Sometime later, she took an opportunity to draw him apart and to express her appreciation for his treatment of her sisters.

He frowned slightly. "I don't take your meaning," he said softly. "I don't believe I am doing anything different than what is usual for me."

"You were not always thus with them," she said.

"I daresay I was afraid of frightening one or all of you. They seem to follow your lead, and you were not always so forthright and charming as you've been tonight. You sing beautifully, by the way."

"Thank you, but Margaret has a better voice and far more control."

"Yes," he agreed slowly, "but I much prefer to listen to you. You have a great deal of presence and a simplicity that I find charming."

She felt her heart begin to strain at its moorings. She couldn't breathe very well either. "Are you flirting with me, Bucksted?"

"No," he stated. "It is not possible to flirt with you. I am merely *trying* to flirt with you. At any moment I don't doubt I shall say the wrong thing and you will snap my head off!"

She blinked. "Yes, I should. I see that you are beginning to know me."

He laughed, then whispered. "I am beginning to know you *and* to like you." With that, with these words burning the edges of her heart, he strolled away.

Damme, he *was* flirting with her, he admitted to himself.

Three

Sometime later, when Bucksted had taken up a discussion with Lady Tiverton and Margaret about the poor in London, Eleanor heard her sister say, "From what Eleanor has told us, the squalor is inconceivable. There are young children in the streets stealing pocket watches and the like from anyone who chances by."

"It is true," Lady Tiverton said, "but it has always been so and always shall."

"Not in our parish. Papa saw to that, along with Mr. Westwell and some others."

"Yes, child, but the Metropolis is a different place entirely."

"I think it is very sad, and were I to live there, I should do something about it. Papa was always telling us that we are obligated to help those less fortunate."

Eleanor drew close since the subject at hand was important to her. Bucksted, who stood near the fireplace, spoke next. "I believe the better path is to set the example and let Providence manage the rest. An example of prudence and hard work—"

"A mere example will hardly carry the day," Eleanor interjected bluntly, "not with the price of grain so exorbitant. And what was it I heard about Providence so recently? Yes, it went something like this, 'A fair share for all, said the elephant while dancing among the chickens.' The poor have neither size nor weight to compete with well-fed elephants, now, do they? And what do you think led to the revolution in France? Many insist the revolt was for equality among all people, but I believe it was because there wasn't enough food in Paris. When people starve, they do not care about anyone's rights."

Lady Tiverton's lips parted in astonishment, and Lord Buck-sted's spine seemed to grow stiffer by the second. She could not mistake the censure in his bearing, even though he remained silent as he stared at her.

"Eleanor!" her mother called to her. "Whatever do you mean by contradicting Lord Bucksted in this fashion? Consider your manners, my dear. Do beg pardon . . . at once!"

Eleanor knew she had been abrasive and inflammatory. Therefore, she offered her apologies, at least in part. "I do beg your pardon, my lady, *my lord,* for perhaps not stating my position with greater tact, but I do not believe setting an example to be sufficient. As for industry, who works harder than much of our laboring poor? They work like dogs for every scrap that is tossed their way, but it is scarcely enough to keep body and soul together. Wages have been far too low for a very long time, and when the price of grain reached the wretched proportion that it has in recent years, I believe many honorable men have been forced to turn to crime in order to feed their families."

Bucksted was white about the gills.

"I see we have a radical in our midst," Lady Tiverton stated with raised brows.

Eleanor turned to her at once. "I am no such thing, I promise you, for I have no interest in forming a government such as the one that killed so many good and decent people as happened in France. But I do think the government would not be unwise to listen to the heart of England instead of just to the pocketbooks of the wealthy."

"Ah," Lady Tiverton breathed. "I don't doubt your sentiments do your heart some justice, my dear." She held Eleanor's gaze for a long, penetrating moment. Eleanor did not flinch as the lady eyed her critically, yet at the moment she had no interest in courting her good opinion.

In the end, Lady Tiverton turned to Lady Marigate and abruptly changed the subject. "I was just admiring your draperies. Moss green is a color I have favored since childhood for, like the moss in our countrysides, everything appears to advantage next to it."

Lady Marigate, her cheeks pink with mortification at her daughter's conduct, launched into a discussion of where she had found the beautiful silk. "Canterbury of all places. I admired it excessively the moment I laid eyes on it. But later, I was told by one of the maids at the inn at which I was staying that most of the silks from that shop have been smuggled into the country from France!"

"Indeed?"

Lady Marigate nodded vigorously. "I was never more shocked, yet the workmanship must speak for itself. It is of the finest quality."

"One hears of all the smuggling taking place because of Bonaparte's embargoes, but how do you suppose the business is managed?"

"I haven't the faintest notion," Lady Marigate responded.

Lady Tiverton lowered her voice, "I hear there is a great deal of smuggling along the coast of Cornwall."

Eleanor could not help but listen to the exchange with trepidation. Anytime the subject of smuggling was brought forward, she felt as though someone had drawn near to her own terrible secret. Her head felt suddenly light and dizzy. Goodness! Lady Tiverton could never approve of a lady who was also a smuggler. Not that she was interested in her ladyship's approval, but the very notion of anyone of genteel birth learning of her activities made her suddenly queasy.

Bucksted approached her. "It is no wonder you have grown pale," he murmured into her ear. "I suggest that the next time you converse with Lady Tiverton, you keep your arguments confined to the merits of Mozart or Handel rather than the heinous policies of a Robespierre or Marat."

She couldn't tell him she wasn't thinking of politics at all, but of smuggling. "I'm sure you are right," she murmured, averting her gaze. Her thoughts had grown so full of her weekly adventures to Broomhill with Martin Fieldstone that she had lost all interest in debating the sufferings of the poor. Never before, not until this very moment, had she experienced even a moment's distress about her decision to take up smuggling to help the poor. Yet, somehow, the evening's conversation seemed to be triggering her conscience.

She was safe enough from anyone knowing the truth, of that she was certain. Martin, who had been smuggling with her from the beginning, was as close as an oyster. He would never tell tales of their adventures. No one else, save one of Martin's stable-boys, knew her secret, not even her sisters to whom she generally revealed every thought.

She stole a glance at Bucksted who was watching her carefully and her cheeks grew warmer still. She already knew enough of his general opinions to realize he would never understand that she had turned to smuggling to solve the financial dilemma her father's untimely death had left behind. If Bucksted was so disapproving of her political opinions, which were mere ideas presented in the safety of a drawing room, what would he think if he knew she was actually engaged in bringing French contraband into Kent as frequently as once, and sometimes twice, a week? He would likely go off in a fit of apoplexy!

How muddled everything seemed now, and so very complicated. A few hours earlier, her world had made perfect sense to her, and every action had had an adequate justification. Everything seemed so simple until . . . She glanced up at Bucksted and realized with a start that everything had seemed so simple until he had kissed her! Whatever could be the meaning of this!

He caught her elbow gently in his hand. "Will you take a turn about the gardens with me?" he whispered. "At least then I can keep you out of mischief, and we might manage to *appear* as though we are very much in love."

Eleanor blinked and strove to reorder her thoughts. She had a part to play in tonight's drama, to pretend to be in love with Bucksted so that Lady Tiverton would be properly humbugged. For the sake, then, of her agreement with him, she took a deep breath and set aside every unhappy thought of her current nocturnal activities.

"I shall do my best," she responded firmly. She permitted him to wrap his arm about hers, and for the sake of their ruse, she leaned close to him and smiled brilliantly up into his face.

This amused him so much that his cheeks began crinkling as he tried not to smile. The moment his back was to Lady Tiverton, however, he grinned hugely, which had the happy effect of ending the terrible tension that had kept Eleanor's chest in a tight grip for the past several minutes.

Once they crossed the threshold of the doors leading into the long gallery, he observed, "Now that I am coming to know you better, I begin to realize how unhappy you must have been these many months and more."

She glanced up at him. "I was," she responded plainly, but added, "However, I must say, now that I am not betrothed to you, I vow I don't think you so very bad a fellow. Besides, I was at fault in keeping my peace. Had I been more forthcoming, you would have learned of my true opinions long before tonight; then you would likely have jilted me!"

"Do you mean this by way of consolation, hoping to make me feel better about the situation?"

"Of course. I was very stupid to have accepted the offer of your hand."

"You are not considering! Whatever my opinion of you *might* have become, I couldn't have ended our betrothal. The bounds of our society are very clear in that regard."

"That is another flaw I think ought to be rectified. If a man offers for a lady, then discovers she is a complete simpleton or horridly ambitious and has no *feeling* for the gentleman at all, why should he be bound to a set of marriage documents? It is against all reason!"

He peered down at her as though seeing her for the first time. "You were mistaken when you spoke earlier. You *are* a radical."

At that, she could only laugh. "Fair and far off the mark, I assure you. I only think our society ought to be more sensible and more generous—hardly radical notions."

"Yes, but it is in your *application* of these *notions* that you transgress the established order. Your mother let it slip earlier today that the gentlemen hereabouts don't favor you all that much. I begin to understand why."

She was not the least offended. "I have too much spirit for them. Papa always said so, and I don't doubt right now you would agree." She sighed. "Sometimes I wish I'd been born a man. Were I such, how much I should champion the poor and work to change the laws of the land. We live in extraordinary times, don't you agree? In the past twenty years, and a little more, we have witnessed a revolution in France—albeit a horrendous one—that literally wiped a monarchy off the face of the earth. And, in addition, the Colonies formed a government never before heard of except in a few ancient theories. Do you think it so wrong of me to believe that England could benefit from at least one or two small changes?"

"You will be labeled a Jacobin if you are not careful!" he retorted. "Whatever can you be thinking to say such things? Already there have been bread riots in different parts of the country. The government won't tolerate such displays with much compassion, nor for very long."

"I don't approve of rioting."

"Now you astound me!"

She frowned at him. "And you, sir, seem determined to misunderstand me. Why wouldn't I oppose rioting when innocent people are always hurt?"

Apparently, he did not disapprove of her opinion in this regard and remained silent. He guided her along the graveled paths where the fragrance of roses was heavily in the air. The gardens off the main receiving room had been designed in a formal manner, in diamond parterres with a white rose tree in the center of each. The low hedges of boxwood were kept neatly trimmed, and the wide pathways were perfect for strolling because the delicate fabrics of the ladies' gowns could move along unobstructed.

Eleanor felt strangely at ease with Bucksted as they walked beneath a half-moon. The entire garden was hemmed in by tall, thick hedges, and only a wisp of a cool, evening breeze was able to steal among the roses. The temperature was perfectly comfortable for her.

As her thoughts rummaged through the discussion of the last few minutes, she finally said, "I could never wed a man who was callous to the sufferings of the poor."

"Ah," he murmured. "I take it that is how you see me?"

"Of course."

"Given all that I have learned of you this evening, I am not surprised."

"You aren't angry then?"

"No. We simply disagree, but I assure you I am not entirely heartless."

She wished that were true, as much for his sake as for hers. Were he not so coldhearted, she felt she might not object to marrying him and even thought in some ways she might like the prospect. At the same time, she felt sorry for him. She believed he had lived so privileged a life that he had no real perspective on what it was to suffer.

Her thoughts drifted to her father and his enormous heart. Was there ever a man more loving, more sensitive to the sufferings of others than her dear parent?

She wiped a stray tear from her cheek.

"Here! Here! What is this?" Bucksted exclaimed. He paused in midstride and caught her chin with his gloved finger. "What have I done now to have brought tears to your eyes? I promise you I have been trying very hard not to offend you, and I certainly never meant to overset you."

She shook her head. "I was thinking of Papa." Her voice broke, and a fresh wave of tears tracked down her cheeks.

"My poor child," he murmured. "I knew your father a little, for he was used to come to Whitehaven often and argue Papa out of another hundred pounds—for the poor, of course."

She laughed a very watery laugh. "Of course. He was always doing so. He said that whenever any of the genteel families saw him coming they would take to their sickbeds as quick as the cat could lick her ear!"

"My father didn't mind. He enjoyed Sir Henry's company, prodigiously."

"Papa had such a delightful sense of humor and was always . . . giving his last shilling to . . ." Her throat ached.

"To the poor?"

"Yes," she squeaked hoarsely.

Her face crumpled up, and he drew her into a tight embrace. "I never meant to make you miserable," he said into her hair. "I meant only good by offering for you. I'm sorry, Nellie. But I begin to wonder if any man could measure up to your father's virtues. From what you tell me, he appears to have been a saint."

She felt suddenly as though she could cry for years, and indeed, one or two sobs did escape her. How strange to think that only this morning she was enumerating Bucksted's faults and here he was wrapping her up in his arms and making her feel safer than she had felt in the past twelvemonth since her father's death.

"There, there," he murmured against her hair, his lips brushing her forehead.

"I've made a mull of everything," she moaned.

"Not everything," he returned.

"Yes, I have," she reiterated, drawing back from him. She pulled a kerchief from her pocket and blew her nose. "I am no saint, like my father. I've jilted you, and now we must pretend to be in love. And . . . and I've done other things." For the barest moment, she wanted to confess that she'd become a smuggler since her father died. The very notion, however, of how disapproving, of how *shocked* he would look, kept her tongue immobile. Besides, no good could possibly come of making a clean breast of something so horrendous. She continued therefore, "And . . . and I gravely fear that I have made an enemy of Lady Tiverton."

He smiled and thumbed her cheek. "As to that, I know for a fact she likes spirited young women, for she has always been one herself. But you might do well not to express your opinions quite so vehemently, at least for the remainder of the evening."

She chuckled and blew her nose again. "I will try."

"I begin to understand you a little, I think. Well, then, what shall we do now, my lady mischief?"

"I don't know. Mayhap I should have been drowned at birth."

He chuckled. "What a wretched thing to say. Besides, your opinions do you much honor, even if your timing is atrocious and your choice of words abominable. We would all benefit from exhibiting a greater kindness to those in need."

"You are being very kind to me just now, and I do thank you, Bucksted."

They had reached the yew arch which led to another portion of the garden, but he did not draw her through. Instead, he turned to her and whispered, "Lady Tiverton is standing in the shadows of the draperies and believes we cannot see her. No, no pray do not glance her direction. I think she may be spying on us, trying to determine for herself whether or not we are a love match. This would be an excellent opportunity to exhibit our *fondness* for one another that she might make a good report to the gabblemongers on our behalf."

He touched her chin with his gloved finger and a shiver went down her neck.

She looked into his eyes, which were shadowed but glittered in the faint moonlight.

"I suppose we shouldn't forgo the moment since who knows when another shall come our way."

"I was thinking the very same thing."

She tilted her head slightly. "Do you know how very handsome you are?"

He seemed surprised. "Thank you, Nellie. That was a lovely compliment."

She smiled. "You are used to hearing as much, aren't you?"

"Not from my unbetrothed, I'm not."

She giggled. Her heart felt light again and she found she was enjoying his gentle banter very much.

"I don't think it will be necessary that I kiss you again. I daresay that were I just to lean toward you thus"—his lips brushed the side of her mouth—"it would appear that I was kissing you indeed."

She felt frozen by the pleasure his lips were giving her, for they were ever so slowly making a path up her cheek and his breath was warm against her skin.

"Oh," she murmured. She was tingling all over suddenly and her mouth had fallen agape because she couldn't seem to drag enough air into her lungs.

When his lips were teasing her earlobe she found that her hand wished to be about his neck, and so it was! How extraordinary!

She had never been enticed in such a manner before, yet why was Bucksted going to such lengths and all for Lady Tiverton?

She took the opportunity to glance toward the window. No one was there.

"We are safe," she murmured. "She is gone."

"Who is gone?" he asked nonsensically.

"What do you mean, 'who'?" She drew back from him. His expression was hazy. "Lady Tiverton, of course."

A crooked smile touched his lips. "Oh, *her,*" he murmured.

She took a step backward. "Were you *tricking* me?" she asked, stunned at the very possibility of it.

He chuckled. "No, indeed I wasn't. I promise you. She was there, otherwise I would not have accosted you."

She narrowed her eyes at him. "You have an odd look about you, my lord. I begin to distrust you."

"Not in a bad way, I hope?" he inquired.

She couldn't help herself. She chuckled. He was flirting with her, quite audaciously, and she was enjoying it.

She wondered about him as he began guiding her back to the house. Was there more to him than she had first supposed? She knew his political sentiments were diametrically opposed to her own, yet he had shown much kindness toward her just now in comforting her.

She said, "Tomorrow, I intend to make a round of visits to some of the sick and indigent of the parish as my father was wont to do when he was alive. Would you care to accompany me?"

He glanced down at her, his brows raised. "Very much so," he responded promptly.

She was pleased. "Excellent. Can you be here by eleven? We could order a nuncheon at the Drake and Fig if you like."

* * *

The next day, Lord Bucksted arrived in the stableyard of Hartslip Manor promptly at eleven. He watched Eleanor inspect a very large basket strapped to the back of what must have been at one time her father's curricle. A stableboy held the horses.

She did not at first see him, and quite took his breath away in a costume that would have been the envy of the most fashionable ladies of Mayfair. She wore a sky blue poke bonnet of gathered silk, lined with white silk under the brim, which set to advantage her shiny black curls presently arranged to perfection about her face. A long pheasant's feather curled from the crown to drape over the edge of the bonnet's brim. Her gown was of a white muslin embroidered in yellow flowers about the hem, over which she wore a cutaway blue silk pelisse folded back at the high waist with pearlized buttons. She presented a picture of summery perfection.

She heard the sounds of his horse's hoofbeats and turned toward him. She cast a gaze of swift appraisal over his chestnut's lines and nodded in approval. "A fine hack," she stated admiringly.

He started. His fine "hack" had imperial lines going back three centuries and had cost his father a fortune. "Thank you," he murmured.

"Jake," she called to the groom, "his lordship and I shall be leaving immediately. You may take his horse to the stables." She turned toward Bucksted, "And don't worry. Jake has an excellent touch with horseflesh."

Bucksted turned to look at the stableboy who was eyeing his mount with obvious admiration. "I have every confidence in your man," he said. He then dismounted, turned his horse over to the groom, and greeted his "betrothed" with a polite, "Good morning."

"It is a beautiful morning, isn't it?" she returned with a soft smile.

As he assisted her in getting into the curricle, he noted she smelled wonderfully of lavender.

"Did you sleep well?" he inquired, as he settled himself next to her. She already had the reins in hand and was entwining them properly about her fingers, when he realized she meant to drive the curricle herself.

He found himself amused. He was himself quite handy with the ribbons and had assumed he would be doing the driving. Would she never cease to surprise him?

"I slept very well, thank you," she said. To Jake, she called out, "You may let go their heads." Once the horses were liberated, she slapped the reins with considerable authority. "And how did you sleep?" she inquired politely.

"Quite well. Your grays are nicely matched."

"They were my father's. I hope you don't mind that I am driving. I thought, since I was familiar with this part of the county, and in particular the places I wished to take you, it would be logical for me to handle the reins."

Once in the lane, the curricle settled into an easy motion as the grays found their stride.

"You've nice, light hands," he commented.

"Thank you. Martin, that is, Mr. Fieldstone, tells me you are a notable whip, so I accept your compliment with pleasure."

"Fieldstone. The name sounds familiar," he said. "Does he live in the vicinity?"

"Three miles to the southwest of Hartslip. His father owns a fine property called Chidding Moot."

"Isn't that the house known for its moat and castellated appearance?"

"The very one."

"Then I have met the senior Mr. Fieldstone, once I believe, at Whitehaven."

"He's a bristly old fellow with shockingly white hair."

"Ah. I recall him very well, now. He enjoys his snuff."

Eleanor knew this to be quite true and said so, then added, "Martin and I grew up together, the very best of friends. I am nearly as close to him as I am to my sisters." She glanced at him. "Do you know this country at all, to the south?"

"Not a bit," he said. "Father's acquaintances are much farther north and to the east." He looked up at the sky, holding his hat down a little. "It is a lovely day, isn't? Such a relief from the constant clouds of coal smoke in London. I find I can actually breathe with considerable ease."

"I enjoyed London during my two seasons before Papa died," she responded. "But it was springtime, and it rained so frequently that even when the smoke threatened to overtake the city, a storm could be trusted to wash away all evidence of it during the next day or so. I imagine summer is not in the least a pleasant time in the Metropolis."

"There is much sickness," he said. "And anyone with a grain of sense will not linger past the end of June."

"Then it is with great pity I think of those who cannot leave at all."

She took a bend in the lane with considerable skill. He shifted his gaze to her and frowned. He felt all his former pique returning, regardless of how beautiful her profile was of the moment. He could not mistake the nature of her remark, or that she was pointing out to him, yet again, how very much at fault he was for not considering the plight of those less fortunate than himself with every other waking moment.

He crossed his arms over his chest, for he thought he understood what she intended by taking him on a trip about the countryside—she meant to educate him. He tapped his foot and pinched his lips together. He wondered when her lectures would begin.

She made no effort, however, to instruct him verbally. She merely pointed out the various farms and villages they traversed as the curricle crisscrossed the lanes leading to, from, and about the King's Highway in a five mile radius to the south of Hartslip Manor. In the process, he saw a number of ramshackle homes, which she said little about except to inform him as to the identity of the inhabitants. Despite his wish to think ill of her, he was impressed with her knowledge of the neighborhood.

Heading north again, a fine country house came into view, a beautiful eighteenth-century brick abode settled on an easy rise and overlooking the River Medway.

"Ah, Lord Westwell's residence," he stated with much satisfaction.

"It is lovely, isn't it?"

"Very much so," he responded. "I have been a friend to Miss Westwell for some time. Do you know her?" His thoughts were full of Daphne and her confessions of love.

"Only a very little. We do not share the same interests, and she is somewhat removed in station."

He smiled to himself. At the moment he was not well disposed toward the philanthropic zealot seated next to him, and the very thought of Miss Westwell soothed his masculine pride. Ah, beautiful, adoring Daphne. How much he began to enjoy the prospect of courting her in earnest, once this wretched betrothal was at an end.

He gave himself, therefore, to delighting in the verdant countryside and commented that however many hovels they had encountered during the trip, prosperity had clearly found its way into this portion of the valley.

Eleanor, however, would have none of it.

"Papa would take you to task for saying such a thing, especially when he made the rounds of the local ale houses and inns every week to listen to the concerns of the people. When the price of grain soared, he and Lord Westwell paid the difference to every baker in a ten-mile radius and made certain that the price for every loaf did not exceed what was reasonable. I cannot tell you how many families blessed these men for their efforts, and as far as I am concerned, if there is one suffering family, it is one too many!"

He had never before heard such a speech fall from the lips of a female. Mostly, they spoke of the latest fashions or the most recent scandalous *on dits*. He stared at her as the curricle rolled along the graveled road.

"I'm not certain, Eleanor, that I can in any manner approve of such interference. These very acts create a dependency that cannot be soon overcome. My father contributes to the poor relief generously, but these funds are managed by the government. By way of argument, I put to you, therefore, what would happen if Lord Westwell were to suffer some reverse of fortune or in any other way be unable to continue his support of all these people who have grown dependent upon him? They would be better served finding other means of providing for themselves and their loved ones than to risk depending exclusively on the benevolence of a neighbor."

Eleanor let the reins go a little slack and the horses slowed their pace. They were but a quarter-mile from the village of Three Ashes and the Drake and Fig Inn where they had earlier ordered a nuncheon. She said softly, "I should like to think that some person of noble heart would rise up to take Lord Westwell's place. When I learned you were the new owner of Hartslip and that your father's own generosity was widely acknowledged, I had hoped *you* would take my father's place. Indeed, I had depended upon it, so you may imagine how greatly shocked I was to discover that your philosophies were so far removed from his and, therefore, my own."

He eyed her soberly. He was beyond mere feelings of pique. He was not so much angry with her as despondent that they had both entered upon a betrothal under such equally impossibly met expectations. "I am sorry, then," he said, not unkindly. "If these are indeed your sentiments, then you must have been more deeply distressed regarding our betrothal than I can possibly comprehend."

He saw her jaw work as she gave the reins a slap. He realized she was close to tears. He reached over and gave her arm a squeeze. She glanced at him and smiled, albeit falteringly.

She said nothing more until the horses had been stabled and they were both sitting across from one another, partaking of the inn's fare.

Undoubtedly because it was understood that the future Marquess of Chalvington would be enjoying his nuncheon at the inn, a great deal of effort had been made in preparing the meal. The roast chicken was succulent, the thin slices of ham rich with flavor, the tomatoes delicious, the cucumber crisp, and the potatoes dripping with butter. A bottle of East India Madeira accompanied the feast.

Eleanor was thoroughly disappointed in the morning's journey. She realized now that she had been hoping for something completely unattainable. She had wanted Bucksted not only to view the efforts of her father and Lord Westwell, but to approve of them and to begin to embrace the possibility of what one man, one person, could accomplish given a little effort, commitment and vision.

Obviously, Lord Bucksted saw nothing to embrace. She had witnessed little in his expression or in his words that indicated he had been moved by her father's and Lord Westwell's deeds. Quite the contrary—he had disapproved of how they had gone about the business.

She wondered if she could ever persuade Bucksted to a different view, or any man for that matter. She was not experienced with men and was, therefore, woefully lacking in the arts which came more naturally to Margaret and Kitty, both of whom had a score of beaux, or even to Daphne Westwell who had been the reigning Beauty since times out of mind.

Daphne was the one who was supposed to make a brilliant match, and so it was that when the Earl of Bucksted, future Marquess of Chalvington, offered not for Daphne but for the countrified Miss Marigate of Hartslip Manor, the entire valley had been in a state a shock for several weeks.

"Bucksted," she stated quietly after the meal and the wine had mellowed her a little, "I wish to apologize."

His brow grew furrowed as he held the glass of Madeira between long fingers. "And what is it for which you are apologizing?"

She leaned forward and met his gaze squarely. "For not knowing how to get on with you. Papa was forever telling me that my manners, my speech were far too blunt and opinionated to be in any degree suitable to society. At the time, probably because he was one of my dearest companions, along with Martin, I had no interest in society. I loved my rather insular occupations by his side, whether we were going about the countryside, as I have with you today, or designing the next thousand square feet of garden at Hartslip."

She watched Bucksted's expression soften a little.

He said, "I must confess that my father was surprised when I offered for you. He even queried quite gently whether I believed myself sufficiently acquainted with you to comprehend whether or not you would make me a *suitable* bride. Do you know what I told him?" She saw that a faint glint of amusement had entered his eyes.

She could not help but smile in response, for she suspected what was to follow. "I think I could hazard a guess, but tell me anyway."

He chuckled softly. "I told him I had already done much to properly instruct you and that you were showing great promise."

"Goodness!" she whispered, covering the lower part of her face with both hands.

"I prated on and on about how conformable you were." He smiled crookedly and sipped his wine. He added, "Yes, about as conformable as a fox staring at a row of sleeping chickens and told not to pounce," he declared, his eyes dancing.

"Oh, Bucksted! It is all too abominable! Your father *knew* me—at least a little—for he came to visit often at Hartslip in the last year before Papa died. He used to call me a minx and pinch my cheeks."

"But you deceived me, silly girl. You would sit ever so politely on your mother's sofa and barely lift your eyes to me."

"Oh, lord, I did, didn't I? I am ever so sorry. By the time you had paid us a second morning visit, I knew the betrothal was a monstrous mistake, but how could I disappoint my family when our need was so very great? Yet, I should have said something then. Indeed, I should have. How will you ever forgive me?" Before he could answer this question, she added, "Me! Conformable!"

She could no longer contain the laughter that strained in her chest. She chuckled, laughed, giggled, and trilled until her sides ached. He joined her, and as together they shared the joke of their betrothal, much of the tension between them fled the dining parlor.

In the end, when she was wiping her cheeks and most of his chuckles had escaped, he said, "Dear God, you must have thought me a pompous, arrogant fool."

"I did. Do you recall the subject upon which you were instructing me during that second visit?"

"Not precisely," he said.

"How to address one's servants in the household of a Peer. My mother kept choking on her ratafia. She was moment by moment in the severest anxiety that I would betray my true opinions to you and thereby ruin the most brilliant match of Medway Valley."

"I cannot conceive how I came to behave like such a coxcomb!"

She sat back in her chair. He did the same. After a moment, she said, "I had not meant to give you offense by taking you about our countryside. But I wanted you to see the effects that the moderate labor of two, quite well-fortuned men could have on a neighborhood."

"*You* were attempting to instruct *me,* this time."

"Yes, in my wholly inadequate way."

"Does the whole of the present effort fall upon Westwell then?"

She felt her cheeks warm a little. "Only in part. I have made it my mission to continue Papa's work, through a number of, er, charitable events." How could she ever tell him how it was that she had been able, in the intervening year since her father's death, to continue paying her father's support of many of the destitute poor?

She had told Westwell that her father had left her an annuity from which she made her contributions, but this was only a half-truth. He had left an annuity for the poor, but it was so small a portion as to be negligible. Shortly afterward, she had taken matters into her own hands and provided the balance for the past eleven months through her smuggling efforts with Martin.

When Bucksted offered for her, she had believed with all her heart that the heavens had intervened to solve the dilemma of how to meet the needs of their joint charity without engaging in smuggling. After all, it was only a matter of time before the illegal nature of her commerce was discovered by the excisemen who patrolled the coasts, then where would she be? Or Martin? Caught and tried for their crimes, or worse, killed!

Lord Bucksted's voice intruded. "Nellie, is something amiss? You've grown very quiet, and you have an unusually serious expression on your face."

She took a deep breath. There it was again, an overwhelming desire to confess the truth to him. Yet, she could not. He would never understand, not in a thousand years.

She responded, "I have wished, from the very day Papa passed away, that there would be some way to do more than I am at present able to accomplish." She smiled falteringly. "Though I must say, the entire situation is not hopeless, for Papa left an annuity on behalf of the poor."

He frowned at that. "I don't understand. Your family has barely two shillings to rub together, and yet he left an annuity for the poor?"

"It is a very small one."

He was frowning into his wine and trying to make sense of what she was telling him. "So you have been busy raising donations and the like?"

She nodded, trusting he would not probe further. Anyone with a grain of sense, who could estimate what local donations were likely to be, or what a charitable fair might reap on behalf of the organizing body, would soon realize that there was a discrepancy between the funds that were collected and the funds disbursed.

He gave a small shrug. "Then I can only presume you are rather successful at your endeavors."

She smiled and hoped he didn't notice how nervous she suddenly felt. "I like to think so."

He still wore a frown, but in the end appeared to believe her Banbury tale. "Well," he said, "it is impressive. I will admit at least that much. Yet, I still hold that to allow anyone to become dependent in such circumstances can only result in future problems."

Eleanor thought of her own difficulties and realized that to a degree she was suffering just the sort of dilemma he was predicting. On the other hand, she saw no other solution. If a wage is frozen, if a man works fourteen hours a day, six days a week, and cannot possibly earn more, if the price of grain rises to astronomical levels, how does that man continue to feed his family?

She posed the question to him. He held her gaze for a long moment then shook his head. "I fear I have no answer."

"Come," she said, rising to her feet and retying the ribbons of her bonnet. "There is something I wish to show you."

He eyed her askance. "Do you risk the gentle nature of our present discourse by doing so?"

She smiled as she took his arm. "Yes, I greatly fear I do, but I still think you will benefit by it."

He grimaced. "I daresay you are probably right. Well, my lady mischief . . . lead on."

Four

The journey required nearly an hour's travel north and northeast during which time Bucksted took the reins. Eleanor was impressed with his precision and control, and told him as much though adding that Martin had already boasted of his prowess sufficiently as to forewarn her that she was in the presence of a complete Nonesuch.

He thanked her for the compliment, but his thoughts appeared to be drawn inward since he seemed disinclined to converse. She left him, therefore, to his ruminations and instead enjoyed the passing countryside, trying to view the familiar terrain from a stranger's eye. What was not beautiful about Kent? she marveled. The June sunshine beat warmly down on the rolling hills of the Weald. Oak woods, which had once been dense forests flowing for miles and miles across the landscape, now lived in lovely islands, dotting the edges of farms and estates in pollarded majesty. Oasthouses gave a quirky, almost playful aspect to the surrounding vista with their conical roofs and tilted tops. Cherry orchards and hopfields abounded.

"We are nearing my father's boundaries," he stated, as they made a wide-sweeping bend in the highway. "There." He gestured with a nod of his chin.

"I know," she murmured. "Do you see the lane on the left? Turn there, if you please."

The rutted road backed the bottom of a rather steep hill thickly wooded with oak, beech, and sycamore.

"I have never been along this track before. What is it you wish to show me?"

"A family with whom I've become acquainted over the past year—the Keynes. I wonder if you know them or have seen them in the village of Glynde Green, north of here?"

"Keynes. The name is not familiar to me."

A mile from the highway, beyond a rambling hedge of bramble, rose, privet, and blackthorn, a low-roofed cottage came into view. In the yard, a horde of children, some very young, were at play, surrounding Mrs. Keynes who held a babe on her lap. Mrs. Keynes was shelling peas and singing. Everything about the dwelling and surrounding land had a tumbledown appearance. "The view is somewhat enchanting in a rustic manner, but what on earth is that smell?" he murmured.

"The lands are marshy, hereabouts. They should have been drained centuries ago. The family is afflicted quite regularly with the ague, which has always led me to believe the cause must be associated with the perpetual damp of the place."

Once Eleanor was recognized as one of the occupants of the carriage, the children began to race merrily toward her, calling out her name. "Miss Marigate! Miss Marigate!"

There was scarcely one with a healthy pallor among them, but Eleanor did not let that keep her from catching up little India in her arms and leading them all to the back of the curricle. She began unloading an almost endless supply of foodstuffs and clothing, which the children gathered up as by habit and began carrying back to their mother.

When the basket was empty, Eleanor followed them to the place where their mother remained seated on an old stump. "How do you go on, Mrs. Keynes?"

"Very, well, oy thank you, Miss Marigate."

"As you can see, the good vicar of Mares End has once more had an excess of donations. I hope you can make use of them."

She knew Bucksted was staring at her for the whisker she had just told. The vicar of Mares End had nothing to do with the largess that came from her own home.

"Thankee, Miss Marigate. I'll sort through it all a bit later. Thankee."

Eleanor turned to Lord Bucksted, who had marched along at her left elbow. "May I present Lord Bucksted? Lord Bucksted, Mrs. Keynes."

"Oh, me lord!" she cried, blinking rapidly, her cheeks firing up with all manner of color. Eleanor thought she knew the reason, but had no intention of revealing to Bucksted that her husband was in the habit of poaching off Chalvington's Home Wood.

He was polite. "How do you do, ma'am? You have a lively, handsome brood about you."

"Thankee, they was all born with quite a bit o' spirit."

One of the youngest, too young to comprehend Bucksted's consequence, tugged on the tails of his coat and lifted his arms up to him. Eleanor was delighted by Bucksted's predicament, for surely the august and quite fastidious heir to the Marquess of Chalvington had no wish to be dirtied by a poor man's brat. She still held young India in her arms and merely watched to see precisely how he would handle the unprecedented event.

"Ahoy, there, little one!" he cried, turning to look down at the boy. In quite an ingenuous manner, he scooped up the little fellow, who was all freckled and toothy, and asked to know his name. Eleanor was stunned. Never in a trillion years would she have thought Bucksted likely to pick up the child, certainly not with such obvious enthusiasm.

"Fwed," the child responded. "I wike yer 'orses."

"Ah, but they are not my horses, they belong to Miss Marigate."

"I want to go fer a wide," he stated solemnly.

This, of course, brought several supplicants stating the same, longed-for wish. Bucksted said, "I'm afraid the curricle is not mine, either. If you wish for a ride, you must ask Miss Marigate."

Eleanor smiled. "Of course you may, so long as John handles the ribbons. Is he here?"

The question did not need to be answered, for the moment she mentioned John, a strong, capable lad of fourteen, two of the older boys were off and running in the direction of a slope of ground which led to a stream at which John fished daily for trout in order to help feed the family. They shouted his name almost as often as their quick feet slapped the earth.

"May I offer ye a cup o' tea?" Mrs. Keynes asked.

"We would be delighted, though we can't stay long," Eleanor responded.

"O' course, ye cannot," she said. "Fer ye have a ball tonight, if I do not mistake the matter." She then winked and grinned.

Eleanor noted that poor Mrs. Keynes had lost yet another tooth. Having borne so many children without the benefit of proper nutrition was costing the young woman, at the very least, her teeth. Regardless, it was clear even to the most undiscerning eye that she must at one time have been quite a beauty. She led the way into the drooping cottage.

Though India seemed content to remain in her arms, 'Fwed' was not interested in tea and demanded to be returned to the earth that he might not miss out on the carriage ride. Eleanor took up a chair by the door, and India leaned into her shoulder.

The house was neat as a pin and clean in every respect. Yet, all the scrubbing, dusting, and sweeping could not remove the smell of the earth and the musty air from the dwelling. Eleanor asked after each of Mrs. Keynes eleven children. She again encouraged the woman to keep the older girls and boys at their studies and to make certain, no matter what, that they continued their schooling.

"I know, I know," Mrs. Keynes said, shaking her head. " 'Tis 'ard, though, when the ague strikes, without warning, leaving even John trembling fer days and days. Still, 'e goes to school. 'E's that determined to do better fer himself. 'E talks all the time about draining the land like yer pa suggested times out o' mind."

"I know. I wish there was more I could do. Was Mr. Keynes unable to gain the support of Mr. Whiting?"

Her lips grew rather stiff. "Mr. Whiting wouldn't listen to 'is ideas even though more than forty acres could become good farmland."

"Well, I am sorry for that," Eleanor said. She asked politely whether or not the bees had been producing as much honey as the Keynes had hoped. After these questions had been answered, and Mrs. Keynes had inquired equally as politely after the health of Eleanor's own mother and sisters, Eleanor finished the last of her tea and rose to her feet. Through the whole of the conversation, India had clung to her in a sweet manner. Holding the child close, she wished Mrs. Keynes well and led the way from the house. She entered the yard in time to see John, quite in his element, snapping the whip and guiding the curricle back to the dwelling.

He was grinning from ear to ear as he hopped down lightly and held the horses' heads until each of his siblings had alighted safely. Afterward, he thanked her for the rare treat, then begged pardon, but said he had to get back to his fishing. He didn't have near enough for dinner to feed everyone yet. He had welts on his face and arms from mosquito bites.

Only as Eleanor was about to climb aboard the curricle did India finally release her. "Good-bye my little precious. Enjoy your whistle. Martin made it especially for you."

Her mother whispered to her, and India said, "Thankee, Miss Mewwygate."

The drive back to Hartslip Manor was a subdued one.

"You are a very generous woman," Bucksted said, after a time.

"I do what I can, but my resources are not at all—"

"I didn't mean that precisely. I was referring to your heart."

She glanced at him, startled. He met her gaze, then smiled ruefully. "Oh, don't stare at me as though you are shocked my horns have momentarily disappeared. I can be *human* on occasion."

"I—that is not what I was thinking. I was merely surprised that you complimented me, especially when I have been given to feeling that you despised me."

He seemed a little dumbfounded. "I don't *despise* you," he argued. "Whatever made you think that?"

"All your lectures. By the time your last visit ended, I was certain you were convinced I was an imbecile. In addition, I am persuaded you do not at all approve of my philanthropic tendencies."

He chuckled. "You do not have *tendencies* of any kind. You have passions."

A smile twisted the corners of her mouth. "I believe you are right on that score, which only makes it the more alarming that you ever thought to offer for me."

"The question, however, remains, do you still despise me as thoroughly as you did yesterday?" he asked.

She heard the uncertain tone in his voice. "Well," she began slowly, knowing full well he was referring to her harsh reading of his character yesterday, "I must say I can hardly think entirely bad of a fellow who would pick up Fred as you did today. I honor you for that, Bucksted. The children are without any family to help them in their troubles or, as today, to offer a little kindness and affection. All are gone. Several relatives have died, and the rest have emigrated to the Colonies."

"Then I am sorry for them, indeed."

"Would you be willing to speak with your father about the land that needs to be drained? Mr. Whiting, whom Mr. Keyne's had hoped to persuade to make the improvements, is your father's tenant."

"I am aware of that fact so now I must ask you, is that why you wished me to see the property?"

"Yes," she stated baldly. "Though I promise you, Mr. Keynes would be aghast if he knew I had taken up his cause."

"I shall speak with Father, but I am beginning to think, Miss Marigate, that it is a very good thing you jilted me. For after only two days in your company, I am already aware of how much labor you would thrust on me, were I to wed you." Since he delivered this speech with a smile which gave the nicest twinkle to his hazel eyes, Eleanor merely chuckled and passed the reins to him.

"Spring 'em," she said. "Or I shall not have sufficient time to dress for our first betrothal ball."

Eleanor dressed for the ball with great care. Lord Bucksted had in the end become such an agreeable companion, as well as a man willing to champion her cause with his father, that she found herself more than desirous of performing well during the course of the evening, as much for his sake as for his parents'.

She had been to Whitehaven once, about two months ago, as a result of having become betrothed to Bucksted. Lord Chalvington had eyed her curiously over the course of a princely dinner in which there had been no less than three complete removes. He had been clearly astonished by her change in demeanor, but to his credit said not a word. He had come to know her well over the years and, just as she had told Bucksted, was used to pinching her cheek and calling her a minx because of her outspoken opinions and lively manners. She had endured the dinner that evening with flaming cheeks, having felt as though she'd been caught in a terrible whisker. Lady Chalvington had been less well known to her, yet was kindness itself in embracing her as a future daughter-in-law.

Her maid, Alice, arranged her black curls in a long Grecian flow, beginning at the crown of her head and extending down the back to end in waves just past her shoulders. A spiraling gold band held her hair in segments reminiscent of the ancient world's style.

Her gown was of white silk and tulle. The neckline rose to a frilly ruff at the back of her neck and descended to a lovely décolleté across the bodice. The style was made high in the waist in the Empire fashion popularized by Napoleon's Empress Josephine. A demitrain embroidered in gold floss gave the gown the elegance the evening's event required. From over her elbows, a red silk shawl draped low behind her, a fashionable accessory which the prevailing trend of the day required to be worn with as much *éclat* as a woman could possibly manage. To carry a shawl well was the mark of a true lady of fashion.

Both her sisters exclaimed over her elegance and beauty. Kitty summed up her feelings. "You *look* like a countess!" she cried.

Eleanor, for all her purpose of deceiving everyone during the course of the evening, still could not help but be pleased by her sisters' approval of her. When her mother clapped her hands in delight, her confidence soared and she began to feel she could indeed carry the day.

The drive to Whitehaven, nine miles distant, required just

above an hour to accomplish since Fulbar, the head groom, had harnessed two pair of quick horses to the light traveling chaise and had instructed the leading postillion to spring 'em.

The highway was adequately maintained, so that only once or twice did Lady Marigate complain of being tossed around like a ball in a cricket match.

When the gates of the fine, old mansion were finally within view, Eleanor could not restrain a sensation of wonder.

Margaret's voice was hushed and awestruck as she breathed out, "And you are to be mistress of this one day? Oh, Nellie, what you could accomplish for the poor and infirm with such a resource as this!"

Maybe it was Margaret's words, or perhaps the sight of Whitehaven itself, but for a brief, powerful moment she knew something like real regret that she was not wedding Bucksted after all. She withheld a sigh as her mind reviewed any number of stupendous projects she could achieve as the Marchioness of Chalvington—a string of orphanages across the kingdom or the establishing of hospitals for the poor in every major city, or . . .

But what errant thoughts were these? She was not going to become Lord Bucksted's wife, and that was that. At the same time, she had every intention of continuing her father's work. She simply had to find some other means of doing so besides either wedding a fortune or continuing the smuggling trade.

The butler led them to an august chamber decorated with so much gilt that the glitter of it once again stunned Eleanor's eye. The formal withdrawing room was decorated *en suite* in crimson damask and trimmed in gold relief at every turn. The stately decor reflected the exalted rank of the inmates of the room. She was struck with the disparity between her somewhat humble home and Whitehaven. It was rumored that the Prince Regent himself often stayed the night at Whitehaven, *en route* to The Pavilion, his summer residence in Brighton.

Thoughts of the Prince, and of the magnificence of Lord Chalvington's home, took her mind to the path to Broomhill near Rye. In this moment, she felt like two separate people, one who longed for adventure and had found it with Martin in old oak casks and bolts of fine French cloth, and the other who might have become a marchioness and ruled over Whitehaven, had she exercised even a mite of sense and refused the temptation to become a smuggler.

A feeling very much like regret threatened her countenance, especially when she chanced at that moment to glance at Bucksted and to remember what it had been like to be held in his arms, to be kissed by him, and to be comforted by him. A real sense of misery grew into a knot in her chest. She felt deep within herself that she had erred, yet the die was cast, her lot was settled, and perhaps had been settled the night she and Martin had first traveled incognito to the coast.

She drew in a deep, steadying breath, promising herself that she would not dwell overly much on what she might have forsaken in rejecting Bucksted, and, instead, concentrated on the personages gathered in the drawing room.

Along with Lord and Lady Chalvington, as well as Lord Bucksted, two young men were present, both of whom were unfamiliar to Eleanor.

Once properly announced, Bucksted moved forward to make all the necessary introductions. A cousin, Mr. Punnett of Berkshire, was one of the men, and the other was a Major Etchingham of the Horse Guards, a son of one of Chalvington's closest friends. Lady Chalvington remained seated in a gilt and crimson damask chair near the fireplace, awaiting their approach.

The marquess immediately took Lady Marigate's arm and led her to a sofa, where he engaged her in conversation. Bucksted glanced down at Eleanor and smiled crookedly.

She was a little taken aback by the expression on his face. "Why are you smiling in that manner?" she asked quietly.

He chuckled, "Because both Etchingham and my cousin look like half-wits ogling you as they are. They have reminded me why it was I offered for you in the first place."

Eleanor felt a warmth rise up her cheeks. She was not used to such compliments. "What nonsense are you speaking now?"

"None, I assure you!" he exclaimed. "You cannot be bereft

of a dressing mirror, nor can you possibly be unaware that you are a diamond of the first water."

Eleanor was completely thrown out of stride. She had never thought of herself as a great beauty, and Bucksted's words were having the rather strange effect of causing her knees to wobble. "Th-thank you, I think!"

He only laughed. "Pray, let me present you to my mother who has been wishing to have a comfortable cose with you these many days and more."

Dinner was a lavish, extraordinary affair again served with three removes. Eleanor was grateful she had kept her stays tightened to only a moderate degree of discomfort, for it was a matter of politeness to partake of a fair sampling of the delights before her. There was pheasant, chicken, ham, roast beef, pigeon, and lamb. The broccoli, peas, turnips, cabbage, cauliflower, and potatoes were sautéed and covered in a variety of sauces. The bread smelled heavenly. Madeira flowed through the whole meal, and conversation was punctuated with expressions of delight and appreciation. Eleanor sat beside Lord Chalvington, and several times—perhaps more than she ought—took wine with him. By the time the meal was concluded, she felt giddy and more content than she had in a long, long time.

If once or twice, especially when Lord Chalvington told her for the fifth or sixth time how pleased he was that his son was marrying Sir Henry Marigate's daughter, she felt guilt ridden, the lively atmosphere at the table would not permit her spirits to remain low but for a few seconds at a time.

The subsequent ball transcended every childhood dream of magnificence and beauty. The ballroom at Whitehaven was even more lavish than the crimson and gilt receiving room. The walls were painted with scenes from Olympus, each trimmed with gilt molding. Eighteen broad steps led up to the ballroom and eighteen down so that everyone could make as grandiloquent an entrance as he or she pleased.

Five blazing chandeliers lit the massive chamber in a brilliant, glittering glow.

Eleanor stood beside Bucksted at the top landing, greeting

three hundred guests who arrived in a steady flow beginning at eight o'clock. She knew but a handful of personages, and those who were unknown to her ranged from the famous Beau Brummell, to a poet just rising in ascendancy by the name of Byron, to the famous patronesses of Almack's. Lady Cowper teased her gently by saying that come next Season, she would surely cast all the Mayfair beauties in the shade.

Eleanor approved of Lady Cowper's gentleness as well as her quiet beauty and the way she leaned up on tiptoe to place an unexpected kiss on Bucksted's cheek. She watched him blush with pleasure, and her heart felt warm and fiery. There was an easy camaraderie among Bucksted and many of his friends, a teasing warmth, which made her long in the oddest way to be admitted into his circle of acquaintances.

Her life in the country, though greatly satisfying, had been quite sheltered. Her father had not been one to visit back and forth among the great houses along the length of the Medway, and his obvious preference for privacy had been respected. Tonight, however, she was able to see quite well how much his hermitlike existence, apart from his philanthropic endeavors, had prevented his daughters from enjoying a much larger and more varied society than they had.

A dollop of sadness entered her enjoyment of the evening. Come Sunday, when she was no longer betrothed to Bucksted, these very acquaintances that were springing up like snowdrops in early spring, would vanish as quickly. How odd that, after all these years of believing she could only be content buried in her gardens at Hartslip or in solving the pressing difficulties of her community, she should discover within herself a need for society she had never experienced before. Odd, indeed!

"You seem distressed," Bucksted commented as he leaned close to her. "Did Mr. Hughes squeeze your hand too tightly?"

She glanced at him and chuckled. "No, indeed! And I do beg your pardon if my expression betrayed my thoughts. I shall not let it happen again."

"I wasn't lecturing you," he was quick to say.

She could see that his hazel eyes were full of teasing and mirth again. She caught her breath. Faith, but he was such a handsome creature, never more so than now, when his every feature was lit with a playfulness she was coming to understand was part of his nature. "I know you weren't lecturing me, goose-cap."

He laughed and introduced her to Sally Jersey, another of the Almack patronesses.

He did not bring up the subject again until they were dancing their first dance together, a waltz, and then not until their feet had come to an understanding of which foot would go where and when. A minute or two saw this essential goal accomplished, primarily because Bucksted was a strong, yet graceful dancer.

"What an easy partner you are!" she exclaimed.

"And you dance the waltz delightfully."

"Thank you. Mama hired a dancing master, a *very expensive* one, from London a few weeks past. He will be glad to know that I was able to learn something from his tutelage."

He smiled and turned her around and around, whirling her about the perimeter of the floor with ease. After one complete revolution beneath the five chandeliers, Eleanor began to relax in his arms. She was able to follow his lead to perfection and the sudden and surprising notion occurred to her that were the waltz to be the sole judge, they were a matched pair.

"What are you thinking now, my lady mischief?" he queried.

Her cheeks grew warm instantly, yet she did not prevaricate. "How well we dance together, or is this how every lady feels in your arms?" Her words, she decided, were the strangest choice and a heat began in her stomach that soon rose in a sweep up to her chest. A profound, yet not unpleasant, dizziness, assailed her.

His gaze grew very piercing of a sudden, and his clasp upon her hand and about her waist grew taut and anxious. "Why? How is it you feel?" he asked, pressing her.

She could hardly breathe. "Very dizzy," she responded, "as though my feet are hardly touching the floor."

"I have had no lady make such an admission to me, save you," he whispered. "Is this how you feel truly?"

"Yes," she responded breathlessly. "I suppose, however, it is merely because you mind your steps so well."

He chuckled softly. "You don't think it might be something else?" he inquired.

"I can't imagine what," she responded innocently.

"Can't you?"

"No." Would she ever regain her breath?

"I have an idea why it is so," he said.

"Oh? And what would that be?"

"You are beginning to be in love with me."

She blinked several times. "But I can't be," she said, her brow feeling pinched suddenly and her heart hammering against her ribs like a blacksmith shaping a flaming horseshoe. She was thoroughly frightened.

He merely laughed again. "Don't distress yourself, Eleanor. I am merely teasing you a little and flirting with you a lot. I don't suspect you of falling in love with me at all. What I think is my father gave you a great deal too much wine to drink, and you have not waltzed very frequently before tonight."

"O-o-o-h," she gushed. "You must be right. Of course you are right. I am so relieved. You've no idea!"

"Why? Would it be such a bad thing to tumble in love with me?" he asked.

She could see the hurt in his eyes, yet still, because too many novel and quite oversetting sensations were still rampaging over her nerves, she cried out, "Of course it would!"

Now she had offended him. "I see," he responded coolly.

"I didn't mean that, at least not in the way it sounded. You know very well that we are not suited to one another."

"I know you do not believe I am fit to be your husband."

She wanted to explain, to tell him that she was not thinking at all of the difference in their views but of other things, of her wretched, wretched adventures with Martin.

"Bucksted—" she began, searching in her mind for some way of making him understand without actually confessing her misdeeds, but at that moment the waltz ended and several gentlemen hurried up to her, demanding the next country dance.

He bowed to her as he moved away, a stiff motion that brought pleasant sensations to sit in a cold pool at the very bottom of her stomach. Would she never learn to mind her tongue in his presence? Why did he have to be so deuced handsome and so pleasant to dance with and so wonderful to kiss? Why was she feeling so confused?

Later, after her feet had begun to ache from so much time on the ballroom floor, she sat down to supper with Bucksted as was expected of her. She immediately apologized for her offensive words. "I didn't know what I was saying, Bucksted," she offered, covering his hand with her own. He glanced down at her gloved fingers and turned his hand over to take hers in a warm clasp.

"I appreciate your saying so, though I know very well that what you said was unfortunately very true." He held her gaze and forced her to consider her words. "We are not suited to one another."

How strange! There it was again, as she looked into his eyes! That odd, quirky sadness she had begun to feel earlier that evening at the thought that in but a few days she would see him no more.

"But neither of us shall say more on this subject, eh?" he concluded.

"Right," she responded promptly. "We can at least be excellent friends."

"Of course."

He was still holding her gaze. She felt mesmerized. The Madeira from dinner was still swirling about her head. Was it her imagination or was he leaning toward her?

"Hallo, Bucksted! And Miss Marigate!" a feminine voice called out.

Eleanor's attention was snapped away from Bucksted as she glanced sharply at the unwelcome intruder. "Miss Westwell!" Eleanor cried. "How do you do? Did you just now arrive?"

"Yes. You cannot imagine what happened! We broke a trace two miles from Glynde Green. We were late anyway because Papa had visitors from the town of Wartling regarding a canal proposal or some such thing, and wouldn't you know it—not a single carriage passed us to bring us hither. Our coachman had to walk all the way to Glynde Green in order to fetch a conveyance for us. In the end, he hired a rather sad-looking brougham to bring us the rest of the way."

"I am very sorry for you," she said.

Daphne's attention turned to Bucksted. "My Lord Bucksted," she cooed. How different her tone of voice was when addressing the earl. Eleanor immediately felt her hackles rise. "Don't you look devastatingly handsome tonight, but then, when do you not?"

Her voice was like honey, Eleanor thought with amazement. Every word dripped over Bucksted as though he were a stale piece of bread in need of a syrupy coating to be palatable. She wasn't sure in this moment whether she approved of Daphne Westwell or not.

Besides, Bucksted was smiling outrageously. "Miss Westwell, I must say those feathers become you." Two purple ostrich feathers, settled in a turban, danced atop her head. Her blond curls dangled to the sides of her face and down her shoulders. Her décolleté was monstrously low, and her muslin gown— Oh, goodness, Daphne had dampened her muslin! Whyever would she do such a thing?

"You must, you absolutely must save a waltz for me. Will you do that, *my lord?"*

These last words were a caress. Eleanor understood something about Daphne in that moment. All the country gossip about her was true! She had indeed set her cap for Bucksted, and appeared to believe that until the knot was tied, she still had a chance of capturing him!

Eleanor glanced at Bucksted. His cheeks had darkened, but not in embarrassment.

"Of course I shall waltz with you, Daph— er, Miss Westwell."

The tenor of his voice had dropped several pitches, his words had been a caress and . . . he had *almost* used the woman's Christian name!

Well!

Five

A half-hour later, Eleanor stood beside her future not-to-be mama-in-law, watching her future not-to-be husband go down the waltz with what Lady Chalvington had described as one of Bucksted's former love interests. She could scarcely attend to her ladyship's conversation, which centered primarily on pointing out several interesting personages and explaining their relationship to the august family of Chalvington. Eleanor's gaze was fixed on the sight of Daphne's clinging muslin gown!

Eleanor felt she responded properly, nodding her head in appropriate moments and murmuring polite acknowledgments. However, on more than one occasion she would swear that laughter was gurgling in her ladyship's throat, yet for what reason she couldn't imagine. She wasn't overly concerned, though. How could she be when all she could really see was the way Daphne was leaning so scandalously into Bucksted and fairly forcing him to hold her more tightly as he moved her around and around and around the deuced, glaring ballroom floor!

"I have never seen Daphne Westwell gowned in such an outrageous fashion!" she cried at last.

She heard that wretched gurgle again and turned to find Lady Chalvington pursing her lips together and apparently trying very hard not to laugh.

"What is so amusing, my lady?" she queried, full of naïveté.

"Well," Lady Chalvington returned. "I hope I do not give offense by saying so, Eleanor, but until this moment I had the worst misgivings that my son had entered into this betrothal without having engaged your affections. Now I can see that I was completely mistaken!"

Eleanor blushed to the roots of her hair. She opened her mouth to protest, then realized she could not do so; otherwise she would risk revealing that she was no longer betrothed to Bucksted. Yet, how astonishing it was that such a simple observation upon a lady's rather reckless costume should cause an intelligent woman, who the Marchioness of Chalvington clearly was, to leap to such a ridiculous conclusion!

She clamped her lips shut and returned her gaze to the ballroom floor. She was suddenly in the worst misery. She hated the sight of Daphne smiling and playing off her fanciful airs, and she was overset that her hostess should actually think, *even for a moment,* that she was in love with her son!

Politeness forced her to remain beside Lady Chalvington until the waltz ended, by which time she wished she could simply disappear into the polished marble floor beneath her feet and vanish forever.

As it was, she had worse miseries to endure, for Bucksted approached her with Daphne clinging to his arm and laughing up into his face as though they'd just shared the most intimate joke in the world. She wanted to slap Daphne silly!

She could barely say anything civil to Daphne, who in turn gushed, "Oh, Miss Marigate! How well Bucksted dances! You are to be greatly envied!" She turned to his lordship, "As for you, Prince of Hearts, I shall leave you to your bride-to-be, for I see Colonel Fitzcombe bearing down on me. Oh, dear! I am to go down a country dance with him, and he inevitably trods on each toe as though it is part of the design of the dance. Dear Colonel!" She called out, letting her arm slide slowly across Bucksted's hand as she prepared to greet her next partner.

Eleanor could only hope that Colonel Fitzcombe extended his ballroom abilities to her ankles and broke them both!

"Eleanor"—Bucksted was addressing her—"will you not take a turn about the halls with me?"

"I should like that very much," she stated, aware that to watch Daphne would give her no pleasure at all.

She bid *adieu* to her future not-to-be mama-in-law, then placed her arm formally on Bucksted's.

When they had passed through two antechambers and greeted at least fifty people, Bucksted led her down the long gallery which held on its walls a number of his ancestors. He pointed them out, naming each one until they reached the last, who bore a striking resemblance to Bucksted. "Henri de Beauchamp. Something of a handsome rogue, don't you think?"

By this time, enough distance had been placed between Eleanor and Daphne so that she felt relaxed with his lordship. "Very much so. You are quite in his mold, I think."

"No," Bucksted responded with a quick frown. "You are mistaken."

"You do not see the likeness?"

"But his eyes are a dark brown!" he exclaimed, taking a step closer to the portrait and peering up at it as though seeing it for the first time.

"And there the dissimilarity ends!" she cried, moving to stand beside him. "You share his shoulders and bearing . . . his chin . . . and that crooked, rather devilish smile which is I believe at the very center of your considerable charm. The strong cheekbones are yours and the aquiline nose, very Gallic, I think, and not so different from your own."

She watched him frown and peer and touch his nose just so. She giggled. "You still do not see the resemblance?"

"I fear I don't, but I will admit to liking the comparison prodigiously. I've always admired Henri. He left all that he had in Normandy and joined the Duke to conquer a new land."

Eleanor considered this. "Yes, but what of all those your ancestors displaced? The Saxons weren't at all pleased with William's eagerness to *'conquer a new land.'* "

"I don't have to account for my ancestors' conduct," he responded promptly. "Only my own, to my king and to my country, during these years of turmoil and war."

She could see that he was sincere and that loyalty was one of his finest components. If only he had a sense of compassion as strong as his sentiments of patriotism.

He turned to her. "You do not like Miss Westwell, do you?" he asked pointedly.

She was a little taken aback. "In truth, I scarcely know her," she responded. "But I will say that I did not appreciate how she draped herself over you tonight."

A strange look came into his eyes. He lowered his voice and his hand drifted along her arm. "Does it really matter, though?" he asked.

She found herself caught, as much by the expression in his eyes as by his voice. The touch of his hand on the bare skin of her arm was fire and ice all at once. Shivers raced up her shoulder and across her neck. "I suppose not," she breathed.

His smile became crooked as he took a step toward her. He whispered against her ear, "You look quite beautiful tonight, Miss Marigate." When he drew very close, she could feel the heat of his body through the silk of her gown.

"Are you wearing oil of roses?" he queried.

She nodded, almost dumbly. She lifted her face to him. She couldn't precisely hear what he said next, something about how well her gown suited her. Instead, a dull roar sounded in her ears. She was thinking back on the kiss they had shared in the garden on the day of his arrival. She leaned toward him, wondering were he to kiss her again, whether the kiss would be as unsettling as before. His lips were but a few inches away now. His expression seemed troubled. His hand drifted over her back.

"I don't think . . . this would be . . . at all wise," he murmured.

"No . . . I suppose not," she responded breathlessly.

He leaned closer yet.

She caught her breath. Her lips parted.

Laughter erupted from just beyond the door. Bucksted's attention was instantly diverted.

He took her arm gently and, turning her about, drew her toward an opposite door.

Eleanor passed through and a rush of cool air dispelled some of the heat of the moment. She found herself in another dimly lit passageway. She drew in a deep breath as the door snapped shut behind the intruders who were now entering the gallery and talking quite loudly.

He whispered, "Come. There is something I'd like you to see."

At the moment, given how her heart was floating so freely within her bosom, she would have gone anywhere with him. Though her mind shrieked a warning that she was in some sort of primordial danger, she refused to heed any such ridiculous prompting. After all, she was with her betrothed. No matter that in a sennight, they would no longer be engaged. Right now, that did not seem to matter one whit.

She walked beside him in complete silence as he guided her down yet another dimly lit corridor, then up a short flight of stairs and into an antechamber which passed through another antechamber lit by only two candles. The chamber beyond appeared to be a study of some kind, but he did not take her there. Instead, he moved to the fireplace opposite a single, moon-drenched window and felt carefully along the wood paneling with the tips of his gloved fingers.

A soft shushing sound drew Eleanor's attention. To the right of the fireplace, a low aperture appeared. Bucksted moved to draw a candle from the wall sconce above and slipped through the small doorway. She followed with great interest.

He held the candle aloft and reached out to feel the panels near the doorway. Another shushing sounded and the panel slid back into place.

"A secret chamber!" she cried in hushed accents. She was thrilled as she turned toward him.

He smiled down at her, then settled the candle on a bookshelf opposite the door. "I thought you might enjoy seeing a haunt from my childhood. Now that I've come to know you a little better, and I'm aware that you are not the shy little miss I had thought you were, I felt you would be intrigued."

"Indeed I am!" she cried without hesitation. "We have nothing so romantic at Hartslip, for Papa and I once made it a mission of ours to review every architectural drawing of the house and search out every suspicious chamber. Since in all former documents and correspondence there was not even the smallest reference to a secret room, we gave up the search a number of years past." She made a slow turn about the chamber and took in the numerous artifacts from his days as a youth—books, a wooden whistle, a slingshot, a cricket bat, and an assortment of fossils and rocks collected from the countryside.

She was struck suddenly by how lonely his childhood must have been, with no siblings to torture or with whom to conspire.

"What is it?" he inquired. "You seem sad, suddenly."

"Oh, it is nothing. I mean, I was just thinking of what your childhood must have been like. Your home, while elegant and quite grand, is also monstrously large. Did you never lose your way, I mean when you were very little?"

He chuckled, "No, never. Nurse was quite attentive. But it is more than that, isn't it?"

"Well," she hesitated, "did you never feel the lack of brothers or sisters, especially in such a large house?"

"I don't know," he responded with a lift of his brows. "To own the truth, I've never given it much thought."

"Well, I should have found it lonely beyond words. My sisters and I brangled of course, but on the other hand, we've always discussed everything, besides enjoying our music together and our reading and, of course, exchanging pattern cards."

His face wore an arrested expression. "You love your family very much, don't you?"

"Of course. You cannot imagine how sad we all were when Papa—" She paused to clear her throat. "You would have enjoyed knowing my father better. He had such an excellent wit and his eyes—"

"Always laughing, weren't they?"

She smiled. "Yes. Precisely."

"I saw him often enough at Whitehaven. My father had always counted him a good friend, a valuable friend. He said no better example existed in the county than Sir Henry's."

Her eyes brimmed with tears, and her throat ached.

He drew a kerchief from the pocket of his coat and drew close to her. His empty hand found its way around her waist—just to support her, mind! The other dabbed at the tears which chose at that precise moment to trickle down her cheeks.

Eleanor was caught up in so many emotions of the moment that she felt all at sea as she let him comfort her. There it was again—his ability to comfort her! The touch of the soft kerchief on her cheek and the warmth of his hand on her waist caused her heart to swell.

Had she been mistaken about Bucksted? Could a man who so gently touched her be as worthless as she had previously supposed? Confusion began to boil in her mind. Her thoughts ran rampant, racing from her former opinions of his character, the disparity in their views about helping the poor, to the truth that she had moved far beyond his reach the very day she'd taken up smuggling. Because her thoughts moved so far afield from her sadness about her father's death, her tears soon ceased to flow.

"There, that's better," he said softly. "I don't think I like to see you cry although your eyes right now are exquisite, drenched as they are and shimmering in the candlelight."

It seemed so natural that he should bend his head ever so slightly and place his lips on hers. Surely he meant just to comfort her a little more, only she shouldn't let him because she was beginning to like him far more than she ought.

Despite her intentions, she leaned into him, her heart straining toward him, her head dizzy with the closeness of him. Her arms found their way around his back. He drew her tightly against him. She parted her lips, meaning to sigh. His tongue entered her so softly. She melted, cooing and breathing in the wonder of what she was feeling.

The candle guttered, and the closed room fell to a thick blackness. Eleanor didn't care. The darkness only caused Bucksted to draw her to him more closely still, if such a thing was even possible!

She felt lost in his arms, in the most marvelous way. Time ceased to exist. Her legs were trembling. Her mind kept drifting as he continued to kiss her—remembering the dance they had shared earlier, recalling the first moment she had seen him so many years ago as a chit not yet out of the schoolroom and thinking he was the most handsome creature she had ever seen, remembering how, in the garden last night, he had almost kissed her again.

What would it be like to be married to such a man, to a man whose kisses were like heaven? For a strong, intense moment she wished for it more than anything else on earth, to be wed to Bucksted!

She was shocked by the thought and clung to him because of it, because such a thing could never be. He kissed her more fervently. She could hardly breathe.

After an eternity, he drew back. She could see nothing. The secret chamber allowed no light to reach its recesses. He held her close and thumbed her cheek gently. He kissed her forehead and the bridge of her nose.

"This is madness," he whispered.

"Indeed, it is," she responded. How odd her voice sounded, as though she were a mere ghost and not herself at all.

"But a good kind of madness," he added.

Her mind began traveling down a rose-strewn path. She saw herself walking beside Bucksted, hand in hand, then arm in arm. He leaned over and kissed her. She called him husband. *Husband!* Oh, my!

She didn't want the moment to end. Once they left the chamber, the secret place of his childhood, the magic would end. He would be merely Bucksted and she a minxish Miss Marigate of Hartslip Manor!

A terrible dizziness assailed her again. Even if all changed and she desired more than anything to wed Bucksted, it could never be possible. She would have to tell him of her nocturnal activities, and then what would he think of her, all tangled up as she was with Martin and smugglers and French contraband!

She nearly swooned. Her knees buckled. He felt her slip and caught her.

"You are frightened of the dark," he whispered.

"Y-yes. A little," she lied.

He chuckled, a low sound that teased her heart all over again. He carefully tucked his arm around hers and led her slowly to her right. She shuffled, unsteady and uncertain of her steps. She heard him searching for the panel which after a few seconds slid open, allowing a rectangle of light to pour in.

A few moments later, she was in the small antechamber taking deep breaths.

He smiled, yet seemed bemused. "I would not have supposed you to become frightened by the dark."

"I wasn't," she confessed. "I—I was just thinking. Bucksted, you shouldn't be kissing me like that."

"You are trembling," he stated. "Come. If we walk a little, you'll grow steadier."

She accepted his arm, though she wished more than anything that she would never have to touch him again. He was dangerous, she realized, for he could make her feel things she did not want to feel. She determined in her mind to set a wall between herself and Bucksted. There could be no marriage between them, no matter how giddy she felt when he kissed her. She—she didn't respect him, for one thing and for another . . . Dear God! How had it come about that she had ever taken to smuggling brandies and silks in the first place?

And why did kissing Bucksted suddenly bring on such a wretched attack of conscience?

As soon as was possible, she allowed the natural flow of the ball to separate her from Bucksted. She had but to dance away the remaining few hours of the *fête* and she would find herself in her mother's coach heading home, heading away from so many dangerous thoughts and sensations.

Three hours later, however, when the ball had drawn to a close, Bucksted ended Eleanor's hope that she would at last be rid of him. He surprised her with his own traveling chariot, and her mother's blessing that he escort her home himself.

Eleanor smiled weakly and thanked him. He frowned slightly as he handed her up into the carriage. "You are quite welcome," he murmured politely in response.

Once inside, she sat stiffly next to him, her head averted. She didn't want to encourage him even in the slightest to think that he could kiss her again. That must all end—now.

He took her hand in his, but she drew it away.

"You are to be shy with me now, Eleanor?" he asked in a voice that forced her to look at him.

The expression in his eyes was boyish hurt. She bit her lip. "This won't do, m'lord. Not by half. You know that as well as I. We are not to marry."

His expression eased up and his lips formed that horridly enchanting crookedness which she was sure could have charmed a dog away from its bone.

She whimpered slightly.

He took her hand again, and this time she didn't pull away. She continued, "It is merely that we are not to marry, Bucksted. And you cannot keep kissing me. It—it isn't seemly!"

Surely he would respond to reason.

"No, it is not," he murmured, lifting her fingers to his lips.

She allowed him to kiss her through her glove. What harm could that do? Oh! How delightful! How tantalizing! She'd had no idea that so much sensation could be experienced through a glove.

He leaned toward her as he kissed her fingers. Her lips were now but a breath away from his own.

The coach, however, slowed at that moment, and the horses jolted in harness. "What is it?" she cried.

Bucksted leaned forward and peered through the front window glass. The coach came to a standstill. He immediately opened the door and leaped down to the road.

The light from the coach lamps was very dim. Eleanor scooted over to the open door and looked out. She gasped. "Who is it?" she cried. She did not hesitate, but wrapped her skirts about her legs and slid to the ground as well. She hurried to join Bucksted who was bending over the still form of a man lying prone on the ground.

"Oy didna think we should pass 'im, m'lord," the postillion called down to him. " 'As 'e stuck 'is spoon in the wall?"

Bucksted placed his hand on the man's back. "No. He's breathing. He's probably foxed. We'll leave him."

"What?" Eleanor cried. Had she heard him correctly?

Bucksted rose to his feet and turned back to her, his expression hard. "We'll leave him where he lies. When I've seen you home, I'll send my servants to fetch the fellow to Whitehaven."

Eleanor pulled her cape closely about her shoulders. "But the air is so cold. What if he should perish?"

"I won't be his keeper, nor will I risk your well-being for a drunken vagrant."

"You don't know that he's drunk, nor that he is a vagrant. He could be an ex-soldier, suffering from an old wound or—"

He interrupted her. "We're leaving him, Eleanor," he stated imperiously. "I'll not discuss the matter further."

He brushed past her, returning to the coach.

She was astounded by his arrogance. "I will not go with you and leave this fellow in the road to be trampled by the next inattentive traveler. *I will not!*"

"The deuce you won't!" he retorted angrily. She watched his gaze slide toward the servant who, when she turned to look at him as well, was staring woodenly into the dark road in front of him.

Eleanor lowered her gaze to the road, compressed her lips, and clamped her hands tightly together. "I'll not go," she reiterated firmly.

"By God, I'll pick you up and throw you into the coach!" he cried, taking a menacing step toward her.

At that, her gaze flew to his. All the sweet communion she had enjoyed with him seemed silly and superfluous in this moment. So . . . he would *command* her, and he would leave this poor wretch in the road. She did not answer him, but settled as cold a gaze as she could manage on him and challenged him with her stare.

Again, his gaze slid to the servant who, Eleanor knew, was discreetly gazing anywhere but at them.

The figure on the road groaned. Eleanor turned toward him.

"Me 'ead," the prostrate man was heard to say.

"There!" she cried, triumphantly. "He is wounded! Now you can have no excuse but to assist him."

Bucksted stared in dismay and fury at his betrothed, who was bending down to the stranger and speaking to him softly. He had never known such anger in his entire life. How could the female be so obstinate and so scatter-brained! And how was it for a brief few hours he had actually begun to believe himself strongly attracted to her? Hah!

The vagrant moaned again, then spoke to Eleanor who was still bent over his prostrate form. She suddenly stood up and backed away from him.

The starlight, though not brilliant, was sufficient to illuminate the lines of her face. She was clearly startled by something the wounded man had said to her. He crossed the distance between them quickly and begged to know what was going forward.

She bit her lip, a habit of hers, before replying, "He begged for a kiss. You were quite right. He appears to be, er, foxed."

"Then we leave him be," he reiterated sharply.

She turned toward him, her face aflame with passion. "I will not! I would rather die before I left any misfortunate creature to perish in the night, in his altitudes or not. 'Tis my duty to give aid to anyone who requires it and yours as well if you would but search your heart."

Bucksted felt something inside his mind snap at this impassioned speech. He did not agree with her, he could not! Each man must be responsible for his actions and not dependent upon others to rescue him from the results of his own conduct—such as passing out on a country road from too much ale.

On the other hand, there was something about the strength of her belief that appealed to him. Was there another lady of his acquaintance who held her ground with such force of will? He didn't think so, nor did he have to agree with her, but by God, he could respect the staunchness of her position. "Very well," he said quietly. "We are yet closer to Whitehaven than to Hartslip. I'll see that the head groom tends to him."

"You needn't do so. We are prepared at Hartslip to care for anyone who comes to us." She lifted her chin haughtily.

He stared at her for a long moment, his gaze locked to hers. He felt her disapprobation all over again and began to be amused.

How was it possible he had ever believed her tractable? He finally threw back his head and laughed at the absurdity of it.

"I don't see what you find so amusing," she stated coldly. "This poor fellow—"

"Pray, no more speeches. I shall call you Saint Eleanor from this moment on, I swear it. That or a vixen sent to torment me."

She appeared adorably confused. He addressed the postillion. "Hold the horses while I toss this man into the carriage. It appears we'll be returning to Whitehaven."

"Very good, me lord."

Six

The following morning, Eleanor sat on the red velvet window seat in her tower room watching her dearest friend, Martin Fieldstone, march to and fro. He was deeply distressed.

"It is become too dangerous, I tell you!" he cried. "Three more excisemen were sighted in Camber, even Broomhill. In Broomhill! Do you know what that means? Someone has told them of our activities, or at least that the ships have been seen on certain moonless nights. We can't do this anymore, Nellie. I tell you plainly, we cannot!"

For the first time since his arrival a quarter-hour past, Eleanor began to feel uncertain. He had made his pronouncement the moment she had stolen with him up to her tower room, that they could no longer continue their smuggling operation, but until now she had refused to credit all that he was saying.

Presently, however, with his freckled face reddened in his distress, she could no longer dismiss his concerns. "But are you quite, quite sure?" she asked. "What does old Romney say?"

"That rumors are running rampant along the coast."

She considered this. She had never placed a great deal of stock in rumors, though she did not say as much to Martin. Instead, she queried, "Do you have the money from the last venture?"

"Yes, yes, of course I do," he responded impatiently, running a hand through his sandy-colored hair. He reached inside his pocket and tossed a packet to her tied up with a burgundy silk ribbon. "Five hundred pounds."

"Five hundred pounds!" she cried. "Why that is nearly twice what we earned last time."

"Yes, you simpleton!" he cried, approaching her and laying both hands on her shoulders. "Because it is becoming more dangerous. Every innkeeper Romney went to last week, disposing of our cargo, revealed that there have been several arrests in the area. The silk merchants were even more forthcoming about news of the excisemen."

Mr. Romney, a weatherbeaten, old man, had been disposing of smuggled goods since he was a lad. He had worked with the most infamous smugglers of Rye during the last part of the eighteenth century and had been delighted to leave his retirement to work with a certain 'Mr. Smith,' as Martin was known to him. Eleanor knew that Martin had complete confidence in Romney, and for that reason she could not ignore his warnings entirely.

"I suppose it would do no harm to temporarily cease our activities," she mused.

He looked at her with a completely bewildered expression on his face. "But, Nellie, you are to be wed in less than a fortnight? You can't seriously be thinking of continuing our operation once you are the Countess of Bucksted."

Eleanor smiled, then chuckled. "That would be ridiculous," she agreed. She laughed a little more and wondered if he could guess the truth of her situation.

Martin stared at her for a long moment. "You are behaving quite peculiarly," he said. Then, quite suddenly, his face flooded with even a little more color. "By Jove, you've jilted him!" he cried.

She nodded. "Yes. I broke off the engagement."

"When? Last night? After the ball?"

She shook her head. "No. The day he arrived."

Martin's face twisted up into a confused knot. "I don't understand. Why . . . then, why did you attend the ball?"

She huffed a sigh. "Bucksted and I came to a new agreement, the details of which would not be proper for me to relate to you. Suffice it to say that I have agreed to *pretend* to be his future bride just for this sennight, until all the arranged events are over.

Then we will stage a quarrel—at some point, I don't know when—and the betrothal shall come to an apparently natural end."

"Good God," he breathed out. "And was this your idea?"

"No!" she cried. "I didn't want this at all, but Bucksted made me an offer regarding Mama—"

"Her debts," he spat out, disgusted. "None of this is your fault, Eleanor," he stated strongly. "If your parent had not succumbed to a desire to purchase every furbelow in a twenty-mile radius of Hartslip, you would never have been seduced into accepting his offer in the first place."

Eleanor was grateful to have a friend who understood her predicament so well, yet at the same time, something inside her wriggled uncomfortably. "Of course you are right. Only, I do wish I had made up my mind several weeks ago. You can hardly blame Bucksted for wanting to play out the ruse for this week, with so many of his relatives and friends arriving from all over England to congratulate him."

The events of last night struck her suddenly in stunning succession—the ball, dancing with Bucksted, seeing Daphne flirt with him, the kiss in his secret chamber, and brangling over the drunken vagrant.

Bucksted had turned the man over to his head groom, and the trip back to Hartslip had been *very* quiet. She had been less than approving of his conduct, and he had still been as mad as a hornet.

Sleep had not eluded her once her head struck the pillow, but because the events of the evening had been as varied as they had been distressing, she had awakened with a dull headache. For some reason, without knowing precisely how, her life had become enormously complicated.

She had been trying to persuade herself all morning that after the week was over, she would be herself once more. Then she would think of how she had felt in Bucksted's arms and she'd begin to wonder if her life could ever truly be the same again. Kissing him as she had, in the blackness of his secret room, had done something to her, changed her, altered her wishes for the future.

Love had never really entered into her mind until now since, just as Bucksted had said, she had never been a romantical sort of female. Her father's occupations of philanthropy and gardening had made up her life as well. She had been content and purposefully occupied, so much so that the normal preoccupation of young ladies and young men with each other had escaped her.

Until now . . .

For a few moments, while clutched in Bucksted's arms, she had actually wondered if she was tumbling in love with him. Of course later, when they had argued over the fate of that poor, poor vagrant, she had realized she could never become truly enamored of Bucksted. They were far too different, too strident in their opinions, to ever love or esteem one another.

Still, it seemed everything was changing and far too quickly for her comfort.

Martin lifted her chin with his fingers and drew her away from her reverie. "He was a fool not to have made you love him first," he said gently, somehow divining the nature of her ruminations. "You will never marry unless you feel quite passionately about your future husband, which leads me to something else I feel I ought to tell you. I'm in love with you, Nellie. No, no, don't protest or say anything of the moment. I've loved you since ever I can remember—your spirit, your love of adventure, your compassion. I suppose what I love most is that you do nothing with only half a heart. Everything must be done completely or not at all."

"Just like you," she returned.

He laughed. "No, I am not such a man. I merely follow your lead. Only tell me, is there a chance, even a smattering of one, that you might be able to love me in return?"

She saw that he desperately wanted her to tell him she reciprocated his sentiments, but she couldn't. She shook her head. "You are like a brother to me," she said, tears filling her eyes. "The brother I never had, but longed for. How can I possibly think of you in any other way?"

He smiled, rather sadly. "You are the oddest creature. Were you so kind when you were jilting Bucksted?"

At that she laughed. "No, I was not. You should have heard the dreadful speech I gave him. I told him I couldn't esteem him and that he thought of no one but himself."

Martin gasped. "You did not? You said as much to the Earl of Bucksted? Oh, Nellie, I would laugh, but I greatly fear you've made yourself an enemy."

"Oh, pooh. He is not such a bad fellow after all. We . . . we just disagree on many things, many important things."

A light scratching sounded on the door. Eleanor directed Martin to stand near the hinges so that when she opened the door to see who it was, he might be hidden.

She crossed the room and drew the door toward her a crack. Margaret's sweet face peeked in. " 'Tis only I," she cried. "Is Martin still with you?"

"Hallo, brat," he stated, emerging from behind the door at the same time.

"Oh! I thought you had come. Only . . . Bucksted has arrived. You probably should leave at once. He will not like that you have been *tête-à-tête* with my sister."

"Thank you for warning us, Megs," Eleanor said. Margaret immediately retraced her steps down the narrow, spiraling staircase.

Eleanor closed the door softly and turned back to Martin. "Are you certain it wouldn't be safe to make just one more run to Broomhill? Martin, I am so close to completing Papa's legacy. Another five hundred pounds would be more than sufficient!"

"No. I tell you it's impossible."

"Does Romney think as much?"

She saw Martin's hesitation and leaped on it. "There! That is all the answer I need. How much longer does he think we can continue our activities in relative safety?"

Martin grimaced. "A few days, at most. But I don't like it! What if . . . ?"

Eleanor waved this aside. "If we were to earn as much from the sales of the next cargo, I'd have enough to fulfill my father's commitments, and that is all I care about."

He shook his head and grimaced a little more. "I know I should be stronger than this . . ."

She squealed and threw her arms about his neck. "This will be the last time—I promise!"

He hugged her. "I never could resist you."

After a moment, she drew back. "Now you must leave before Bucksted finds you alone with me. Megs is right, he would not like my being alone with you. After all, as far as the entire county is concerned, I am still to become Lady Bucksted and ought to attend to every propriety until the betrothal is formally dissolved."

Martin shrugged. "Seems to me I ought to stay. Why don't you seek him out and bring him up. I'd love to tell him what his darling little bride has been up to for the last year."

"Oh, you odious man! Now leave, before I tell Mrs. Whiting that you kissed her daughter in the orchard last year. She would see to it that the pair of you were married before the day was out!"

He placed a dramatic hand over his heart. "Faith, but you terrify me! All right, I shall go! Only pray, never mention Mrs. Whiting or her offspring to me again."

She led the way down the staircase and teased him. "I think you ought to marry Miss Whiting."

"What? A farmer's daughter? My father would flay me alive and feed me to his pack of hounds before ever consenting. Besides, I've come to comprehend her ambitions, and I shall not be that foolish again."

"I'm glad to hear it," she said. "Miss Whiting clearly had set her cap for you." She was giggling as she reached the broad heavy door at the base of the stairs and pushed it open.

She was still smiling, though not for long, when she stepped into the entrance hall and found Bucksted staring at her and Martin. A warmth stole into her cheeks. She felt as though she had been caught stealing peaches from the vicar's orchard again.

"Hallo, Bucksted," she called to him. "You are acquainted with Mr. Fieldstone, are you not?"

"Your servant, Fieldstone," he said, bowing stiffly from the waist.

"My lord," Martin responded, speaking with mock politeness. "And may I offer my congratulations? It would seem you've stolen a march on the rest of us."

Bucksted's eyes narrowed.

She glanced up at Martin, whose cheeks had darkened, and recognized the rising of his temper. "Oh, come down off your high ropes, Martin. You have to be leaving now, remember?"

He pinched his lips together and turned to glare at her, but she would have none of it. She hooked his arm and led him toward the door to the terrace that he might take a short route to the stables. He obeyed her, only grumbling slightly as he marched beside her. She gave him a gentle push through the doorway.

He stunned her, however, by turning back and placing a kiss on her lips before he left.

The door closed, and she remained standing mutely, staring at it. Whatever had Martin been thinking, to have kissed her in such a fashion? What must Bucksted be thinking at this moment? She almost dared not to turn around.

Bucksted felt the kiss as though Mr. Fieldstone had struck him hard across the face. He understood then that whatever the supposed relationship between Eleanor and Martin, the latter obviously thought he had some sort of claim upon her.

He watched her turn around slowly, her cheeks aflame. He began to walk toward her.

"I cannot imagine," she said, her hands clasped tightly in front of her, "whatever possessed him to kiss me."

How unwaveringly she met his gaze. "Nor can I," he stated. He was uncertain of his sentiments of the moment, but his next words, which seemed to roll unbidden off his tongue, clarified at least some of them. "I can only suppose that you have told him of our ruse. However, might I suggest that until we have broken off the engagement entirely, in a sennight or so, that you prevail upon your beau to leave you in peace?"

His arms felt stiff as he walked toward her. He watched her lift her chin.

"I shall certainly ring a peal over his head once I have occasion to speak with him again. I was never more mortified. Martin has never taken such a liberty with me before, in case that is what you were thinking."

So the chit felt compelled to elucidate the situation for him. He was pleased, though he didn't understand precisely why. At the same time, for some inexplicable reason he could not bear the thought of Eleanor's lips having been trespassed upon by anyone other than himself. He thought perhaps such remarkably territorial feelings sprang from the fact that he was betrothed to her, even if for a scant few days more.

When he reached her, she still stood with her hands clasped in front of her. "So, you have been friends with Mr. Fieldstone a very long time," he said, softening his voice a trifle.

At that, as though responding to the timbre of his voice, her features gentled. She no longer looked like a cat ready to spring at him with claws extended. "Since I can remember," she responded. "We are nearly of an age, and he has been like a brother to me. His father's property marches along Hartslip's southern boundary. The two share a common oak wood, beautifully pollarded, a perfect place to play at highwayman and in which to build tree forts."

Something inside his chest began to grow warm. "What? No playing at dolls and stitching a hundred samplers with which to adorn the nursery?"

"I daresay I did as much of that as any young female, but whenever I could escape my governess—which was more frequently than I ought to have—Martin and I would enjoy the very best of adventures. You can have no idea!"

He wondered if there would ever come a time when Eleanor Marigate would cease to surprise him. And how had he ever thought her such a gentle female? He recalled the moralizing letters he had sent her and the two rather stilted visits he had paid to her once they were betrothed, how he had prosed on and on about his family's lineage and the seriousness of the duties she would be taking on once they were wed. With such a history as she had known—building tree forts of all things!—his notions of what their marriage ought to be must have threatened her happiness entirely.

"More and more I begin to comprehend why you have jilted me," he stated. "You must have thought me a prosy old bore."

The flush that covered her cheeks quite instantly made her sentiments known. "To own the truth," she said quietly, "when I accepted your hand in marriage it was with many of Martin's accolades ringing in my ears. For all his recent display of hostility toward you, he is a great admirer of your abilities. I had thought at the time, when Mama was pressing me to respond to your generous offer, that a man who has been known to drive a mail coach in a blinding snowstorm could not be an entirely worthless fellow. I was stunned when I received your first letter—"

"And the many which followed, no doubt."

"Devastated," she said, lowering her gaze.

So much disappointment was writ in her countenance that he found himself uncertain of what to say next. He cleared his throat and cast the conversation in a different direction, "My father has decided to hire that fellow we brought back to Whitehaven last night."

She lifted her face to him, a sudden glow in her eyes. "He has?" she gushed.

She was so easy to comprehend. Her face revealed every thought, every emotion. He realized he could never be in doubt of her mind, though sometimes with unpleasant effect. Right now, however, the fact that his simple pronouncement had so pleased her seemed to bring a sunbeam straight into the room.

"Yes," he responded a bit reluctantly. "We had a long discussion about it after I arrived home. He was waiting up in the library, sipping a brandy. He had nothing but praise for you, for your conduct at the ball, no airs or simperings, a great deal of confidence and poise, and a certain complete disinterest in rank that really pleased the old man."

"You seem disgruntled, almost as though you don't approve that he approved of me," she said with spirit.

He could only laugh. Everything she said kept him off balance. "That is not what I intended for you to construe, my lady mischief. If I seemed perplexed, it is only that I am wondering what a mystery you are. You appear to think my father's compliments would have been given about anyone, but there you are out. He does not offer praise so openhandedly, so that when he speaks words of tribute, trust me he felt you were everything he said you were. And the worst of it is, had you behaved last night the way you have with me for the past several months, or at least up until two days past, he would have had serious doubts about your abilities to one day rule at Whitehaven."

"He said as much?" she queried, clearly dumbfounded.

He inclined his head. "Yes."

Eleanor was stunned. "I understand, then, why you frown at me as you do now. I don't know what to say. I have learned to be who I am at my father's knee. He was never, as he used to say, a respecter of persons. But I have begun to wonder, Bucksted, how it was you would ever have wanted a woman to be your wife who had not a word to say for herself."

He had begun to wonder the very same thing. "Well," he began lamely, "I can only justify the stupidity of at one time holding to such an opinion by saying that I take my duties to my future rank and home with great sobriety of purpose. I wish to be, one day, the excellent man my father is."

She regarded him for a long moment, her green eyes searching and questioning, perhaps as though trying to make him out. Her expression was soft, quizzical, and utterly beautiful in the morning's glow. At last she smiled and took his arm. She turned him toward the doors leading to the staircase and beyond. "Did you still wish to go to the fair today?" she asked.

"Only if we do not have to bring home every drunken vagrant we stumble across."

She giggled and his heart lurched. He had half-expected her to fly into the boughs at his words. Instead, she chuckled. He wished, for just a moment, that he had known her in London for a Season or two, just as she was now, without the least pretension of being a quiet, manageable female. Would he have fallen in love with her? Or would he have despised her for her outrageous conduct and admissions of childhood scrapes? Or was it possible he had offered for her because he had suspected her hidden depths?

She left him in the care of the butler who brought him some refreshments at her command, a tankard of ale and a plate of cheese, fruit, and soft rolls. The trip to the fair, which was being held west of Headcorn, was some ten miles, and a little sustenance, he realized, was precisely what he needed.

As he took a pull of the ale, he shook his head. Somehow, this wretched engagement was beginning to have complexities that disturbed him. Why did she have to be so beautiful, for instance. And why did she have to laugh with just that bubble in her throat as though she'd been amused for a century or so and was just now ready to share her amusement with him. And why did she somehow have to divine that a fine ale and a plate of food was precisely, of the moment, what he needed?

During the drive to Headcorn, Eleanor demanded to know every particle of Bucksted's conversation with his father about the stranger they had nearly run over on the highway. It seems they knew the man, a certain Mr. Borde, who had lost his family to scarlet fever, including his wife some years past, and who had had trouble since keeping employment even though he was known to be a man of considerable leadership and skill. Lord Chalvington had given him the post of assistant gamekeeper whose primary function was to keep poachers out of the Home Wood and to dismantle the traps set for game.

Eleanor praised his father's actions.

He gave a slight tug on the reins as a rather sharp corner approached. "And are you not going to applaud my efforts?"

She could tell he was half-teasing. "You merely came to your senses," she stated primly. "Why should I praise you for that?"

He chuckled in response and, once the horses gained the corner, gave a brisk slap of the reins and called out to them in a commanding voice.

The day was pretty beyond words, and Eleanor lifted her face to the bright sunshine, which peeked more often than not from behind a scattering of the most beautiful puffy white clouds. It was a day made for the pleasures of a fair if ever there was one.

As Bucksted's curricle drew closer to the fairgrounds, at which several horse races promised to form the central attraction, Eleanor's heart began to thrum. The cool breeze on her cheeks could do nothing to stop the rush of heat to her face. She loved nothing more than all the liveliness and excitement present at a local fair.

Every manner of person imaginable attended such an event, making it so different from the mild social gatherings she frequented with her mama and sisters. More than once over the years, she and Martin had stolen off to the Clifton races or to nearby fairs, dressed in clothes more suitable for the lower classes. She had always enjoyed herself prodigiously, though keeping an eye to avoiding any who might know her. The fabulous truth was, however, that persons of genteel birth had no interest in any woman wearing faded black bombazine and a straw bonnet adorned with a strip of gingham. She couldn't recall even one occasion on which someone with whom she was acquainted had even so much as glanced in her direction. It would seem the class distinctions of her society were as much a protection against recognition as any clever disguise with a wig, powder, and rouge might have proven to be.

She had frequently pondered the prospect of actually attending a fair dressed as she was when she and Martin made their weekly trip to Broomhill to collect their smuggled goods—as a young gentleman. However, she felt this would be going a bit beyond the pale. As she glanced up at Bucksted, she wondered what he would think of her garbed as a young man of fashion. Merciful heavens! He would likely faint!

She queried, "Did you never dress up as, oh, say a tradesman or a farmer for the purpose of disguising yourself while attending a fair or the like?"

He looked at her, his brows raised. "Of course not!" he retorted. "Whyever would I wish to do something like that?"

She was right. He would be shocked. She decided she couldn't resist. "Well, I have done so."

He started, jerking his head toward her, his mouth agape. "You what?"

"Well, I was seventeen at the time and game for any lark, as Martin always used to say—"

"So, it is Fieldstone again, is it?"

"No, no, I won't let you fault him. The idea was mine, although he took to it quite readily."

"I am beginning to think that you will never cease to shock and amaze me. Did you enjoy your adventure?" By this time, they had reached the outskirts of the fair, and Bucksted began carefully navigating his way around a variety of conveyances.

"You cannot imagine how much fun it was."

He was silent for a moment. "I should imagine," he began thoughtfully, slowing for a passel of children who had suddenly appeared from behind several carriages, "that to lose the constraints of one's social position could be an exhilarating experiencc."

"It is," she pronounced.

He responded with a chuckle and a bemused shake of his head.

He drew his carriage next to an old weathered barouche. A boy of about twelve ran up to him. "See to the 'orses, govner?"

"Yes, thank you," he said. He reached into his waistcoat pocket and flipped the lad a coin. He helped Eleanor descend and addressed her, "Well, my lady mischief, what do you wish to do first?"

"The Gypsies!" she cried. "I must have my fortune told—*again!*"

"Are the results ever the same?" he asked, laughing.

"Of course not, but the mere idea of it enchants me so much that I find I cannot resist!"

He took hold of her arm and wrapped it in his. "And it is you I find enchanting."

Eleanor was nearly thrown out of stride as she glanced up at him. "What flummery!" she cried. "You may say anything to me today, Bucksted, but I will not permit you to pitch even the smallest bit of gammon!"

He chuckled again. "How unkind!" he cried, playfully. "Besides, I am only trying to flirt with you a little." He drew her aside to let a pack of rowdy young bloods pass by, the majority of them already half-foxed. She was grateful for the attention.

"Well, were I to flirt in response, then," she said, once he had put them both in motion again, "what should I say?"

He considered this. "I think normally a female would respond with something like"—and here he put his voice into a falsetto—"Why how very gallant of you, Lord Bucksted. I vow I've never heard such flattery in all my life, and you speak it so prettily."

She laughed outright. "You know, you can be very amusing!"

"Thank you," he murmured, again in a falsetto.

She giggled and sighed and giggled a little more. Faith, but this sort of raillery was much to her liking as were the movement and life and sounds all about her. She grew deeply content as she took in the smell of horses and leather, the sounds of children squealing or crying as many were, the undercurrent of hundreds of voices murmuring in conversation, the rising screams and dipping groans of a crowd watching horses run a race, the music of the Gypsies, the very dim sounds of a small orchestra playing country airs, the loud penetrating voices of women selling ribbons, and men calling to passersby to purchase their wares, play at their games, or view their entertainments. But mostly—and here she had to be honest with herself—she loved the feel of walking beside Bucksted, with their arms wrapped tightly together as though they were securely bound by invisible ropes. In this moment, she felt she was beginning to comprehend why people longed for the married state. There was something absolutely lovely about her arm being physically joined to Bucksted's as they paraded about the vast fairgrounds.

They found an intriguing Gypsy, an old, dark woman who told Eleanor she would have a dozen children, live to be eighty, and enjoy being married to a tall man with dark brown hair. Previously she'd been told she would have seven, nine, ten, and fourteen children, and that she would live to be forty-eight, fifty-two, thirty-three, and ninety years old. She glanced up at Bucksted, noting, however, that there was one element of the prophecies which had never wavered—her future husband would have dark brown hair.

She said as much to him. He responded, "Well, that relieves my mind on one score."

"And what is that?" she queried.

"You will *not* be marrying Mr. Fieldstone."

She could only laugh, something she seemed to be doing a lot in his company.

She glanced at him. He was smiling softly. In the warm sunshine, his hazel eyes glittered. "You have incredible eyes, Bucksted. Has anyone ever told you as much?"

He seemed a little taken aback, "Are you now trying to flirt with me?"

"Not a bit," she responded crisply. "I am merely stating a fact and inquiring if anyone else has noticed the color and brilliance of your eyes."

"Now my eyes are brilliant. Faith, my love, you are putting me to the blush."

She giggled again.

She saw Punch, several peep shows, and dancing dogs. But when a pistol-shooting game came into view, she demanded that he show her the skill of which Martin had boasted so very frequently.

He did not hesitate to oblige her. "Shall we wager for it?" he suggested with a hint of a smile.

She shook her head. "I am far too anxious to witness your skill. Fire away and let me see if Martin boasted properly of your abilities."

He smiled and began. He felt the weight of several pistols and after several minutes of careful examination made a selection. He loaded the weapon and primed the pan. "Does this pistol list either to the right or left?" he inquired of the proprietor as he gazed down the barrel and took aim at a piece of paper dotted with a black circle the size of a tuppence.

The man grimaced, "Nay, govner. She's the best of the lot. Ye've chosen well."

Bucksted relaxed his body and turned to level an eye on the man. He said nothing more, but waited patiently for the proprietor to open his budget.

The man shifted on his feet and coughed slightly. "Well, there be some wat says the pistol balls might lean a bit to the left."

"Ah," Bucksted responded. He again took up a careful stance, raised his weapon, and fired.

The air exploded and smelled singed of a sudden. Eleanor peered at the target carefully and saw that he had hit his mark true.

"By Gawd!" the proprietor cried. "A bit of fine shooting if ever I seen it! Pierced the target dead center. By Gawd!" He ran to retrieve the mark. The hole was, just as he said, as near to the center as could be.

Eleanor took the paper and marveled. "No wonder Martin says you are a Nonesuch."

The proprietor stared at the man. "Might you be Bucksted wat shoots at Manton's in the City?"

Bucksted nodded.

"Why, might I shake yer hand, me lord, fer I've 'eard of ye fer nigh on ten years now." He turned to Eleanor, "The finest shot in England, he is."

Eleanor glanced up at Bucksted, who seemed a little embarrassed by such a tribute. "I begin to believe it's true!" she cried, smiling.

Bucksted shook the man's hand and received as his prize a lovely porcelain doll with long blond curls. As the proprietor began to boast of Bucksted's skill in a loud voice, the earl quickly took Eleanor's arm and drew her away.

"You would never have struck me as a man who would run from praise," she said.

"Were it deserved, I daresay I wouldn't, but there are any number of men equally as capable as I."

"I find that hard to believe," she murmured.

When he bestowed the lovely doll on her, she thanked him. "You do not wish to save it for your daughter one day?" she asked.

He glanced down at her in surprise. "Why would you say that?"

"Oh, I don't know. I suppose I can envision you, at some

distant point in the future, with a child on your knee, a little girl perhaps, sporting very long curls, who looks up at you admiringly. Then I see you telling her all about that wretched Miss Marigate, with scarcely a proper manner about her and a tongue so untameable as to be worthy of removal, whom you once had the good fortune to escape wedding. In the end, you present her with this very doll as proof of my existence."

When he threw back his head and laughed, she added, "You might also be able to use the entire episode as a sort of improving lesson for her."

He frowned slightly as he looked down at her. "I'm not certain about that. The more I know you—and may the gods forgive me for saying so—the more I begin to like your forthright manner of addressing me." He then hurried up this speech with, "But pray, I beg you, don't take this as permission to unleash again every vile opinion you have of my character, for I promise you I shall be smarting from your previous lashing for at least two decades to come."

His eye was full of too much laughter and teasing for her to take him entirely seriously. One thing she knew for certain, however, she was beginning to like him, as well, and a great deal too much for her own good!

Seven

A few minutes later, after Eleanor had teasingly admired Buck-sted's prowess with the pistol, she felt her legs attacked by what proved to be young India Keynes. She quickly drew the child into her arms and queried, "Where is your mother and the rest of your family?" She glanced around, but saw no one familiar to her.

The child pointed into the crowds, and she followed the line of her finger. After a few steps, the remainder of the family came into view, Mrs. Keynes's visage contorted into an expression of deep distress.

"India!" she called out.

"Mama!" the child called back. "I found 'er! With her papa." She was referring to Bucksted.

The error was an honest child's mistake, but one that made Eleanor meet Bucksted's laughing gaze with a smile of her own.

She then addressed her friend. "How do you do, Mrs. Keynes? You remember Lord Bucksted, of course?"

"O' course, me lord. And a good day to ye both." She dipped a brief curtsy, such as she could manage with one babe over her shoulder and another cuddled on her hip. "We been plannin' t' come t' the fair fer over a year now. I did so want me little ones t' have a bit o' fun."

"I'm so glad you were able, then," Eleanor remarked.

Fred squeezed through the legs of one of his older brothers and held his arms up to Bucksted. The earl hefted the child into his arms and asked him if he'd seen the bears yet.

"Aye," Fred responded. " 'Twere two huge uns!"

"Aye, that they were," Bucksted responded readily.

Eleanor watched him in some fascination. Whatever opinions she might have previously held of him, this much was also true—he had a way with children. She saw him in a few years, just as she had told him, dandling his own toddlers on his knee, playing at hide-and-seek with them, reading to them and probably scolding them often. He would be a good father, she mused.

Something within her heart swelled at this thought. Most of the young gentlemen she knew would fairly kick young children out of their paths before they would bend to play with them or even to acknowledge them. Not so with Bucksted. When more of the children crowded round them both, he very kindly asked their names and ages, information each was happy to provide.

After a time, Mrs. Keynes apparently decided her offspring had harassed the patient earl enough. She began calling them to her and directing their attention elsewhere. It was at this moment that Bucksted reached into the pocket of his breeches and withdrew his purse.

"Do but look what I have," he announced. "A Gypsy gave me several pence and said that I was to pass them along to the first group of children I encountered. If I followed her instructions quite strictly, then my wife, once I was wed, would treat me with great kindness the rest of my days. I suppose, then, these must belong to you?" In his hand were enough pence for each child to have one.

"Oh, Ma!" Fred cried. "Can we 'ave the Gypsy's coins?"

Bucksted glanced at Mrs. Keynes who appeared distressed. "Indeed, you must take them," he pressed her, extending the few coins toward her.

She stared at them, fully cognizant of the gesture, yet reluctant. Eleanor watched the woman's pride wrestling with her desire to see her offspring have a good time at the fair.

"These are just for the children, mind," he added coaxingly. "Nothing for you, I'm afraid. The, er, Gypsy was quite adamant about that. The whole thing had something to do with a prophecy about my wife bearing me a great number of children, which I do indeed long for. Pray, then, don't refuse these coins and jeopardize my future happiness."

Mrs. Keynes looked around at her hopeful yet silent brood. This act had clearly been endured more than once in the course of her life, and more than once such kindness was refused. "I know I oughtn't," she began with a frown, "since I don't want me children believing in so much superstition, but for your sake, I suppose I ought to oblige."

The children released a few cries, squeals, and even one or two huzzas into the air. Bucksted gave her the coins. She in turn passed them out to her offspring who instantly scattered like chaff in the wind to whichever amusement had appealed to them most. Mrs. Keynes, her youngest children still clinging to her, thanked Lord Bucksted very sweetly for the, er, Gypsy's generosity and finally gave in to India's plea to be taken to see the Punch show.

Once her dark, worn skirts had disappeared into the crowd, Eleanor said, "That was beyond kind, Bucksted, and so cleverly presented. She would have refused otherwise, I am convinced of it."

"I would have in her situation. No one likes to be reminded of their lot in life, especially when that lot is so very low."

"Indeed," she murmured. Again, she looked up at him, wondering about him. She would never have expected him to have given coins to the children. The thought crossed her mind that he was perhaps trying to impress her, wishing to raise himself in her esteem. This, however, she dismissed. Bucksted was many things, but he was not interested in courting a good opinion for any reason.

Eleanor spent the remainder of the afternoon with Bucksted at the fair. Every possible amusement was searched out and partaken of, including several sets of country dances enjoyed beneath a pretty canopy at the eastern edge of the grounds. Bucksted had purchased several bits of trumpery for her, as well as a silver filigreed comb for Margaret and several silk ribbons in varying shades of rose for Kitty.

When he at last brought her home, she was delightfully fatigued and expressed her enjoyment of the day's adventure with a smile and a kiss placed on his cheek. "Thank you, Bucksted. I had a wonderful time. Are you certain you wouldn't prefer to keep the doll?"

He chuckled softly. "No, thank you. I should like you to have it, knowing that once in a while you'll settle your eyes on her pretty golden curls and think of me and of the afternoon we enjoyed together one beautiful June day."

"How very romantical!" she cried playfully. She started to descend the curricle, but he caught her arm and prevented her from doing so. Something in his expression gave her pause, as though he was looking into the future and willing her to do the same. What was he thinking?

A westerly wind slipped around her shoulders and a chill went through her. Was the future calling to her even now? A future *with* Bucksted? After all, the doll, then, would belong to both their children.

But what nonsense was this?

She had no intention of seeing the betrothal through. Surely he felt the same. So, why did he gaze at her as though he wanted her to hear his thoughts, to understand them.

He said, "I wish that I had known you in London."

Her smile faltered, "Bucksted, you would never have approved of me, nor would any of your famous hostesses whose virtues you are constantly extolling."

"I cannot agree with you," he said. "Except for a mild tendency to speak your mind a trifle strongly, everything else about you is near perfection."

"You can't mean that!" she cried, laughing.

"I do mean it." He spoke almost fiercely.

Her heart began to quake. She felt in danger somehow. She was entirely unused to the flirtations of men, having always kept such entanglements at arm's length. If Bucksted had somehow decided he wanted to see if he could wiggle his way into her affections, she could only admit at this point that he was succeeding.

"There is much about me, however, that you do not know," she said at last. "That is what I am referring to."

He leaned toward her. "I wish to know everything about you," he responded, his voice low, his breath upon her cheek. "Even if we are not to be wed, I confess I am intrigued by you."

She had to leave. She had to break this spell he was casting over her. "I must go. I refuse to listen to any more of your nonsensical speeches." She quickly climbed down from the carriage with the ease of a young lady who had been wont to do so her entire life.

A second more, and she disappeared inside.

Bucksted watched the door shut behind this strange creature to whom he was presently *not* betrothed. He felt confused and exhilarated at the same time.

Just now, when he had pressed her about being *near to perfection,* he had both meant it and yet not. He knew a dozen females far more poised and elegant in person and speech than Eleanor Marigate, he knew a dozen who were more accomplished on the pianoforte, he knew a score infinitely more versed in the various means by which a woman could entice a man; yet, for all this, he had never before been charmed by a woman as by this mischievous, outspoken female who had jilted him.

She had appeared completely taken with him as he flirted with her and teased her and whittled away at her resistance. He began to believe he truly could win her affections and restore his wounded pride. On the other hand, he hadn't given his original designs even a moment's consideration the entire day. He had simply been caught up in the pleasure of her company.

Good God! Was it possible he was in danger of losing his heart to this country maiden?

He laughed at the thought. No. That would be quite impossible.

He set his team in motion and felt their weariness as the leader stumbled forth in harness. "Only a few miles left, old fellow, and then you'll have a satchel of oats, a long rest, and as much grazing as you please."

* * *

Eleanor rested for an hour before dinner and was sufficiently recovered from the day's enjoyments to give a quite satisfactory account of her trip to both Margaret and Kitty. The ladies exclaimed over Bucksted's gifts, properly remarking on his ability to shoot a pistol well and finally murmuring their hearty approval that he had given money to the poor Keynes children.

"You will not be seeing him this evening, then?" Kitty asked.

"No," she replied. "Today held enough amusement for one day, and besides, I will need to recuperate for tomorrow night. From the little Bucksted told me, the island *fête* at Whitehaven is destined to be unsurpassed."

"The island," Kitty said dreamily.

"Oh, yes, the island," Margaret agreed. "I can hardly wait."

Shortly after dinner, just after Eleanor had set her foot on the first step of the staircase, she was caught up short by one of the footmen who presented a missive to her on a silver salver. She recognized the handwriting at once, and her heart instantly added a score of beats to its usual rhythm.

She hastened up the stairs, but waited until she had shut the door of her bedchamber before breaking the seal. The letter read, "Eleanor, I regret to inform you that my plans have changed, and if you wish me to deliver the gift as promised, I shall have to do so at noon tomorrow."

Old feelings of excitement and danger returned anew. She felt as though she might jump out of her skin. The letter was from Martin, of course, and the words were a code. *Noon* meant midnight and *the gift* was of course the latest shipment from France.

She folded the letter into a tidy square, then secreted it in the pocket of her gown. She found herself grateful that Martin had acted so quickly. Since their conversation earlier that morning, she had begun to fear he would set aside her wishes and refuse further shipments.

Ah! Another smuggling run! She could hardly wait!

She crossed to her wardrobe, intending to retrieve the clothes she would be wearing for the night's venture, when a different sentiment altogether assailed her—one almost of regret.

For some reason, her mind was suddenly full of Bucksted and the pleasant time she had had at the fair in his company. What would he think of her, were he to discover the truth—that she was a smuggler?

His words came back to her, prickling her conscience.

Everything about you is near to perfection.

He had seemed to genuinely hold this new opinion of her, she had seen as much in his eyes—no dissembling there!

She felt very queer as she considered the earl. The thought of Bucksted learning the truth about her made her heart squish up into the size of a walnut. For some, quite incomprehensible reason, his opinion was hourly becoming more important to her, and she understood his mind well enough to know that he would never condone her activities even if she was smuggling for the purpose of fulfilling her father's legacy.

She gave herself a mental shake. She couldn't allow her concerns for Bucksted's opinions to deter her from her objective—not now when she was nearly within reach of her goal. If Romney could sell tonight's merchandise for another five hundred pounds, she would have all the money she needed to sustain Sir Henry's philanthropic commitments.

Time to make her preparations. She dropped to her knees and opened the doors of the wardrobe. She removed the false wood floor of the old cabinet and withdrew a set of Martin's cast-off clothing which he had lent her for each run to the coast. Later, he would see that the same set of clothes was laundered and pressed for the next smuggling run.

She replaced the board, shoved the clothes beneath her bed, and rang for her maid. Within a half-hour, the entire household would know that poor Miss Marigate had the sick headache again and would not be seen about the house until late the following morning.

Her mother, as was her habit, came to inquire after her, expressing her concern yet again that she suffered too many headaches for a young woman and requesting to be permitted to summon the doctor.

As was Eleanor's habit, she refused the ministrations of a physician, insisting that any number of her friends suffered as she did and protesting that Margaret had had the headache only a fortnight past.

"Yes," her mother agreed, plucking at her paisley shawl. "But if you recall, there was a large gathering of clouds in the north, and within the hour the storm drenched the countryside."

She smiled wanly at her mother. "There is scarcely a cloud in the sky, so I cannot blame the weather, but I promise you I am not ill beyond this annoying headache. Please have no fears for me on that score."

Lady Marigate frowned. "You poor thing. It was perhaps the sun, then. You were at the fair for too long a time today. I shall speak with Bucksted about his having taken you in an open carriage. I am not at all disposed to think so much air and sun is of use to anyone!"

Eleanor bit her lip. She hadn't felt quite so well in years and was of the opinion that the day's traveling, and a little of the company perhaps, had given her such a marvelous vigor. Presently, she required every dramatic facility to keep her excellent health from her parent.

She closed her eyes and winced. She laid a hand aside her temple. In weak accents, she said, "Pray, Mama, do you think you could extinguish the candle now? The light— Oh, I am so miserable."

"Of course, my pet. Did you take your laudanum?"

"Yes," she lied, and winced a little more.

"I'll leave you then," her mother whispered. She leaned over and placed a kiss on her daughter's cheek. The heavy smell of jasmine wafted over Eleanor's face. "Good night, my dear."

"Good night, Mama."

At midnight, Eleanor stole down the servants' stairs. The household, keeping country hours, was entirely asleep, as she had expected it to be. She quit the manor by the kitchen door and made her way along the shadows cast by the dwelling and past the maze to cut quickly through the hedge that led into a narrow field of flax bordered on one end by a stream and a narrow path. The smell of wildflowers and wild roses was thick in the air. Her every sense was heightened.

The oak wood opened at the end of the path. A recent shower and subsequent sunshine had enriched the air with the pungent, heady fragrance of the ancient trees. She spied Martin in the shadows.

"My God," he called to her in a forced whisper. "You always take me by surprise in your breeches, coat, and top boots. Yet, still pretty by half!"

She recalled their conversation of yesterday and felt a blush rise on her cheeks. She didn't think she could bear a return to the subject of his affection for her. "Hallo, Martin! So you will still call me pretty even though I am dressed as a man!"

"Yes," he responded baldly. "Are you certain you won't reconsider my offer?"

"And what offer would that be?" she asked teasingly.

"Good God! Did I not make that part clear? I know I told you I loved you."

"Regardless," she said, her heart warm with affection for him. "My answer would still be no, must be no."

He sighed, then smiled softly upon her. "I do wish you every happiness, Mutton. You know that, don't you?"

"Of course," she said, giggling at his use of what she had always felt was a truly wretched pet name. "And I wish as much happiness for you, Chops."

He smiled but his forehead crinkled. "I hope I haven't overset you by my declaration."

"No," she murmured. "I'm only sorry that I don't return your affection, at least not in that way."

He nodded. "I beg you will not repine. I never thought you could love me, though I must admit I am enormously relieved to find that you will not be wedding that jackanapes. I was beyond worried, for I could not imagine how he could ever make you happy."

Eleanor again recalled the day spent with him at the fair and found herself uncertain. He had made her happy today. Not that it mattered one whit, of course, only that even if she were to wed him, she no longer believed she would have been entirely miserable.

"Well, I suppose we should be on our way," Martin said.

The first leg of the journey took them to Romney's farmhouse near East Guldeford, at which the old man helped Martin exchange his fast curricle and matched pair for a large wagon and four massive farm horses. In the wagon was a heavy canvas sheeting, several yards of strong rope, and a strong litter used for transporting the cargo from the beach to the cliffs above.

Romney assured them that all had been quiet in the area for the past two days and that though he had heard enough gossip to be convinced the excisemen were still working in the vicinity of Rye, the generous fog that had rolled into the coastal regions would help them get the contraband safely away.

Once aboard the serviceable wagon, Martin kept to old cart tracks and infrequently used lanes, avoiding the King's Highway as he made his way to the coast in the direction of Broomhill.

The smell of the sea grew pungent in the thick fog. Martin walked the horses along a wooded road, then paused at a bend. He descended from the wagon, handing the reins to Eleanor, and moved an old log and scattered brush from an ancient cart track that would lead through the final distance to the cliffs.

Eleanor had helped Martin create the hiding place which could not be seen from the belt of grassland, a mere ten feet in width, separating the wood from the cliff. A moderately wide path led to a rocky beach below.

Eleanor pulled on a pair of thick leather work gloves and quickly descended from the wagon, with Martin following behind. She paused at the edge of the wood, waited, and listened. Her face was already wet from the salty fog. She listened a little more. The only sound she heard was a distant and quite gentle rhythmic beating of waves against the shore. The smell of the sea was sharply in her nostrils.

Her blood quickened. The muscles of her stomach grew taut and firm. She glanced back at Martin and smiled. He carried the makeshift litter of strong oak poles and canvas over his right shoulder. He chuckled softly and whispered in her ear, "You might at least pretend you're not enjoying this!"

She giggled. He gave her a push, and she darted across the grass and leaped down the familiar path.

The fog obliterated the stars and the moon—a perfect night for smuggling. She paused at the base of the path and peered toward the sea. Somewhere in the distance, a schooner was anchored, but not even the faint glow of a ship's lantern could be seen through the mist.

She made her way to the right, feeling her way to the familiar spot where the cargo would be waiting in a dark cove, already paid for by Romney in a secret meeting earlier that day at Rye.

When she reached the beach, she dashed toward the cove and found the contraband hidden behind a wall of rock that jutted out at the edge of the cove.

The task of moving the contraband required a great deal of time since Eleanor's strength was considerably less than Martin's. The kegs of brandy were laid side by side on the canvas litter and carted up the hill two at a time to the wagon. Eleanor's muscles ached in the best way as she made trip after trip. Only the leather of her gloves prevented her hands from becoming pocked with blisters.

The silks and lace were easier to manage since they were rolled into long bolts.

By the time the last of the cargo had been hauled to the wagon and secured tightly under canvas and rope, Eleanor's legs were aching like the devil. She wiped a film of perspiration from her brow. She had just opened her mouth to proclaim their success when the pounding of hoofs forced her to remain silent.

Excisemen.

Her heart instantly doubled in size and she could feel every heartbeat in her throat. Martin ran to the leader's head and held the bridle in a taut grip. His soft murmurs kept the horses quiet.

Oh, God. Martin had said there was more danger now than ever before. Would they be caught? Now? Tonight?

The pounding drew nearer. Eleanor squeezed her eyes shut. She felt ready to cast up her accounts. She could not begin to imagine what would happen to her family were such a scandal to burst upon the Medway Valley, not to mention how such a scrape would affect Bucksted.

Yet, they were protected by the careful position of their hiding place, concealed by the thick wood and protected from the lane by the old log and fresh shrubs Martin had placed behind the log. Maybe they would be safe. Maybe.

She could hear voices now, which became a shouting. "We've missed the turnoff!" one man cried.

"I told ye, 'twas three miles back! I sawr it meself!"

A drawing up of horses followed, along with several shrill whinnies of complaint.

A moment more and the horses were pounding off in the direction they'd come.

When the thundering of hooves diminished, then vanished altogether, Eleanor realized tears were streaming down her cheeks. "Oh, for heaven's sake!" she murmured in disgust.

Martin came to her and placed an arm about her. She could feel he was trembling as well. "I thought we were done for," he whispered. "I would never have forgiven myself if you'd been caught. Thank God, this is the last venture. There must have been a dozen men in that group."

"A dozen at least," she murmured. "But what do we do now?"

"We must wait for a long time—dawn perhaps. They'll be patrolling all night."

Eleanor fell asleep in his arms and only awoke when she felt him stir. "We'll go now," he whispered.

The air was cold and damp. Her bones ached. The horses complained when he put them in motion.

"It's nearly four. I'll be able to get you home just past dawn.

Do you think you can manage to get into the house without being seen?"

"Of course." She'd been able to do that since she was a child. The real questions on her mind were whether she would look completely refreshed for Lady Chalvington's island *fête* that evening and whether Buckstead would notice any telltale evidence of her night's adventure.

Eight

Her mother could not have chosen a better gown, Eleanor mused as she regarded her reflection in the long, gilt looking glass. From the first, when she had learned that the evening's entertainment would involve an island, dinner *al fresco,* and a string quartet, the affair held beneath a high-ceilinged tent, she had been *aux anges* about the prospect of the unusual *fête.*

Now, as she held wide the diaphanous skirts of her white silk and tulle gown, embroidered all over with delightful cherries, she was convinced the evening would be all that any young schoolgirl's imagination could conjure up in the most brilliant of daydreams.

Her sisters were ecstatic as well and had been exchanging jewelry, bits of feathers and lace, ribbons and bows for the past two hours, all in the hopes of creating the most perfect coiffures and fashionable ensembles possible. Eleanor was no less affected by the occasion.

She peered closely into the mirror, noting in particular the hint of bluish shadows beneath her lower lashes. She pinched her cheeks. She smiled. Regardless of the telltale signs of her night's adventures, she felt certain no one would suspect her of anything except a little weariness from the pleasures of her betrothal week.

She twirled in a circle, her maid clapping her hands in complete approval of her appearance. She dipped a playful court curtsy, then prepared to gather up her sisters and depart.

* * *

The island was lit with a score of bobbing Chinese lanterns. From the edge of the lake, where the party of twelve revelers prepared to enter several rowboats, Eleanor thought she had never seen anything so pretty. "They are like glowing butterflies," she cried, "weaving about in the breeze as they are!"

Bucksted, who had hold of her arm, leaned his head close to hers. "Are you pleased?" he whispered, his breath warm on her cheek.

"Very much so," she gushed. "We all knew the idea was extraordinary, but your mother has quite outdone herself." The faint strains of Mozart struck the air suddenly, and Eleanor's arms were quickly covered in gooseflesh. "I shall perish with the delight of it!" she cried.

Bucksted chuckled. "You ought to come to London next spring," he said. "If you think this is anything to be desired, you would be astonished to see the manner in which every hostess strives to cast all the others in the shade. The masquerades are pure adventure."

She turned to him. "How you tempt me!" she breathed out.

He smiled down at her, his hazel eyes warm in the dusky light of early evening. Leaning closer to her still, he whispered, "I only wish I could be the one to introduce you to the delights of society, for I am persuaded that though you profess to enjoy your cloistered existence, you would thrive among tonish life."

She couldn't help but tease him a little. "And I am persuaded," she responded, also on a whisper, "you would likely wring my neck before the first *fête* was over."

"Never," he murmured hoarsely. He caught her gaze and held it quite purposefully. His expression was so solemn, yet, at the same time so intense. What did he mean by it? she wondered. Her heart pounded in her throat.

"Bucksted!" a male voice called out. "Give the lady your hand and help her into the boat! We are all waiting!"

Eleanor turned, quite crimson-cheeked, to look into the face of Bucksted's cousin, Mr. Punnett, whom she had met at the ball two nights ago. He was a dashing gentleman some five years the earl's junior. His hair was blond and brushed in gentle waves about a cherubic face. She thought him a fine man with sensible ideas and a pleasant, easy manner of address. He added, "There will be sufficient time for flirting with your betrothed later."

"Enough of your impudence!" Bucksted responded jovially. He then assisted Eleanor into the last of several small boats, the former of which were already easing their way across the shallow waters to the festive island.

Servants were readied on the nearest shore to hold the boats steady and to assist the guests in alighting with as much dignity as could be managed. The rocking of the small craft caused a number of near tumbles and one or two waist graspings and arm holdings which sent any number of feminine squeals and giggles into the cool evening air.

Bucksted glanced at Eleanor as their own craft gently struck the slanted bank of the island and came to a slightly jolting halt. He was mesmerized by her and had been so from the moment she had arrived at Whitehaven. Indeed, from that moment, he had felt as though he'd been caught up in a dream.

He remembered that he had been laughing at something Colonel Fitzcombe was telling him about Golden Ball Hughes when the butler announced the ladies from Hartslip Manor. He had turned just as Eleanor entered the room. A strange sensation had come over him, as though her presence had brought a warm breeze blowing through the stately crimson and gold drawing room. Every sense had become heightened as he watched her. His blood seemed to quicken in his veins.

Now, as he glanced at her, sitting beside him in the rowboat, he realized with a start that his initial intention of winning her heart—for the strict purpose of later breaking it—had completely drifted by the wayside. His thoughts were centered on how radiant she appeared in her cherry-embroidered gown, how the soft, evening light played so beautifully on her every feature, how she was always so full of life and joy. Even at the fair, she had entered into every silly amusement with enormous enthusiasm. He drew in a deep breath, striving to understand and to control the powerful feelings that were rising in his chest.

Good God! Was it actually possible he was beginning to be in love with her? Oddly enough, the idea did not irritate him as much as he might have supposed it would.

He supported her gently about the waist as she rose to her feet. When the boat waggled, his grip tightened. He knew a strong desire never to let her go.

She met his gaze and her brow puckered. "What is it?" she queried softly, as his cousin jumped from the boat. "You seem, I don't know—distressed, or at least, distracted."

Her words drew him out of his reverie. "I was thinking of yesterday, though I assure you I am not in the least distressed."

Eleanor was fully caught by Bucksted in this moment. He seemed to be speaking many silent things to her. She wasn't certain what to make of him, for he was staring at her with the oddest light in his eyes, just as he had earlier, on the opposite bank. She would have moved her feet, shifted a little to begin her own disembarking from the small, unsteady craft, but she felt suddenly drowsy and satiated as she stared into Bucksted's eyes. He was feeding her soul with a dozen unspoken wishes and unrehearsed proclamations.

If only they were alone, she mused, then he might address her in *spoken* words. Perhaps, then, he might even kiss her.

From a distance, she heard a burst of laughter and was brought back to earth again, or at least to wood and water. She smiled and turned from him, finally giving herself to the servants who held her firmly and drew her onto the bank.

When she brushed past a weeping willow, a view of the lights from the Chinese lanterns and several oil lamps emerged. Three exquisite tulle-draped canvas tents, long strands of ivy cascading from the top of each, met her gaze. Already, four couples were going down a country dance beneath the tent which housed the quartet.

The ladies who danced were dressed in fancy silks or intricately embroidered muslins and floated about on the careful, practiced arms of their partners. The gentlemen were teasing and flirtatious. Was there an eye that was not shining with delight in that moment?

Bucksted drew her immediately to join the dancers, and the next half-hour was a laughing progress down at least two dances.

Iced champagne cups were passed round, the quartet played continuously, the air never seemed to grow chill and unwelcoming.

Later, Eleanor sat beside Bucksted on a thick woolen blanket and ate of cold chicken and asparagus salad. The lacy, drooping branches of the weeping willow hung over their secluded spot. Though she was some distance from her sisters, indeed, from the rest of the party, still she watched her siblings for a time, enjoying the happiness much in evidence on each countenance. Margaret sat on a chair, several of which had been provided for any who did not wish to sit on blankets, and Kitty lounged easily with Mr. Punnett at her side. Kitty's eyes were aglow.

Eleanor could not recall in the past twelvemonth seeing her siblings so enlivened and content, and for that reason she found herself grateful she had agreed to Bucksted's scheme after all.

"Your cousin seems to be an exemplary fellow," Eleanor stated. "Probably one of the most charming I have ever met."

She turned at that moment to watch Bucksted whip his head in Kitty's direction. A frown creased the bridge of his nose so suddenly that Eleanor was taken aback. "What is it?" she asked.

He abruptly reverted his attention to her, letting the frown slide from his face as quickly as it had come. He opened his mouth to speak, then closed his lips.

The most obvious reason for his displeasure coursed quickly through her mind. "Is it because Kitty has no dowry?" she asked. She had little doubt that would be his answer.

"No," he responded quickly. "No, I promise you that is not my concern in the least. I was not thinking of Kitty and her prospects, but rather of my cousin's. I'm afraid he's poor as a churchmouse."

She smiled, and her heart eased up. "They are only conversing. I shouldn't be too concerned. Kitty is a remarkably sensible young woman."

At that moment, another young man came to take up a place opposite Kitty and immediately engaged her in what appeared to be a lively conversation. Eleanor watched Bucksted breathe a sigh of relief and wondered if there was something he wasn't telling her.

She asked him about his family and only had to prompt him a little before he began to talk. He and his father had always been the best of friends. He and his mother got on as well. They were very close, the three of them. He said, "You asked me the other night whether I had missed having siblings, and though I said that I had not given the matter much thought, I was a little surprised later to learn how my mother felt about not having borne more children."

"Indeed?" Eleanor queried. She felt honored that he was sharing such an intimacy with her.

"I'm telling you this because it concerns you. Mama was watching you at the ball. You were dancing with Colonel Fitzcombe—or at least *trying* to dance with him."

She chuckled. "Poor, inexpert Colonel Fitzcombe."

He continued, "At any rate, Mother had tears in her eyes as she watched you. I asked her if anything was amiss. She sniffled a little, then said, 'I hope Eleanor will have everything she wants, I mean, all the children her heart wishes for.' I knew—I didn't have to ask—that she was thinking about her own circumstances and not yours. 'How many did your heart wish for, Mama?' I queried. She paused for a moment before answering, 'A dozen, at least. I had wanted to hear the halls of Whitehaven ringing with all the laughter and squabbling that only a passel of children can bring.'

"I was shocked. I had meant only to tease her a little. I never in my life suspected she had suffered such a disappointment. I had always thought perhaps she might have missed not having a daughter but a *dozen* children!"

"Isn't it odd," Eleanor said, "that we can live with someone our whole lives and still not know them, or all there is to know about them? Papa had been gone some five months, and Margaret and I fell into this enormous argument about whether or not he liked peas. She insisted he hated peas, but I was adamant that they were his favorite vegetable. Mama confirmed he despised them." Her voice broke a little, and he covered her hand with his own. She sighed. "I still miss him so very much. We were like books and words together, he and I."

He squeezed her hand. "I'm so very sorry, Eleanor. I can see how much you loved him. Your father had such a fine reputation. He was a man of great worth and dignity, and was greatly admired."

She nodded. "Everyone loved him. He seemed to know how to live properly. I don't mean just in a moral sense, for he was all of that, but he had such humor and liveliness, he was competitive but fair, and he carried around a dozen axioms which he spit out with unflagging regularity like, *Get over rough ground lightly, Nellie,* and *Don't spit in the wind,* really one of my favorites, for I was always tangling up my life in exactly that way."

"What way?"

"Being foolish about things all the while thinking I was so clever." She felt self-conscious suddenly as she recalled how close she and Martin had come to being caught last night.

He leaned toward her. "You've paled!" he cried. "What maggot just got into your brain?"

She laughed, almost hysterically, at his choice of words. "What maggot?" she exclaimed, trying to divert his attention away from the hue of her complexion.

"Sorry," he responded. "That did sound a bit coarse. It's just that you suddenly seemed frightened."

"Did I?" She searched about quickly and said, "I suppose it was all the talk about my father. The year since his death has been so strange, so difficult."

"Yes, of course," he responded quickly. "Well, I don't want to see that particular expression again, so I will be happy to change the subject." He asked then about her mother, and since Lady Marigate was, in many ways, an amusing woman, she had many anecdotes to relate.

The conversation broadened and deepened, from family to their respective parishes, the difficulties of manor life and maintenance, his childhood wish of working with steam power, hers of ending poverty in her neighborhood.

The evening breeze blew all about Eleanor's face and uncovered limbs. She drew her silk shawl over her arms and tucked her feet more closely beneath her gown. She was feeling a trifle chilled, yet could not bring herself to end the comfortable cose since every syllable passing between them seemed of precious significance.

When she finally shivered despite her efforts otherwise, he drew very close and slid his arm about her. "We are betrothed, after all," he murmured, by way of excuse.

The heat of his body caused hers to relax. She was warm once again. She looked up at him and met his gaze. What a mistake, for there was something in the look of his eyes that set her heart to beating wildly. A truly wicked thought shot through her mind: *If only we were completely alone!*

She felt herself blush, but in the darkness of the evening knew that such a circumstance would be invisible to him.

He dipped his head close to hers. "Did I compliment you on your gown? It is quite lovely." He spoke in a whisper. His breath on her temple sent a shivering of gooseflesh tickling her neck and cheek.

"Yes," she responded quietly, finding it suddenly difficult to breath. "At least four times."

"Hardly sufficient," he murmured.

Oh! Did his lips brush her skin ever so lightly just above her eyebrow? She tingled all over. She wanted him to do it again. Hastily, she responded, "Very true. Not sufficient at all." She waited, breathlessly.

"I have been remiss, then," he murmured. "You look radiant tonight, Nellie."

Oh! There it was again! How soft his lips were, how warm, how moist! She leaned toward him. He covered her hand with his own. She drew in a deep, silent, yet rather ragged breath and closed her eyes. A willow branch swirled in the breeze and its long, drooping fingerlike leaves drifted over her shoulders.

He continued his praise, "Your gown could not fit Aphrodite

even one fraction better than the way it clings to you. You've a lovely figure. All of Olympus must be quaking at Venus's jealousy."

She giggled, but leaned closer to him still. "You are being nonsensical."

"Do you object?"

"Of course not."

"Should I continue? I have a great deal more that I could say to you."

"Oh! Continue then!" She decided in that moment that something strange and exotic was happening. Perhaps the Fates had whisked them away to another land where they were indeed betrothed and very much in love and so could be this ridiculous and this content and this amorous.

His fingers slid over hers languorously. She leaned her head against his shoulder. "My little angelic beauty," he murmured, "do you know that in the sunshine your dark locks gleam a vivid shade of blue? How does it happen that black hair can glimmer like the waters of a grotto at midnight? You are enchantment to me, a mystery, a strange creature that has cast a spell over me. Are you part Gypsy, my lady mischief?"

She looked up at him from the nest of his shoulder. His eyes held her in a mesmerizing stare. Her lips parted. She could barely breathe. "I am no Gypsy," she responded.

"Oh, but you are, and more. No one has eyes like yours, though if they are not Gypsy eyes then a Gypsy must have empowered you in some manner with a dangerous potion. Surely." His voice was deep and every murmured word a song to her heart. The melody she had been hearing since childhood, the words she had never known until now.

"You are the Gypsy," she responded softly. "*You* are practicing your wicked craft now, telling me such whiskers and the like while I recline here, in your spell, believing them all."

She heard his intake of breath, a soft swoosh that melted her heart. Was he as transfixed as she was, caught up in this wonder as she was? She wanted him to kiss her. His fingers made a long journey from her hand up her arm to her shoulder, to finally catch up her chin. He was a breath away.

He placed his lips on hers and in some odd way she felt he was kissing her for the first time. The magic of the evening swirled over her, the seclusion of the island and the gentle teasing and laughter coming from the dancing tent, the darkness of the night which surrounded them both like a velvet cloak, the sweet cunning of his words, the gentleness of his touch, the comforting warmth of his body. His lips felt like heaven, warm and moist and soft.

She had never thought kissing could be so sweet or gentle, yet at the same time begin a passionate raging in her body that seemed at once fierce yet benign. He would never hurt her. The thought swam through the liquid parts of her mind. He would love her in this way, as one determined to drink slowly from the cup. His lips became a warm pulse, and the fleshy softness of his tongue engaged her more deeply in the mystery surrounding them.

She took his tongue and tasted him. He moved against her, seeking a greater closeness. His hand slid over her cheek and nestled at the back of her neck. He moved so deeply into her mouth that she felt completely joined to him. Her soul drifted from her chest and began to move over his soul, mingling her deepest thoughts and hopes with his. She dreamed of living her life with him, forever and ever. She felt suddenly bound to him, to his life, to his hopes and his wishes, to his fears and his heartaches, to his inexpressible places of meanness as well as his heights of gallantry and nobility, all because of a kiss!

He drew back suddenly. "You were touching my mind," he stated, staring at her almost in horror.

"You had invaded my soul," she responded, equally in horror.

He drew back his hand. He stared at her, into her, willing her to read his thoughts.

"We aren't to be married," she whispered. "We shouldn't be doing such things as this."

"I know. For a moment there, I thought I could go on kissing you until dawn."

"For a moment, I would have let you." Tears brimmed in her eyes. She didn't understand what was happening to her. She felt terrified and overset.

"We should join the others," he stated at last. "Good God, Eleanor, I never meant to . . . to torment you or to make you think that—" He broke off, an expression of complete consternation on his face.

"That what?" she asked, laying her hand gently on the lapel of his coat. He caught her fingers in his and kissed them tenderly.

"That I would take advantage of a female in this way. It is despicable. Will you forgive me?"

"Truly, Bucksted, there is nothing to forgive. I gave as much as you."

He nodded, his face contorted with something that seemed like anguish. He rose suddenly to his feet and extended his hand down to her. She gained her feet unsteadily, weaving against him. He caught her about the waist. The awkward slant of the land as it eased downward toward the gentle lapping water caused her to fall into him. He drew her, quite suddenly and unexpectedly, into the shadows of the weeping willow.

His lips were on hers again, only this time in a fierce, demanding kiss that robbed her of breath. She flung her arms about his neck, leaning wickedly into him. He possessed her innocent mouth as he had before, only there was something desperate about the way he kissed her now, desperate and time-robbed.

She felt his need and responded in kind to the transient nature of the joining. She could never kiss him again, not like this. When would she? How could she ever permit him to violate her in this manner again? She was not betrothed to him. She would never be his wife. Only a wife should permit such . . . Oh, he was gentling now, yet fire seemed to be raging over her entire body.

This is passion! her mind cried. She felt passionate in Bucksted's arms. How had this happened?

"Miss Marigate?" a voice called in this distance.

Her mind was foggy with yearnings and hopings. She wondered how Bucksted could possibly speak when he was kissing her so thoroughly. Her hand slid from his neck and down the lapel of his coat. His chest was broad. Her fingers traced the shape of him through the fine cloth of his coat.

"Miss Marigate? Bucksted?"

Now why was Bucksted calling his own name, and how could he when his lips were still touching hers so wildly.

"Bucksted!"

The earl drew back sharply, and Eleanor nearly lost her balance again. She blinked several times, and saw, some twenty feet away, Bucksted's cousin. He stood below a branch which was hung with several Chinese lanterns. His expression was visible in the faint glow of light that surrounded him. He was vastly amused.

"Miss Marigate, this is our dance. You promised me a waltz!"

"Indeed I did," Eleanor responded, her voice strangely hoarse.

She curtsied in an embarrassed and quite unnecessary manner to Bucksted and pushed past him. Her knees weren't working very well. She picked up her skirts a little and concentrated on keeping her balance.

Oh, dear! What was happening to her, and how would she ever be able to face Bucksted again!

Nine

Henry Punnett was nearly half-foxed, Eleanor realized as he missed his steps yet again and laughed outrageously because of it. His brow was a sheen of perspiration, and his cheeks were ruddy with heat. She could not be angry with him, however. He was too sweet, even in his sloppy movements, and far too apologetic, even in his laughter, for her to do more than smile and help him take up his place again.

When the dance finally drew to a conclusion, he led her on, half-stumbling feet away from the tent, the quartet, and the rest of the party toward the lake's western edge. A cool breeze blew, and as he blinked several times, still holding her arm rather tightly to keep his balance, he began to regain his composure. "That is a deuced sight better!" he exclaimed. "By Jove, I should not have insisted on going down that country dance with you. I do beg your pardon, Miss Marigate. You must think me a fool!"

"I think, Mr. Punnett, you've had too much wine!"

He threw back his head and laughed. "No wonder Bucksted loves you so very much. You're very droll, besides being quite the prettiest female I've seen in years!" He hefted a sigh and directed his gaze toward the dark lake and the star-studded sky. She felt an odd tremble pass through her. "Oh, God," he groaned suddenly. "What is to become of me?"

Eleanor was startled. She glanced up at him and saw that his face had become suddenly rumpled with misery. "What is it, Mr. Punnett?" she asked.

He shook his head. "No, I can't burden you with my absurd, schoolboyish troubles, not during an evening of celebration. Come! Let us return to the tent. Colonel Fitzcombe has been longing to dance with you. He says as much every time he casts his eyes in your direction."

He turned to go, but she stayed him with a tug of her arm against his. "I shan't return until you tell me what is troubling you. I've been told I have an understanding ear. So . . . speak, Mr. Punnett, else I shall be quite discontented with you."

He looked down at her, his expression serious. "I wish that I could have met someone like you years ago. How much better my life would have progressed, I've little doubt of it."

"You are far too young to be regretting your life, and if you continue speaking in such a manner I will begin to believe you are given to theatrics." She laid the challenge in the air and watched him closely. His expression did not change except to grow even a little more serious.

"I was in love once," he confessed, "several years ago when I had just turned twenty. She was the sweetest, most endearing creature. Her dowry was sufficient to give us at least a modicum of gentility for—and I have no qualms in revealing this to you—as my father's third son, I've never had even a feather to fly with. At the time, I was preparing to enter the church, as younger sons are wont to do. My mind, indeed the sincerity of my heart, was set on such a course. My bride would have been an admirable vicar's wife, but alas, her father would have none of it. His ambitions were far greater for his daughter than my fortunes would ever allow."

"I'm so very sorry," she murmured. "Such a case as yours, unfortunately, is not uncommon in our day and age. I pity you—and your lost love."

Bitterness swept over his face and countenance. His shoulders slumped. "Easily spoken, when you are to wed into one of the largest fortunes in all of England."

She was a little taken aback. She wanted to tell him that it was no such thing, that the betrothal was a sham, so that he might accept her sympathies more readily, but she was under a firm obligation to keep her peace. However, she certainly had an opinion on the subject, which she did not hesitate to express. "The Chalvington fortune notwithstanding, Mr. Punnett, I do know what it is to be without prospects as you should be aware. My family's misfortunes are generally known in these parts."

She willed him to read her mind, that her acceptance of Buck-sted's offer had been entirely forced on her.

He eyed her carefully. "Good God!" he whispered. "Do you tell me yours is not a love match?" He seemed genuinely shocked. "Yet, when I see the pair of you together . . . Ah, well, if this is indeed the state of things, then I am sorry for you. I spoke hastily before. Pray forgive me."

She smiled. "There is nothing to forgive between friends. I only hope in future you shall not find me entirely without empathy for your plight."

He bowed slightly. "I shall never do so again." He then took a deep breath and faced the westerly breeze once more. The stars flickered and blinked. He seemed noble in that moment, his shoulders well laid back, his nostrils flaring slightly, as though he bore many burdens, yet refused to be a burden on anyone else.

"If only . . ." he murmured.

"If only what?" she inquired.

He clucked his tongue. "Oh, it's nothing."

"If only what?" she pressed him.

He glanced at her in his childish way. "I wonder, Miss Marigate, if I might importune a favor from you, a very small one I assure you?"

"Tonight, Mr. Punnett, with the breeze so gentle on my face, you may ask anything of me, and if it is in my power I shall give it to you."

He smiled. "You are an amazing young woman."

"No more flattery, if you please. Now, how may I serve you?"

He lowered his chin and leaned very close to her. "It is the most ridiculous thing, of course, but I find my pockets are quite to let, and there are still two months to go in the quarter. Do you think, I mean, could you find it in your heart to . . . ? Oh, but I ask far too much of you. I presume too much on the sweetness and generosity of your temperament. Forget that I have spoken."

Never in a hundred years would Eleanor have believed that Bucksted's cousin would beg money of her. She felt oddly numbed by his request, and for the barest moment realized that were she to become Bucksted's wife, this would not be the last of those requests. She couldn't remain silent and said quietly, "I fear you have made your request to the wrong person. I have nothing to spare you. In a sense, even my brideclothes have been given to me by Bucksted, such is my condition."

"Good God!" he cried. "Did you think I meant to ask a loan from *you!* I am such a sapskull. I have bungled the whole of it! Miss Marigate, I would never ask funds of a lady. I was hinting that you might lay the matter before Bucksted. For reasons I cannot mention at present, I have been unable to gain his assistance."

"Then you have asked him before?" She felt her heart grow very still within her.

"I have hinted," he said with a smile. "Bucksted has always tended to ignore me because he is my senior by several years."

Mr. Punnett had only hinted then. Ah, she understood. Bucksted was not precisely the most perceptive of men. "Does he have a notion of how much you would require?"

"Yes, that much I believe he understood in our conversation of yesterday. He was, and rightly so, quite distracted. My cousin seems to be in something of a glow these days."

"Indeed?" she inquired.

Her mind flittered back to a half-hour prior, when she was locked in his arms beneath the concealing willow tree. She had never felt so wild before in a man's arms, so filled with desire and every hope for future bliss. Was it possible the miracle of love had happened to her and to Bucksted as well, and at the very moment when neither was searching for love?

Yet, it seemed so impossible, especially because Bucksted would never understand nor forgive her for having taken to smuggling as she had. That much she knew of him.

For this moment, however, she wouldn't dwell on the impossibility of loving Bucksted or being loved by him. Tonight, she would pretend that she was a simple, dignified miss who was just beginning to know the ways of Cupid's arrows, and she would enjoy Bucksted's company.

She turned in the direction of the dancing tent and saw that the earl was guiding Margaret through an old-fashioned, yet quite charming, minuet. Margaret was moving almost gaily, and Bucksted's expression was all that was amiable and intent on pleasing. Her heart began to swell and melt all at the same time. He was, in so many ways, though quite unexpectedly, her ideal.

She turned back to Mr. Punnett. "Of course I will ask on your behalf."

He took up her hands in his and clasped them fervently. "Thank you, Miss Marigate. Thank you so very much. I begin to think you are an angel."

At that, she could only laugh, especially when she thought of her activities with Martin of the night before. No, Bucksted's appellation was far more suitable. *My lady mischief.* He had called her that on more than one occasion.

But not tonight. Tonight she would be Mr. Punnett's angel.

Eleanor waited to approach Bucksted about his cousin's request. After turning Mr. Punnett over to Kitty's willing hands, she danced with Colonel Fitzcombe and the rest of the gentlemen of the party each in turn.

As the hour approached ten, she was just curtsying at the end of a country dance to a Mr. Long when Bucksted drew everyone's attention.

"To the boats!" he cried. "I have been informed that the fireworks will be displayed shortly on the eastern shore."

A burst of applause ensued along with a great deal of squealing and giggling as everyone ran to the boats.

Bucksted helped all the ladies to clamber aboard, along with the proper gentlemen to row them onto the lake. One of the boats quickly seated six people, Mr. Punnett insisting Kitty and Margaret not be separated. Since the ladies glanced at Eleanor, she quickly realized the entire scheme had been purposeful, to result in leaving a boat for just Bucksted and herself.

She blushed at the very notion of it and could not meet Buck-sted's gaze. Yet, she could not be anything but content with the arrangement. Ever since he had kissed her so boldly, she had been wanting to be alone with him once more.

He steadied the boat for her, and with great care, she took up her place. He followed after, picked up the oars, and guided the rowboat a few yards onto the lake, the dangling branches of a weeping willow sweeping over her back. Within seconds, the fireworks began, a blue scattering of powder and glitter that shat-tered the night sky and became a magnificent, colorful reflection on the lake.

Eleanor exclaimed her delight. He caught up her hand and pulled her toward him. "You will be much more comfortable leaning against me," he said.

She instantly acquiesced and was soon seated on his leg, his arm about her waist supporting her. She wrapped her arm about his neck quite unself-consciously and craned her neck into the sky as the next rocket shot into the air.

She squealed her delight as many of the ladies were doing. The gentlemen, too, were lifting their own huzzahs into the air. All, in fact, except Bucksted.

Eleanor turned to look at him, wondering why he was so silent, and drew back a little that she might look into his eyes. "Are you not pleased?" she asked.

The expression in his eyes, however, made her forget all about the rockets and the glitter and the smoke-filled air.

"I am pleased, very much," he said quietly into her ear, "though in this moment I must confess it is not because of the fireworks."

She could not mistake his meaning. He gave a strong tug on her waist, pulling her against him in a crushing embrace. She flung both her arms about his neck and kissed him as though there was no tomorrow.

Fireworks continued to sing and burst in the air, but she re-mained oblivious to them all as Bucksted kissed her fiercely, just as he had earlier. The boat floated backward and rocked into the shore of the island again. They were hidden by overhanging willows once more. She wanted to slide down into the boat with him and remain there forever.

"I wish we could stay on this island," he said between kisses. "Just the two of us, tonight, forgetting about the future entirely."

"Yes. Oh, yes, Bucksted," she breathed out.

He kissed her for a long time, long after the fireworks had ended and the guests had rowed ashore.

Eleanor wasn't certain why she stayed with her betrothed who was not her betrothed. Perhaps because the future loomed too close, knowing that once the evening ended and she returned to her home, the magic of the moment would dispel and she would be without a bridegroom yet again.

"We should return now," he said at last. "Though I daresay I don't need to tell you how much that notion displeases me."

She sighed. "What will all your friends be thinking, and my sisters as well?"

"That we are being foolish lovers who are to be married in a few days."

Her throat constricted. "But we are not to be married."

He placed a finger beneath her chin and turned her to look at him. "No, we are not," he murmured.

She saw something in his expression, something hopeful and appealing. She wondered what would happen were she to suggest that perhaps she had been mistaken, that she very much wanted to wed him after all. Her heart began to pound in her breast at the very thought of it. Should she suggest such a thing to him? What would he say? What would he think of her? Was she being stupid, forgetting what he really was? How would she ever explain her many excursions to Broomhill in the company of Martin? Would he ever forgive her for it?

She opened her mouth. She wanted to bring forward the subject. Her throat ached with the unspoken words.

"What is it?" he asked.

His eyes were demanding she speak.

"Bucksted!" A voice carried across the waters. Mr. Punnett, again.

Relief poured through her. She needed to ask Bucksted about

helping his cousin. She wouldn't have to discuss the other matter at all.

"We must go!" she cried. "M-my sisters have probably been waiting this half hour and more!"

He nodded. "Yes, of course," he said. "Only, I wish you would tell me what you were thinking just now."

She shook her head and smiled faintly. "It doesn't signify," she responded, "though I wish you to know how very much I've enjoyed being with you, yesterday and today."

"As have I," he responded. He released her with something of a crooked smile. "Perhaps we can speak of this another time, when my cousin is not waving at us and making a spectacle of himself."

She chuckled, for so he was.

As he began to pull toward shore, Eleanor decided the moment was perfect for broaching Mr. Punnett's dilemma. She gently suggested he help his cousin, currently in distress, since at the beginning of the quarter his cousin would be able to repay him in full.

Eleanor had little doubt, especially given the sweetness of their recent embraces, that he would acquiesce and Mr. Punnett would soon be at ease again. However, she was not prepared for Buck-sted's abrupt change in expression, demeanor, and tone of voice. "What?" he cried angrily. "Do you tell me you are asking for money on behalf of my cousin?"

Eleanor felt the heat of his anger burning her cheeks. "Yes," she responded, unsettled. She explained, "He approached me this evening, very embarrassed of course, and informed me of his straitened circumstances. Why are you glowering?"

He shook his head and pursed his lips rigidly together. "Pray forget that he importuned you in this manner, Eleanor. He had no right to do so, to take advantage of you as he has."

"He did not *opportune* me and in no way has he taken advantage of me. He merely spoke of his current need in a very humble manner after I prompted him to do so. Though he did not say as much, I could see that he has become quite desperate."

"As men of his stamp usually do," he said curtly, pumping

the oars in the water and moving the boat more swiftly forward.

Eleanor regarded Bucksted, inwardly grimacing. In this moment she felt used, not by Mr. Punnett's honest request, but by Bucksted's sudden alteration in countenance and character. He had reverted to his normally callous view of the world and of those about him. He clearly had no compassion for his cousin and apparently not the least understanding of what it was to be impoverished.

She wanted to say something to him, but so much anger rumbled around in her head and in her chest that her vocal cords were swollen with far too much feeling. She drew in a deep breath, then let it out in a soft hissing sound.

"You are angry!" he exclaimed suddenly.

"Yes . . . very," she returned.

"Why?" he cried. "What reason do you have to be angry with me?" He appeared dumbfounded.

She couldn't believe he could be so obtuse. "Why do you think?" she retorted cryptically.

"I haven't the faintest notion!"

"Of course you haven't," she said facetiously. "For you always hold precisely the right opinion on every subject and about every circumstance. Only let me ask you this, have you ever conceived of what it is like to never be beforehand with the world, to have to scrape together every tuppence to keep hearth and home together?"

His mouth dropped open, and one of the oars slid from his grip. He thrust his arm quickly into the water to retrieve it, soaking his coat and shirt to the elbow. "How dare you," he murmured. His eyes flashed in the darkness of the night. "How dare you continue to make your judgments without the least knowledge of the situation."

Her anger evaporated with such words, and in its place was only disgust—for him, and for herself because she had let him kiss her so thoroughly only a few minutes past.

"I wish to go home," she responded quietly. "I daresay you and I have nothing more to say to one another."

* * *

Eleanor tossed and turned on her bed seemingly all night. She replayed the evening in her mind a hundred times, the general pleasure, the entire event from beginning to end culminating in a wretched argument with Bucksted which had yet again revealed his character to her. Every time she reviewed the final moments in the rowboat, she cringed and shrank and finally wept with frustration and sadness. How could one man be so cruel, so indifferent to the sufferings of those about him? Such a man would never make a proper husband. *Never!*

He had marched her solemnly to her coach, where he left her with sleeping Margaret and drowsy Kitty. The ride home had been uneventful save for Kitty's yawning remark, "You look fagged to death, Nellie! Don't worry, you shall see your bed very soon."

Her bed, however, had proved a torturous compilation of writhing feathers, sheets, and blankets. A bed of nails could not have been more agonizing.

Once or twice the nagging thought rose in her mind that perhaps she had been mistaken in some manner. Yet, try as she might, she could not conceive of how. She had not been wrong to make Mr. Punnett's request for him. Her heart had been innocent in purpose. And poor Mr. Punnett was obviously in dire need to have laid his troubles bare before her. She could fault him for nothing since she understood his despair so completely.

No . . . no. Bucksted was entirely at fault. His was the blame. His was the heart which lacked compassion.

She finally fell into a deep sleep and slept until ten. Summoning her maid, she was surprised when Alice arrived at her bedchamber and handed her a missive. Her heart leaped into her throat. Perhaps Bucksted had written to apologize to her, perhaps he had decided to help his cousin after all.

She was excited and hopeful. She sat up and broke the seal instantly, but the signature at the bottom of the letter disabused her mind completely.

The missive was from Henry Punnett.

Dear, dear Miss Marigate

I will always be grateful for your efforts on my behalf. Unfortunately, Bucksted was unmoved by your plea. I, for one, should have stormed heaven and earth to have obliged the woman I loved and whom I was soon to make my wife. How Bucksted could be unaffected by you, I shall never comprehend. Yet, I don't mean to defame my cousin's *noble* and otherwise upright character. He simply cannot comprehend what it is to live in poverty as some of us are *forced* by *Fate* to do.

Regardless, I shall always hold with great affection and feeling the simple fact that you acted on my behalf.

I shall forever be at your service.

Yours, etc.
Henry Punnett, Esquire

Rage boiled up in Eleanor, hotter than even the night before. "Alice!" she cried. "My riding habit, at once!"

"Y-yes, Miss!" Alice responded, her eyes as wide as saucers.

The ride to Whitehaven lathered her horse, Maiden, and it was with some relief she turned the animal over to Lord Chalvington's head groom. He took one look at the steaming coat and called out, "John, walk this horse down to the orchard and back!"

Knowing then that Maiden would be well cared for, she turned toward the house. She entered the mansion through the morning room and was startled to find Lord and Lady Chalvington at breakfast.

"Oh!" she cried. "I do beg your pardon!"

Amusement shone in Lord Chalvington's light blue eyes as he rose to greet her. "Miss Marigate!" he cried. "I shall not forgive my son for failing to inform us that you were expected this morning."

"Oh, but I wasn't expected," Eleanor explained, a blush now burning on her cheeks. "I—that is, I had something of great import to discuss with your son, and that is, I must speak with him at once. Something quite urgent has occurred and . . . and I rode here immediately. I took the liberty of riding my horse directly to your stables. Maiden was quite lathered by the time I passed through the gates of Whitehaven." She wanted to disappear into the woodwork. Whatever must they think of her in this moment, with her stammered explanation as to why she felt it appropriate to storm their home on a beautiful June morning!

"You were very right to have done so," Lady Chalvington said gently, settling her fork on the side of her plate. "Won't you join us? We have just begun our repast, or if you are not hungry, perhaps a cup of coffee or tea?" She gestured toward the sideboard which was nicely laid out with several dishes. Two footmen flanked the walls ready to assist them.

"Thank you, but no. I—I only want a word with Bucksted." She was fairly certain her cheeks were by now the color of ripe tomatoes.

Chalvington glanced toward the door of the morning room, a small frown of perplexion on his brow. "Why don't I escort you to the library where you can wait for him? I'll see that he's brought to you."

"Thank you," she breathed out. "I would be most grateful." He gathered up her arm and wrapped it warmly and affectionately about his own. He ordered one of the footmen to inform Bucksted that Miss Marigate was awaiting him in the library. He then led her from the chamber, all the while prattling about this and that in order to spare her the necessity of speaking.

She doubted a millennium would be sufficient to express her gratitude to him for having treated her dreadful arrival as a welcome visit.

When Chalvington led her to the library, he turned toward her, raised her hand to his lips, and kissed the back of her hand in a sweet manner. "Don't be too harsh with the lad," he said, his eyes crinkling with amused understanding. "He's never been betrothed to a woman of spirit before, and all his former *interests* were determined to defer to his every word. He has yet to comprehend the value of a lady who will speak her mind."

"Oh," she murmured. He had given her a compliment, but in

just such a way that she didn't know precisely how to respond. Finally, she said, "I'm sure he's been a very good son to you, my lord."

That only made the Marquess of Chalvington chuckle, after which he bowed formally and left her to her own devices.

The library was an elegant, square chamber, flanked by small-paned windows which faced northeast. A beautiful morning light filtered into the room at a lovely slant, just creeping beyond panels of rust velvet to the side of the windows.

In the center of the room was a tall table for map reading, and beside it a globe of the world. She began to contemplate her situation and especially her impetuous flight to Whitehaven. What a ridiculous figure she must have cut, entering the morning room as she had! Her cheeks began to burn anew!

She spun the globe gently, pushing the Atlantic Ocean with the tip of her finger. Her movements were absentminded as the ball went faster and faster.

A hand slammed down quite suddenly and stopped the spinning. "You will break it," Bucksted said.

"Oh!" Eleanor cried, glancing up at him. "I did not hear you enter!"

"What are you doing here?" he asked. She could see he was not in the least repentant for his actions last night and even seemed quite peeved that she had dared to enter the sacred halls of his ancestral home.

"I came to speak with you on a very important matter," she retorted hotly.

"Indeed?" he queried. "And what would that be? Have you discovered some other relative of mine who is presently out of funds and requires my assistance?"

She narrowed her eyes at him. "You needn't be sarcastic, my lord. It doesn't become you."

He leaned toward her. "I don't give a fig whether it becomes me or not!" His expression was wholly challenging.

She pursed her lips, settled her hands on her waist, and tossed her head. "Whether you care or not, there is something I left unspoken last night, and it must be said."

He crossed his arms over his chest. "And pray tell what might that be? A new cataloging of my faults or just a fresh raking of your former complaints of me."

"Mr. Punnett wrote to me. I take it he left Whitehaven to return to London last night?"

"Evidently."

"Did you not even speak with him before he left?"

"No. He understood my mind. Words were entirely unnecessary!"

"Oh, but you are abominable and heartless. The worst of it is you haven't a mite of understanding of his predicament or the continual distress of his situation."

"Nor do you," he retorted.

"You forget. I have lived as he is living now."

"No, you haven't." His voice was cold and flat.

She shook her head at him. "How can you be so obstinate, so unwilling to consider the sufferings of those who have so much less than yourself?"

"I am sick to death of your wailings about how I haven't a grain of compassion for those less fortunate. I think there's something you need to see. Right now!" He stepped toward her and grabbed her arm.

"Let me go, you beast!" she cried. She tried to jerk his hand away, but he was unforgiving in his determination.

"I will not. You may strain and struggle all you like, get yourself bruised black and blue for all I care, but I will not let you go and you *will* come with me."

She stopped wiggling about and looked up at him. She was shocked by his violent attitude. "You are hurting me."

"Come," he stated menacingly.

There was only one thing for it. Clearly he'd gone mad, and she must now pacify him by doing as she was bid, else she was unlikely to escape with her life.

She followed meekly beside him as they quit the library, mounted the stairs, and moved into a small chamber in which were situated more books, a desk littered with various papers, a tall wing-back brown leather chair which was drawn up in front of the desk, and a second matching chair in the corner by the window.

He drew her roughly around the side of the desk and fairly shoved her into the chair. "Sit!" he commanded her.

She adjusted the long train of her dark blue velvet riding habit about her feet and said, "All right, I'm sitting. What do you want of me now?"

He flung a hand toward the clutter on his desk. "Because of your wretched words last night, I have spent the last several hours going through all of these, making notations of figures and separating the worst into that pile on the far right." Here, he reached across the desk and picked up the stack, then continued, "These are the many demands for payment I or my father have received in the past six months from Mr. Punnett's creditors. *You,* Miss Marigate, will now spend the next hour or two or three doing the very same thing, or by God I'll wring your neck. For I'll not sit by another minute and have you accusing me of that which you know not!" He threw the letters in front of her with a vengeance.

Eleanor felt all the blood drain from her face at the mountain of receipts, letters and scraps of vowels began to swim in front of her eyes. "Good God," she breathed after glancing at several of the items, "is your cousin a . . . a gamester?"

She turned to look at Bucksted, who had moved to stand by the window, the morning light spilling over his blue coat and buff breeches.

"Precisely," he muttered, unwilling to look at her.

Eleanor sat very straight in the chair for a long moment as she lifted one receipt after the next and read of Punnett's obligations. She then drew the chair forward and adjusted her riding habit a little more. "Will you procure me a pot of tea, Bucksted? It would seem I shall be very busy for *an hour or two or three.*"

She did not look at him. He walked briskly past her and disappeared into the hallway. She settled in to sort through Henry Punnett's *trifling* affairs.

Bucksted returned after a time, bearing the tray himself. He prepared a cup of tea for her, with a little milk and sugar and a plain, strong cup for himself. He pulled the chair by the window forward and watched her work.

She made a neat list of every receipt, marking those with a tick which had been accompanied by a nasty letter demanding payment or threatening prison for Mr. Punnett.

At the end of two hours, she totaled the figures. Even though she had been several times overwhelmed by the enormity of this or that debt, she was still astonished to find that the sum came to over eight thousand pounds which included several recent gambling debts.

She presented him with her compilation. "I misjudged the situation entirely," she said quietly. "I beg you will forgive me, for the extent of my hostility as well as the terrible words I said to you. You were very right to take me to task."

He glanced at the final sum, then set the paper on the table. She had expected him to gloat, but in the end he seemed very sad. "I grew up with Henry, Hank as I was used to call him when we would run amuck about the neighborhood. He was game for any lark. He received an inheritance two years ago, a tidy sum, over fifteen thousand pounds. My father begged him to see it invested, secured for his future, but he would have none of it. From that time he lived very fashionably indeed. However, his spendthrift ways caught up with him. These began arriving six months ago."

"Then he lied to me as well about wanting to marry a certain young woman and . . . and about his wish to become a vicar?"

"Half-lies, I'm sure. When he was younger, he expressed an interest in the church because he fancied the livings which he was convinced my father would give to him once he took holy orders. The lady you mention, whose name would be better left unspoken, was willing to marry Henry based on these prospects. What Henry didn't understand was that my father already had several fine men employed in the livings within his command. He had no reason, no desire, to remove them for Henry's sake. When Henry confronted him about them, there was a terrible row and his *beloved,* when she learned of Henry's turn of fortune, ran off with a baronet from Sussex with three thousand a year."

Eleanor considered the history for a long moment and finally murmured, "Poor Mr. Punnett."

"Now why the devil do you say that!" he flared. "Your compassions must have some bounds, Eleanor, else they will become useless. Henry suffers from a want of character."

"I know that," she said in defense of her soft heart. "I was expressing my sadness not over his want of fortune, but just as you have said, his want of character. He will know a great many hardships, worse than poverty, I fear, in years to come. I don't doubt he will very soon be in debtor's prison."

Bucksted shook his head. "My father has already decided to settle his debts."

"Ah. He wishes to avoid the scandal?"

"It's not that. He feels guilty I think. Henry has always been a favorite of his, and for as many years as I can remember, Papa would settle a debt here and one there, but nothing of this magnitude."

"You must listen to me," she said. "Henry ought to face his problems now, not later. Let him spend some time in Newgate Prison. Help him furnish his room, but don't pay a farthing more."

He stared at her, disbelieving, for a long moment. "This, from you?" he cried. "It is incredible."

"I am not wholly without understanding," she retorted.

He eyed her carefully for a long moment. "You are thinking of your mother, aren't you?"

"Yes, and that had she not cast all caution to the wind I would never have accepted your offer of marriage as I did. Bucksted, I—I would very much have liked to have met and come to know you under much different circumstances." Her mind drifted quite suddenly to her smuggling activities. "*Much* different circumstances."

He chuckled. "Nellie, I believe that is the nicest thing you have said to me yet."

Ten

That evening, just prior to the musicale at which the famous Catalani was to perform, Eleanor watched Bucksted with hungry eyes. Most of the guests had taken up their seats, with the exception of Daphne Westwell with whom Bucksted was presently flirting quite outrageously. He stood very close to her, a circumstance which caused Eleanor's fingers to curl up into strange little claws. With some effort, she relaxed each digit. Daphne was simpering, turning her head this way and then that in slow movements, like a cat stretching in a patch of warm sunshine. She unfurled her fan and hid a trill of laughter behind a spread of feathers and lace. Her eyes sparkled like gems and never left Bucksted's face for a moment. Eleanor was disgusted.

Bucksted was smiling now and so lost in his conversation with Daphne that he did not hear the violinist tuning his instrument and the other musicians following suit.

Eleanor felt sick inside as she watched the woman flirting with Bucksted and Bucksted obviously responding with interest.

Something within her heart had changed since the previous day when she had made the accounting of Mr. Punnett's debts. Bucksted hadn't railed at her for her mistake; he had been humble and obviously concerned for his cousin's future. He had displayed his character to her in that moment, and she had been thinking of little else since.

Her cheeks grew warm with embarrassment. She had truly misjudged Bucksted, even from the beginning. Yes, perhaps he had erred in his initial courting of her and in his stupidity in thinking that he could mold any female to his liking. These, however, she had begun to think of as the follies of untried theories.

Presently, her own follies were sitting rather heavily upon her shoulders. Why, for instance, had she not seen through Mr. Punnett's ploy? Why had she thought so well of him without knowing anything about him, yet at the same time had been determined to believe ill of Bucksted?

Why, indeed?

Perhaps she was afraid of Bucksted, of her growing feelings for him, in a way she could not precisely understand. Her gaze was still fixed on Daphne and how she was making him laugh. Her heart thrummed in her throat, and her neck ached. She felt ridiculously like crying.

She was losing him!

But this was nonsense! She had never possessed him in the first place, and once the betrothal week ended in but three days, she would probably never see him again.

She was so overset by these thoughts that she averted her gaze entirely and concentrated instead on the palm which flanked the stage in front of her. The next moment, the famous Catalani stepped from behind the curtain and moved to the center of the stage.

A rippling of enthusiastic applause brought the extraordinary songstress to a bow before her appreciative audience. Only then did Bucksted guide Daphne to her seat, then take up his own next to Eleanor.

She did not look at him—indeed, how could she?—but rather kept her gaze fixed on the woman who now began to let her throat swell with song.

Lord Bucksted could not help but be satisfied as he crossed his arms over his chest and smiled. He was a man and as such enjoyed the attentions of beautiful women. However, that was not what gave him such marvelous pleasure in this moment. He could scarcely keep from chuckling as he thought of how his bride-to-be had responded to his flirtation with Daphne. He had been watching her furtively as she glared at Daphne more than once and finally averted her gaze altogether.

He believed he had nearly succeeded in the very thing he had set out to do, win Eleanor's heart. Of course, he could not be completely certain, but the pained expression on her face even now gave strong evidence that she was not indifferent to him.

Only . . . what did he want to do with such sentiments as Eleanor was exhibiting? Several days ago, his desire had been to see her heart broken to the same degree she had injured his pride on the day of his arrival at Hartslip. Only . . . was that what he still wanted?

He glanced down at her. She held her chin stiffly and refused to look at him. Faith, but she was exquisite even when she was miffed.

He recalled the way she had looked yesterday when she had stormed at him in the library, oh-so-contemptuously, about his unwillingness to give succor to his cousin. She had not exhibited even the smallest fear of him, and had shown decidedly no interest whatsoever in trying to impress him. He had known for a bare moment, when her eyes lit with passion and her complexion with a beautiful flame, the strongest, most powerful desire to take her up in his arms and kiss her for an eternity.

Then his own anger had flared, and he had forced her to review Mr. Punnett's debts. Now, as he watched her, as Catalani's magnificent voice flowed over him and around him, he reached over and took her gloved hand.

How quickly a blush suffused her cheeks! She glanced down at the hand covering hers. He watched a tear well up in her eye. He squeezed her hand. He willed her to feel the excitement he felt at being with her as the music swelled and filled the ballroom. The chandelier above began to hum. She slowly turned to look up at him.

His mind seemed to grow full of her thoughts. She was returning his sentiments, matching them to a shade. Who, then, had conquered whom? Would she want him, though, in a forever-after way, or did she still think so poorly of him that she could never relent and become his wife? Then again, did he want her to be his wife, this woman who had only begun revealing herself to him a few days past?

Eleanor felt the tight pressure of his hand through the remainder of the concert. She was undone by it. She didn't know what to think. This was no playacting on his part, of that she was sure. He was pretending nothing for the benefit of the onlookers. He wished for something from her.

She felt herself both possessed and the one who possessed. How was that possible? What was Bucksted thinking? Was it in any manner likely that he still wished to wed her? No, that was unthinkable when she had so abused him, not just yesterday but on his arrival a few days past.

She didn't know what to think, and her neck still ached as she turned away from him and tried, albeit in vain, to concentrate on Catalani.

The remainder of the concert and the brief supper afterward did not allow for serious conversation. Eleanor was disappointed, but her own fatigue from the week's events, including the horrendous night of smuggling, was beginning to tell in every part of her. She was physically tired and equally as worn out from trying to guess at Bucksted's sentiments and from wondering just how she would ever be truly content again once he had returned to London or wherever else the year's events would take him.

She bid him good night as he handed her up into her carriage. She sat by the window and for some reason extended her hand to him before he shut the door. He took it and holding her gaze placed a fervent kiss on her fingers.

She wanted more than just that kiss. She wanted to speak with him, to ask the questions uppermost in her tortured mind, to caress his face with her hand, to look into his eyes and try to determine, if she could, the precise state of his sentiments.

At last, he released her and closed the door. The postillion set the horses in motion, and very soon the darkness of the night swallowed up her carriage.

Later, she lay in bed very much awake for a long, long time. She reviewed over and over every aspect of her relationship with him, the strained, truly wretched beginning, all his lectures, and the dullness of his letters. She considered her own silent concession to becoming his wife so that her mother and sisters might be comfortable again. She remembered waving down his coach, and seeing him emerge so tall and handsome, so stunned by her conduct, so ready to take her to task, and then so completely dumbfounded when he came to understand she was jilting him.

She recalled the kiss in the garden, the kiss in the secret chamber, the several kisses on the island, and the way he had looked at her during Catalani's concert. Warm waves of something very close to wantonness flowed over her at the thought of how much pleasure the quite innocent act of kissing had brought to her.

Therein, she decided, lay the heart of the matter. Bucksted had aroused a passion within her that had never come alive before. Only Bucksted, whom she had been determined to hate, had done so. Only Bucksted who, in three days, would no longer be her groom-to-be.

She wept into her pillow as she thought of life without him. And yet what would life with him entail? She would always set up his back, and he would undoubtedly grow even more clutch-fisted, not less, as the years wore on. But what did any of that matter when . . . when she was a smuggler! Even if she admitted her love, even if he professed a love for her, even if somehow they could agree on issues of importance, how could Bucksted ever accept as a bride a female who had been engaged in the smuggling trade for the past year?

The entire situation was *hopeless,* she sniffled due to the melancholy of her thoughts—for even if she considered the possibility she had tumbled in love with him, she could never completely respect him and—and besides, why would he ever want to marry such a wicked female as she!

She awoke the following day with puffy eyes and spirits that seemed to have drooped all the way to her silk slippers and which enjoyed being trod on step after step.

Her mother asked if she was bilious. Margaret begged to know in a whisper if she'd come the crab with Bucksted and now he was mad at her. Kitty came closer to the truth, "Oh, Nellie," she breathed out, "don't tell me you've actually formed an attachment to Bucksted?"

Eleanor's brow was crinkled as she spoke, and never had she looked so youthful.

"No—yes—oh, I don't know!" she cried in response. Tears leaked from her eyes, and she brushed them away angrily.

Kitty clapped her hands, "But this is marvelous. I have thought for some time, at least since his arrival here, that you were wondrously suited to one another."

Eleanor regarded her in surprise and blew her nose. "Why do you say that?" she asked, stunned.

"Well"—Kitty considered, pursing her lips studiously—"I suppose it is because of the way he looks at you when you but enter a room. Honestly, Nell, it's as though the sun only began to shine in that moment. He sees you, and then his eyes smile in that way of his . . . you know."

She knew precisely what her sister meant. "They do?" she queried, disbelieving.

Kitty nodded. "And then there is the way you dance together, as though you'd been doing so since time out of mind instead of only a scant few days."

"He is quite skillful."

"I saw him stumble while guiding Miss Goudhurst about the floor at Lady Chalvington's ball."

"You did?" She could not credit he could ever do so.

"But then you know what Miss Goudhurst is," Kitty responded, laughing. "Her ankles are nearly as thick as her knees!"

Eleanor laughed outright, and she hiccoughed, then giggled a little more. After a moment, she cried, "Oh, Kitty, I am lost." Suddenly, the tears gushed a little more and wouldn't stop.

Kitty, always sympathetic, put an arm around her elder sister's shoulders and kissed her cheek. "How can you say that? Do but think! If you have now tumbled in love with the man you are to marry how much more could any woman wish for?"

This only made Eleanor cry harder as she turned her head and buried her face into Kitty's shoulder. She let herself be comforted for a few minutes, then finally drew back to blow her nose. "You've been very sweet to listen to my silly weepings and wailings. I think, though, that I ought to begin preparing for the *al fresco* nuncheon. I daresay I must look a fright."

"Only a very little," Kitty murmured, "though if you were to wear the light blue silk, I am convinced the lovely color would enhance your complexion more than a plain muslin."

Two hours later, Eleanor walked beside Bucksted as he guided her along a path toward the Home Wood. She wore the blue silk, just as Kitty had recommended, but felt that her restored appearance had more to do with the fact that Alice had placed cold compresses over her eyes for an hour before she dressed for the outing. Even so, she felt entirely subdued.

Bucksted complimented her on her gown and on her appearance generally. When she responded with a very quiet, "Thank you," he paused in his steps and gently drew her to a stop as well.

"Is anything amiss, Eleanor, for I vow since your arrival you have been uncommonly quiet. Your demeanor has put me fully in mind of the two occasions upon which I visited you previous to this week. I don't hesitate to say I tremble at the thought of it."

Eleanor couldn't help but smile, though tremulously. She glanced up at him, catching a full view of his handsome face from beneath the brim of her wide, straw bonnet.

"I—that is, there is something troubling me, only I don't know where to begin . . ." How could she tell him that she knew she would miss him dreadfully once the last ball of their betrothal week came to a conclusion on the following evening.

He took hold of her arm, "Only what, my lady mischief? Please tell me what is troubling you?"

"Only I was thinking of the future a little. I . . . I hope that we shall meet occasionally once, well, once we have staged a quite furious quarrel and ended our betrothal." She tossed her head, hoping by doing so that the gravity of her heart might not be fully exposed.

"I try not to think of the future overly much," he responded evenly. "At least not today. I prefer to think of the expansive blue sky overhead and the smell of the woods before us. Oak and fir, both so strong, so pungent. Do you care to accompany me a little ways into the wood?"

He was obtuse. He did not hear her soft hints, even in the least. All he thought about apparently was the fragrance of fir, and he probably meant to collect a few acorns as well. She sighed. "If you wish for it," she said resignedly.

"Indeed, I do," he responded emphatically.

Before she moved into the wood, however, she turned around and glanced back at the mansion and the rest of the family party.

"Whitehaven is so beautiful," she murmured.

"Yes, it is," he agreed.

Two of Bucksted's female cousins had attended the *al fresco* nuncheon along with their children. A neatly scythed lawn, the labor of several gardeners, rose in a steady grade toward the wood behind her. The distance from the mansion was probably the length of a quarter mile. Several of the children were flying kites and squealing as they ran down the hill, trying to get them to soar aloft. The scene was utterly idyllic.

Made of white stone, Whitehaven was a beautiful diamond, glinting in the sunlight. A long procession of servants marched from the house, bearing tables and chairs and service ware for nuncheon.

Lord Chalvington was resting, of all things, on his wife's lap.

"Look at your father," she said.

He leaned over her shoulder and, dipping beneath the broad brim of her hat, whispered against her cheek, "He is probably snoring by now."

She chuckled. "Do but look how your mother strokes his forehead. Was theirs a love match?"

"Yes," he whispered softly, his lips suddenly touching her cheek.

Gooseflesh rippled down her neck. Tears brimmed in her eyes again.

He slipped his arms about her and held her close. "I wish things had been different for us, Eleanor," he said.

Her heart swelled and began to hammer against her ribs. She wanted to tell him that she thought perhaps she had erred and wouldn't mind marrying him after all, but she couldn't. In part because she wasn't certain this was true, but also because she was quite simply afraid to say anything so bold to him. What would he say in response? She truly didn't want to know. Oh, blast! It was all so hopeless!

"Come," he whispered after a few minutes. "The wood is nearly as pretty as this vista."

She turned with him, her heartbeat slowing, her spirits drooping once more.

She walked slowly beside him. The path was clearly marked and ambled in a leisurely direction both across and up the hill toward the west. Sunlight dappled the spongy, leaf- and needle-laden trek. The fragrance of oak and fir, just as he had said, permeated the air thickly.

He did not offer even a mite of conversation, and she had no interest in speaking of anything, so the walk became a quiet communing.

At last, he said, "There is a lovely glade which overlooks much of the downs. We are nearly there."

He had to push aside several branches of fir before the path opened up to a view of rolling downs and a scattering of trees. In the distance a silver-blue ribbon wended its way through a verdant valley.

"Oh, its beautiful, Bucksted, truly. I'm so glad you brought me here." A breeze redolent of grasses and mulchy earth swept over her, some of her sadness drifting away on it.

She looked up at him and smiled. He released her arm and slipped his about her waist. With his other hand, he drew apart the ribbons of her bonnet.

"What are you doing?" she cried, her heart feeling light for the first time all day. Surely he meant to kiss her—again.

"I want to see your hair." He lifted the bonnet from her head. Then, stepping very close, he drew her into his arms. She could feel the brim of her bonnet against the backs of her legs. "Now tell me something, my pet. Have you been crying?"

She scowled up at him. "You weren't supposed to have noticed and certainly were not to have mentioned the matter to me."

"Quite thoughtless of me, I suppose," he said softly, but his brow was puckered. "Only tell me, have you?"

She smiled wanly. "Just a little, nothing to signify, I promise you. I'm just, oh, I don't know, missing you, your company."

"What do you mean? We are together right now."

She smiled, but again a whole host of tears threatened her countenance. "Yes, we are." She looked up at him and met his gaze. She wanted so much to speak of the confusion she felt in her heart. She wanted to know if he was feeling a similar ambivalence, but she was too afraid to ask. She was frightened of the possibility that the answer would be far from what she wished, nay even longed to hear. A sudden breeze buffeted the skirts of her gown. "But we won't always be together."

A crooked smile touched his lips. "Yes, that much is true. One day I shall pay my debt to nature as we all shall."

Such a cryptic response. She blinked at him, uncertain what to think. "That is not what I meant."

"I know. But I daresay if I begin to think what . . . what my life shall be like next week, I shall begin to cry as well. And to own the truth, though I'm certain you would be careful not to reveal as much to anyone, the 'truth will out' and then where should I be? 'Have you heard,' the gossips will exclaim. 'Bucksted is become a watering pot!' "

Eleanor giggled.

"There, that is very much better. I've not seen such a long face on a female before. My mother thought you might be suffering from the headache."

"She did?"

"Yes. She instructed me to discover if it was true. Yet, how odd to learn that you are sad because once we end our betrothal you shan't see me anymore."

He had spoken her heart aloud. The winds seemed to catch up his words on light wings and fling them all about her head. She felt dizzy. His lips drew near. "Oh, Nellie," he whispered against her mouth, "what is to become of us?"

He pressed his lips gently to hers. She leaned into him, wrapping her arms about his neck. He pulled her tightly against him, the rim of the bonnet still striking her at an odd angle. His kiss deepened. She parted her lips and allowed him to penetrate the soft, intimate recesses of her mouth. As before, she felt joined to him in some magical, mystical way.

A soft groan sounded in her throat. He placed one arm about her shoulders and held her closer still. He kissed her harder, almost desperately. She was overcome with familiar sensations of passion, the way she always seemed to feel in his arms. She was lost to the feel of the earth under her feet and to the cool breeze blowing from across the downs. She was floating. They must be floating together.

She forgot herself entirely as she hugged him tightly. "Bucksted," she murmured again and again as his lips began to play over hers.

"Nellie," he breathed in response.

The word "love" played through her mind in an exotic tune she had never thought would really be played for her. She had always felt like the shell of a pianoforte, without resonant strings within to receive the strikes of Cupid. How dull she had always been until now, until these past few days when she had found herself enraptured by Bucksted's embrace. Her knees felt weak, her limbs trembled, her stomach was running riot. She was dizzy, exhilarated, and content all at the very same moment.

How could she let him go? How could she let him drift out of her life, especially when she had only so very recently come to know him? How could she live the rest of her days without him?

She drew back slightly. Her lips felt wondrously bruised, and a shimmering of tears put Bucksted in the softest, dreamiest focus. "Why didn't you kiss me like this the day you offered for me? I vow I should have gone anywhere with you then."

He laughed and shook his head. "I was a complete simpleton not to have done so. I wanted to. You had taken me into the garden. You were so quiet, yet so extraordinarily beautiful. I have often thought of you in that moment. I recall that you turned toward me, looking up at me with a dozen questions in your eyes. You seemed so sad. Yet even in your sadness you possessed a radiance I am unable to explain. I believe now that is what drew me to you in the first place, not my absurd belief you were a *conformable* female. Eleanor, I hope I don't cross some dreadful line at this time by telling you that, even after all the wretched things you've said to me, by God, I think I've fallen in love—"

A sudden, powerful noise, the boom of a gun, erupted not thirty feet away in the Home Wood.

Eleanor jerked at the unexpected sound. A shouting began. A man called out, "Halt! At once!"

"What the devil!" Bucksted cried.

"What is it?" Eleanor exclaimed. "What has happened?"

Another booming of a hunting rifle ensued.

"I think there can be only one possibility. The gamekeeper has caught a poacher!"

Eleven

Eleanor hurried along beside Bucksted, heading back to the expansive lawns on the northern slope behind Whitehaven. Every few seconds she expected to hear yet another discharge of a rifle, so that even at the sound of a crackling branch beneath her feet she would jump.

Bucksted matched his pace to hers, though with his long stride she was certain he could have outdistanced her in a trice. She could see he was tense and uncertain as to what had happened. Only once did he comment, "The poachers have been a scourge in our woods for the past several years."

She glanced up at him, the hostile tone of his voice not lost to her. She felt obliged to say, "I am not in the least surprised, with the price of grain as high as it is."

He met her gaze, his brow wrinkled. "So, you will be at that again?" he queried.

"You cannot disagree that many are forced to poach to sustain their families—hardly a crime."

He opened his mouth in astonishment and finally said, "What you are suggesting, were we all to justify our conduct in such a manner, is another word for anarchy.

"I am not justifying this man's conduct, only explaining it, even sympathizing with his plight."

"Well, I am glad to hear that!"

Eleanor fell silent. She let her gaze move to the footpath in front of her, her jaw growing rather rigid as she marched quickly beside Bucksted. Old sentiments returned, quite strongly. She was reminded once again of Bucksted's rather cold heart. The disparity in their views once more asserted itself, and so it was with each step she took, much of the delirium of his recent embraces drifted away.

When she finally emerged from the woods at the edge of the lawn, she found that thirty yards away a crowd had gathered about a man kneeling while another bound his hands behind his back with a rope. Upon drawing closer, Eleanor saw that a trail of blood was dribbling down the kneeling man's cheek. His clothes were terribly worn, the simple garb of a country laborer without his smock. His hat was pulled down over his eyes. She wondered who he was and whether she might be acquainted with him, since she knew many of the poor about Whitehaven.

"Just as I thought," Bucksted muttered. "A poacher. We've finally caught one of them. I have you to thank for that, you know."

"What?" Eleanor cried. The very thought of it made her feel queasy.

He flung an arm toward the group and said, "The gamekeeper—there, the one binding the man's hands. He's the one you insisted I employ here."

Eleanor felt herself pale. The punishment for poaching was quite simple, the man would be brought before the local magistrate and, if found guilty, hanged for his crime.

Bucksted immediately fell into conversation with his father about what was to be done next.

Eleanor couldn't believe a poacher had been caught. She felt terrified for the man. She met the gamekeeper's eye. He seemed rather triumphant. Bucksted congratulated him and thumped him on the back.

She rounded the group so as to see the poacher's face more clearly. She wondered again if she knew him.

Bucksted commanded him to stand up. He struggled to gain his balance with his hands tied as tightly as they were.

She could see the side of his face now, but with his hat slouched over his eyes and the blood covering up his cheek, she wasn't able to determine his identity. She moved a little more to the front of him.

Lord Chalvington dispersed his family from about the unfortunate man. Several of the male servants now approached, stoney-eyed. Was there a workingman who did not sympathize?

One of them pulled the poacher's hat off. By then Eleanor had made her way to a point directly in front of the man. She met his dazed eyes and gasped. "Oh, no!" she cried.

Bucksted glanced at her, a little stunned by her outburst.

She whirled around, her hands pressed to her cheeks. She began walking swiftly toward the house. Tears were already running down her cheeks. She stumbled and fell to her knees on the lawn, then picked herself up and began to run.

"Nellie!" she heard her mother call. "Kitty! Follow your sister. See what is amiss!"

She ran into the mansion, feeling wild and panicked inside. Her only thought was that she must inform Mrs. Keynes at once that her husband had been captured by Chalvington's man. When she reached the entrance hall, she commanded a footman to bring round Lady Marigate's traveling chariot. She climbed the stairs by twos and only vaguely heard Kitty calling to her.

When she reached the lady's withdrawing room, she quickly removed her pelisse from the wardrobe as well as her traveling bonnet, which she switched for the broad-brimmed summer hat.

Kitty was breathless when she appeared in the doorway. "Nellie, whatever are you doing? Have you gone mad! Everyone is in such a state because you are behaving so oddly. Lady Chalvington thinks perhaps you've had too much sun! Wh-what are you doing? Where are you going?"

Eleanor stared at her youngest sister. "Do you know what they do to poachers?" she queried.

Kitty frowned as though studying the matter judiciously. "Well, I suppose they hang them."

"Precisely."

"It is terribly unfortunate, but that man was breaking the King's Law."

Eleanor's shoulders slumped. Even her sister hadn't a mite of understanding. "He will be dead after the hanging," she stated bluntly. "He will no longer be able to provide for his family."

"You don't even know that he has a family. He's probably one of those terrible fellows who sells the meat to the London markets."

"I know him, Kitty," she stated quietly.

Kitty's mouth formed a silent oh, and her fingers covered her lips. "Who is he?" she asked after a profoundly quiet moment.

"Mr. Keynes. He has a wife and eleven children. They live in a hovel near a very marshy tract of land not far from Whitehaven. I know them all very well. I know that Mr. Keynes works day and night to care for those he loves, but that Mr. Whiting, Chalvington's tenanted farmer, has refused to offer the assistance he needs to drain the lands allotted to him. I know that they suffer badly from the ague because of the noxious air. I know them all." Tears smarted her eyes once more.

"Then it is no wonder you are so distressed. I do beg your pardon, Nellie. I had no idea."

She finished buttoning up her pelisse and walked toward the door. "What concerns me more is that, without so much as a shrug of your shoulders, you dismissed his hanging as though it were no more significant than if you were having kippers rather than eggs for breakfast."

"I am sorry, Nellie. I . . . I just don't have your sensibilities and poaching *is* contrary to the law."

Eleanor knew she couldn't persuade her sister to think outside these boundaries, but added, "Should you have a chance to look at Mr. Keynes before he is taken away, I wish you to notice how thin he is. Does he look like the sort of man who thrives off of stealing the bounty of his neighbor?"

Kitty frowned and blinked. She bit her lip. "I will look at him," she promised, "and I will think about what you've said. You remind me so much of Papa in this moment. I am truly sorry if I offended you."

"There, there!" Eleanor responded. "I didn't mean to make

you cry. Pray tell the others that I have gone to fetch Mr. Keynes's wife. She will want to know what is going forward."

"I'll tell the others."

By the time Eleanor left Whitehaven and returned with a very subdued Mrs. Keynes beside her, the *al fresco* nuncheon had been devoured by the family, the youngest children were lying down for afternoon naps, and the elder ones, all of whom could swim, were rowing boats to the island on the westernmost reach of the property.

She met Bucksted in the courtyard of the stables where, it turned out, Mr. Keynes was being held prisoner until such time as the local constable could be summoned to take him to Glynde Green. He arrived not ten minutes after Eleanor took Mrs. Keynes to her husband.

"What will happen to him?" Eleanor asked as she took up a place beside Bucksted.

"Mr. Ripple, the constable, is discussing the matter with my father. I shouldn't wonder but that he will be taken to the village and locked up in the roundhouse at Glynde Green until such time as he can be tried for his crime."

"When will that be?"

"A sennight, perhaps more."

"He will be hanged."

"Undoubtedly," Bucksted said seriously.

"You will not be saddened by such an event?"

He turned toward her. "I knew from the moment I learned the identity of the man and that you were so closely connected to the family that this was how it would be, but, my child, you must understand . . ."

"I'm not your *child,*" she answered quietly.

He took in a deep breath. "No, you are not. I meant it as an endearment, but I was wrong to have employed a phrase that could only be applied to a very *conformable* young woman, which you are not." He was smiling a little, but his eyes were full of sadness. He continued, "You have more than once shown me your deeply compassionate heart, which does you much honor. Surely, in this case, however, you must admit that Mr. Keynes was caught in an unlawful deed and must, by the very nature of protecting our entire society from such reoccurrences, be punished. Where would we be if it became known that every scapegrace were allowed to do what he wished with merely a slap on the back of his hand for his crimes?"

"I know your opinions. Why then do you place your arguments before me? Do you expect me to agree with you?"

He lifted his brows. "Of course. It is only logical, a natural sequence of right thinking which must lead every sensible man or woman to such a conclusion."

"I wish everything were so simple for me," she responded. She then took his hand and said, "Come with me for a moment, will you?"

He nodded somberly, and she led him to the stables. At the far end, Mrs. Keynes was lying in her husband's arms, sobbing. The man's eyes were still glazed from the wretched turn of events the day had brought him. He neither looked at them nor in any other manner acknowledged their presence or even his wife's except to pat her shoulder in a dull manner.

"Of course she is overset," he whispered.

"But what else do you see, Bucksted. Pray *look* at them! Recall what you saw at their home a few day's past, what do you see now? Can you not see his sunken eyes and the hollows of his cheeks?"

He merely shook his head and turned away. She followed him back to the cobbles of the courtyard.

"It's called poverty, Bucksted," she stated to his back. "Such as you nor I have ever, nor will ever know. And not a genteel sort of poverty as many endure, for these at least have sufficient coal, bread, and honey to survive from winter to summer and back again. Mr. Keynes does not eat because all goes to his children. Theirs is a stomach-gnawing hunger."

Bucksted whirled on her. "He broke the law. Do you understand? *He broke the law.*"

"That is not the point," she countered firmly. "What other choice did he have?"

He threw up his hands and ventured into the house.

Eleanor remained on the cobbles, intending to take Mrs. Keynes home once her husband was removed from the estate. She approached Lord Chalvington and the constable whom she knew quite well to be a hard man whose decisions always fell on the side of the law.

She pleaded with both of the men anyway. She spoke for a long time, giving a history of the family and of her association with them, of Mr. Keynes's long-held hope that he could see the marshes properly drained, of the despair the family would endure were his crime to result in the usual punishment, ending finally in a plea that he be released under her care, that she would take the whole family to live at Hartslip until she could see them on a ship to the Colonies.

Lord Chalvington spoke, "Your sentiments speak greatly for your generous character, Eleanor, as they must for any woman of fine sensibility. However, I cannot make an exception in this man's case. It would not be fair to the many who have died in former years because of a similar crime. Until the law is changed, I will not be party to any such abuse of power. In this manner, I am in complete agreement with my son."

Her hopes were dashed on these words. She excused herself and went to the stables, where she comforted both Mr. and Mrs. Keynes, learning from them that the assistant gamekeeper had long harbored a deep resentment against Mr. Keynes. "Borde knew I took game from Whitehaven's woods. Most 'ereabouts do. 'E followed after me this morning. 'E said as much after 'e shot me face and dropped me to the ground."

Eleanor recalled the moment she had commanded Bucksted to bring Mr. Borde to Whitehaven. What a great irony, she thought, that one man's blessing, and that from her own hand, had become another man's misery, as much from her own hand as if she'd lifted the rifle herself!

* * *

Eleanor took Mrs. Keynes back to her home and addressed the oldest children. She promised them she would do everything in her power to free their father and that they mustn't give up hope. Her own father, beloved as he was in the county, had had many powerful friends, and she would not cease her efforts until their father's life had been spared.

The faces gathered about her were solemn, several tear-stained. She promised to send round a basket from her pantry before the sun set, and on those words she left the unhappy household and returned to Hartslip.

She spoke with Cook first, telling her of the Keyneses' wretched misfortune and encouraging her to take as much from the larder as possible to see the mother and children through the next day or so.

" 'Tis a great sadness," Cook moaned, shaking her head and blowing her nose. "A fine family, the children as respectful as those of any noble household in the valley. Tsk. Tsk. If only yer papa was here. He'd 'ave the situation mended in a trice."

Eleanor did not attempt to promise she could do the same, for she wasn't yet certain what she could do. She thanked Cook for her kind attention to the matter, then retired to her bedchamber for a long think.

After an hour of heavy cogitations, she knew what she had to do. The family needed money to leave England, and leave England they must! That meant she would have to take money from her fund. It also meant she would have to make at least one more smuggling run to the coast. But she wouldn't think about that just yet.

As for Mr. Keynes, she also knew exactly what needed to be done, but she could barely voice the thought in her head—nonetheless aloud—without quaking in her slippers.

For a long moment she pondered the possibility of begging Bucksted for his help in her schemes, but she soon dismissed this avenue. She and the earl disagreed far too strongly, and on too many topics, for him to be of any use to her now. She knew he was a man who would defend the law to his death while she was a woman who felt the injustices of the law ought to be circumvented when the stakes grew far too high to be in any manner tolerable. If a certain sad longing accompanied these thoughts she quickly set them aside. She had far greater concerns to tend to than the melancholy of her own heart. She had a life to save and a family to send abroad.

She sat down at her writing desk and quickly penned a note to Martin, asking him to meet her in the oak grove at nine o'clock that evening. Somehow, she would persuade him of what they had to do next. She then drew a tin from the secret compartment of her wardrobe and withdrew eight hundred pounds—an enormous sum, but what would be needed to secure passage to America.

Afterward, she had the horses hitched to the traveling chaise and drove to the town of Headcorn, where she purchased thirteen tickets to Bristol by the next two mail coaches. Then, she drove to Mrs. Keynes's house, gave her the tickets, as well as the money, and told her in great detail the plan she had formed for them all. They were to pack their belongings, pile into the wagon, and travel to Headcorn to await the arrival of Mr. Keynes.

"But, Miss Marigate!" Mrs. Keynes cried, staring white-faced at the enormous sum which had just been placed in her hands. "What do ye mean by all this?"

"Why, I intend to help Mr. Keynes escape from prison and to see the rest of you safely to Bristol and thereafter, to the Colonies. Your family is unknown in Headcorn, and if you are discreet, no one will be the wiser."

"But—but, I canna accept this money."

"You can and you shall!" Eleanor snapped. "And I'll hear no refusals, not now, nor ever. I'm only doing what my father would have done in this situation, and I know that were he standing before you, you wouldn't think of refusing. Besides, you must give all your thought to the future of your children and forget for now about your pride."

Mrs. Keynes was decidedly taken aback. "Aye, miss, just as ye say."

"That's better—thank you."

Mrs. Keynes grimaced, "But will not the constable follow after us and prevent our leaving?"

"I don't think so," she said. "No one truly wants to see your husband punished, and I'm certain all the villagers will remain silent when it is known he has escaped. You see, Lord Chalvington could not permit your husband to go unpunished because that would have set a terrible example for the rest of the parish. However, he is a good and a noble man, and when he learns your husband has escaped I believe with all my heart he will not permit anyone to pursue the matter."

Mrs. Keynes sat back in her chair, her chin growing quite determined. "I will do all that ye've said. Thankee, miss." Tears brimmed in her eyes.

Eleanor elucidated her hastily sketched plan. Mrs. Keynes listened attentively and finally said, "So, ye wish that I be at Glynde Green, with a gig and pair, no later than half-past midnight?"

"Precisely."

"I'll be there, make no mistake."

Eleanor watched with great satisfaction as Mrs. Keynes's features became quite set and determined. She then called for her eldest son and immediately began instructing him as to the night's forthcoming events.

Eleanor left her home, satisfied that her plan would prevail.

That evening, at eight o'clock, Lord Bucksted sat at the oak desk in his office, where only two days past he had watched Eleanor methodically review all of his cousin's debts. He was in a brown study and nearer to feeling blue-deviled than he had been in his entire existence. He wished over and over that he had never taken it into his head to offer for Nellie Marigate. Even now he could not conceive whatever it was which had persuaded him to do so! He must have been mad as Bedlam because for the life of him he could not understand how he had made such a wretched error in judgment.

He dropped his head into his hands and groaned. What was he going to do? Even the question was ridiculous because all he had to do was get through one more evening with her, the final ball of the betrothal week, and he would be rid of her forever. Only . . .

Only . . .

Dear God, when had it happened that he had actually tumbled in love with the wretched, belligerent, opinionated, headstrong, impetuous chit! Was ever a man born who had been so completely knocked over by Cupid as he?

He laughed outright, shook his fist heavenward, and generally made bullish sounds which only ceased when he heard his father's voice in the distance calling to some servant or other. A moment later he heard a rapping on the door.

"Come," he barked.

The Marquess of Chalvington entered the chamber with a twist to his lips and an amused light in his eye. "One of the maids thought you might be exceedingly ill for she heard you groaning quite 'fiercelike' as she told me."

He leaned back in his chair and shook his head yet again in complete exasperation "What am I to do with her, Father?"

Lord Chalvington chuckled and took up a seat in the leather winged chair. "Beautiful day today," he murmured absently as he glanced toward the window. He then turned back to his son. "As to your dilemma, I haven't the faintest notion. She is a handful, I'll grant you that."

Bucksted turned his chair to face his father and said quite seriously. "She jilted me on Monday, the very moment I arrived at Hartslip."

Lord Chalvington's silver brows shot up in surprise. "Indeed?" He appeared both shocked and amused. "You mean just this past Monday?"

Bucksted nodded.

"But I don't understand. Why, then, did the pair of you continue on?"

"My pride, my abominable pride, of course. I couldn't bear the thought of the scandal it would create, what with so many of my friends, acquaintances, and family prepared to attend the events of the week."

Lord Chalvington frowned. "She must have been greatly overset."

"She was."

"How then did you persuade her to enact this charade?"

"It wasn't difficult, not with her mother having accrued any number of tradesmen's bills in the past few weeks—Eleanor's brideclothes."

"Ah," Chalvington murmured. "You bribed your bride-to-be, eh?"

"Precisely. The trouble is, I am at this completely hopeless place of having fallen in love with her, yet dreading the prospect of marriage to her and at the same time doubting she would have me anyway!"

Chalvington drew in a deep breath and let out a hearty sigh. "Isn't it a fascinating truism that the very moment you feel you can master your life, some hysterical unknown raises its ugly head and spoils everything?"

Bucksted stared at his father, and a gurgle of laughter began to rise in his chest. "You've no idea. I . . ." He began to laugh, "Good God, I thought she was conformable."

"Son," Lord Chalvington said, shaking his head, "how could you have been so bacon-brained?"

"Have you never heard anything so absurd?" He could no longer control his laugher. He howled because it was beyond absurd. He explained in fits and starts how quiet she was the day he'd called on her to offer for her.

His father joined him, and together they laughed until both were wiping their cheeks.

"You were clearly never in her company for any extended period of time, then," Chalvington stated.

"Never. Last summer, when I saw her in Three Ashes, I found myself caught by her beauty, even enchanted. Since I had been incredibly inept at falling in love with any of the usual, gentle London misses, I thought I would extend a hand of compassion toward her, toward her family since you so esteemed her father, and make up for their many losses since I was the new owner of Hartslip."

"You've a good, if misguided, heart, and I'm proud of you for that."

Bucksted chuckled once more. "I shall never forget that conversation we had when she waylaid my coach before I arrived at Hartslip."

"She stopped your coach? In the lane?"

"Yes. Her hair was quite lopsided from running. I believe she may have been watching for my arrival from one of the tower rooms."

Chalvington shook his head.

"I immediately began to give her a severe dressing-down for I yet held the strong belief that she was *interested* in my opinion. That was when she told me she couldn't marry me. She was sorry for it, but she didn't esteem me."

Chalvington whistled. "No mincing words there."

"Hardly. I was never more stunned or angry. I felt strongly inclined to give her a solid thrashing, especially for daring to cross my own conceited self-opinion."

"There is no question now that she is the proper wife for you. I had my doubts at first, when you told me how she gave every evidence of being willing to wait upon your every word, but now I am fully convinced."

"Did you never suspect that I was such a despicable fellow?" Bucksted inquired.

Chalvington grimaced. "My son, we are all despicable and caught up in our own conceit, especially when there are so few about us willing to speak the truth because of the Chalvington rank and fortune."

Bucksted fell silent, letting his gaze drop to the floor. "If we are to marry, if she will have me, I daresay we will quarrel nine days out of ten."

"You mean as your mother and I do?"

Bucksted shot a hard look at his father. "You do, don't you?"

"Yes, and very frequently your mother is right, more often than not. However, I promise I shall flay you alive do you ever say as much to her."

Bucksted nodded and sighed deeply. "If only Eleanor could love me."

At that Chalvington uttered a crack of laughter as he rose to his feet. "She does, m'boy, make no mistake. A female of her stamp does not fall so easily into a man's arms unless her heart is engaged."

He smiled, though crookedly. "She does at that," he said, his heart lighter than it had been since the poacher was caught earlier that day. "Only, how the devil do we get beyond this business concerning Mr. Keynes?"

"That will be a tough one, but I daresay you'll sort it out."

His father left him after that to his own ruminations. He remained in his chair pondering the extraordinary nature of love having found him after all. He was charmed, but full of misgivings. He wondered if it would ever be any other way.

Only one thing became clear in his mind through the chaos of his thoughts—he must speak with her. He glanced at the clock. The hour was late, past eight already. Still, if he rode his strongest horse, he could be there by nine. Surely she would not be abed by then.

He made his decision swiftly. He would go.

The hour could not have been but a trifle past nine when he reached the outskirts of the oak grove which bordered the eastern and southern end of Hartslip Manor. The ride had done him a great deal of good, and in truth he now savored the thought of laying before Eleanor the state of his heart and his desire that somehow they find a way to go beyond their differences and make a true and biding union together.

He turned north, heading toward the manor gates. From the corner of his eye he caught movement in the grove, a white, bounding line which, as he concentrated on it, became the flounce of a gown beneath a black cape.

He drew his horse to a halt and stared at the strange sight. His mind worked in lightning flashes of understanding so that to draw a conclusion required but a handful of seconds—a lady was meeting someone in the grove clandestinely. He nearly spurred his horse forward, unwilling to interrupt what was probably a romantic liaison when he was struck with the possibility that he might know *the lady.*

His heart leaped and thrummed in a horrible manner until he felt faint. His horse responded to the subsequent erratic pulses of his knees and turned almost in a full circle. Bucksted dismounted and tied the reins to a nearby thornbeam shrub.

Somehow, he knew that Eleanor was the lady making her way into the woods.

Eleanor found Martin seated on a fallen log and holding the reins of his horse in hand. He did not seem to notice her approach, apparently deep in thought. His head was bent, and his chin almost rested on his chest. If she hadn't known better she would have thought him asleep.

She rounded the log and slipped her hands over his eyes. She giggled as he grasped her wrists and pulled her hands away.

"Enough childishness!" he barked. "I'm in no frame of mind to be delighting in your playfulness, for I can only suppose you've some madcap scheme in mind."

Eleanor sat on the log next to him. "Don't come the crab, not now, not tonight, for I have solved the deuce of a problem. You have heard about Mr. Keynes?"

"Yes, of course. The entire county must know of his capture by now. But, Nellie, what are you about? Why have you sent for me?"

She minced no words. "We must return to Broomhill."

"Good God, Nell! You know we can't. I nearly got you killed last time. I can't do it again. I won't!"

"You have to. We must return." She then explained about having used a great deal of her money, both in purchasing tickets for the family to Bristol as well as giving Mrs. Keynes passage fare to the Colonies. "Keynes will be hanged, otherwise," she pleaded. "And you know I was saving that money for Father's charities."

"I know," he murmured, his head still slumped between his shoulders. Even in the dappled moonlight, she could tell he was frowning deeply.

"Chalvington was resolute, Martin. He would not hear of releasing Mr. Keynes, so there was only one thing to do, or rather, one thing yet remaining to be done." She willed him to guess at her schemes.

He lifted his head and met her gaze. "Oh, Nellie, what are you about now?"

She smiled fully. "Tonight, at midnight, I intend to free Mr. Keynes from prison."

He stared at her. "By yourself?"

"Why not?"

"Of all the absurd fleas that have teased your mind over the years— Nellie, I begin to think you're not playing with a full deck."

She laid a hand on his arm. "That may be very true, but you must understand, I have been acquainted with Mr. Keynes, with his whole family, for nigh on eight years. I couldn't let him perish at Tyburn Tree."

Martin was silent apace. Finally, he spoke resolutely, "I'll help you free Mr. Keynes, but I'll not return to Broomhill."

"I don't need your assistance in freeing Mr. Keynes. As for Broomhill, I have given that situation a great deal of thought. What do you think about arriving, oh, say, an hour before dawn? The patrols will have become soaked through because of the early morning drizzle and will be inclined to give up their watches in exchange for a rum punch at a local alehouse, don't you think?"

Martin paused, then said, "Very likely."

Eleanor heard the hopeful note in his voice. "Besides, a laden wagon, traveling about the countryside in the first light of day, would not be in the least unusual."

"No, it would not." He sounded resigned. "But why must we go so soon? Why not wait until Romney tells us the patrols have moved to another stretch of coastline?"

"Because I'm using all I've saved recently for the Keynes.

The rest is safely invested, but the vicar is expecting at least three hundred pounds in two days for the households that Papa sustained all those years. I can't—I won't—let him down." For some reason, she thought back quickly to something Bucksted had once said to her about what would happen were it suddenly impossible for charitable funds to be paid? It would seem he had spoken a prophecy.

"I could loan you the sum," Martin said, "and you wouldn't have to repay me for—"

"Never!" she cried. "Don't even think about it. I won't be beholden to you, Martin, not in that way."

"No," he agreed on a laugh, "you'll just have me risk my neck in Broomhill."

"Oh, come!" she cried. " 'Tis not like you to be so henhearted! Besides, we escaped easily enough last time. I am convinced we shall do so again, so long as we follow my plan. Arriving near dawn will solve everything. I am convinced of it!"

"I'll do it, on one condition. If Romney insists it is become too dangerous, then we shan't make another run until it is safe."

She laid a hand on his shoulder where a shaft of moonlight had settled. "Agreed."

He overlaid her hand and smiled halfheartedly. "I am a fool to oblige you," he said.

"You are a man with a generous heart, for you know very well that every tuppence we make from the run will go to the poor. And once the annuity is completed, a score of families will benefit for many years to come."

She leaned forward and placed a sisterly kiss on his cheek. He caught her arm. "Nellie," he murmured hoarsely. "You know how I feel about you, how I've always felt. Tell me there's a hope that we might— Oh, the devil take it!"

He rose abruptly from the log, pulled her up with him and drew her summarily into his arms.

Eleanor received his kiss with a jolt of surprise. For that reason she did not immediately pull away. When she had collected herself, however, she gently extricated herself from his tight grip. She had no intention of wounding his pride or of destroying even in the slightest the wonderful camaraderie she had enjoyed with him for years. However, sharing a passionate kiss was going beyond the pale.

Lord Bucksted felt his neckcloth constrict about his throat. In the listing shadows of the moonlight, he watched Eleanor Marigate stare lovingly into the eyes of that ridiculous whipster, Martin Fieldstone. The soft luminescence of the grove turned a strange bloody hue as the lovers slowly disentangled themselves from what anyone could see was a passionate kiss and embrace.

He had arrived at a place of hiding some few minutes earlier and had watched in stunned disbelief as his bride-to-be playfully placed her hands over Mr. Fieldstone's eyes. Even then he had been nearly beside himself with rage at her antics. Such a game of covering Fieldstone's eyes might have been considered harmless in the full light of a burning sun, but in the middle of the night, in a darkened, shadowy forest, he could only construe the worst of motives to the nocturnal *tête-á-tête*—a lover's assignation!

He had been able to catch only a few words of the conversation, something about midnight and later Broomhill, which he knew to be a village on the coast. He could only construe that the pair was planning an elopement at midnight tonight.

So, this was the truth then—his Nellie was in love with Fieldstone and meant to marry him as soon as she could get rid of her betrothed!

Rage roiled in his chest, so fiercely it was all he could do to keep from making his presence known with a running attack. He wanted to plant Mr. Fieldstone a facer, demand satisfaction of him, then strangle Eleanor Marigate.

He turned away from the intimate scene, fearful of what he might do to either of the young lovers, and returned to his horse. So much of Eleanor's conduct now made perfect sense to him—her anxious wish to be freed from the betrothal, her bouts of hostility toward what she termed his ungenerous conduct, the peculiar way she would fall silent after he would kiss her. And to think he had been nearly certain she was tumbling in love with him! What a bacon-brained idiot he had been, indeed!

He guided his horse back through the shortcut which led toward Whitehaven. He was in a dark, sullen temper and was not surprised when occasionally his horse would look back at him in some curiosity. "Pay no heed," he said at the horse's last flick of the head. "I've merely been cuckolded."

He was halfway to his home when he decided he was not through with Eleanor Marigate. If she intended to humiliate him by eloping tonight with Fieldstone, she would first have to answer to him. In fact, they both would!

Twelve

Eleanor completed her habitual bedtime routine, even going so far as to yawn several times for her maid's benefit. With the candle beside her bed snuffed, she listened intently as the rest of the house, by stages, fell asleep.

When the garrets overhead no longer creaked and had been silent for over half an hour, she stole from bed and quickly dressed herself in an old riding habit of worn red velvet, a gray wool cape, and a straw bonnet decorated with three feathers and an artificial purple violet. On tiptoe she made her way to the kitchens, a wondrous tingling of excitement rippling all over her as she pilfered the cupboards of an apple, an apricot tartlet, and a cup of Cook's cherry brandy. This fruitish feast she handed over as a bribe to the stableboy who already had her horse saddled and waiting for her at the end of the oak grove.

He immediately curled up next to the stone wall, wrapped himself in a blanket and set to enjoying his repast with much enthusiasm. When she returned, she would find him in the same place, as usual, awaiting her arrival in order to slip burlap socks over each of the horse's hooves by which to return him silently to the stables.

She set off toward Glynde Green in high gig, feeling guilty for taking so much pleasure in an event that should have given her a fit of palpitations. She wondered briefly if there might be something wrong with her since she loved her adventures so very much. This she dismissed with a shrug of her shoulders. Tonight, if nothing else, she was saving a man's life. What could be nobler or more important?

Nothing, she decided and so, for the next several miles as she alternately loped and trotted her horse toward the village which held Mr. Keynes in an ancient roundhouse, she did so with a smile.

Bucksted had fully expected his bride-to-be to turn in the direction of Chidding Moot, Fieldstone's home. Instead, she headed northeast along a cart track familiar to the inhabitants of the valley and used infrequently by carriages. Even in the small hours of the morning, an occasional coach could be heard rumbling along the King's Highway parallel to the lane. Clearly, Miss Marigate did not want her movements observed. Only, where was she going?

He followed at a discreet distance, keeping to the shadows of the hedgerows and only topping a rise if he could do so beneath the spreading branches of an oak or chestnut tree. On one final rise, he came to comprehend her destination, and his heart began to beat strongly—Glynde Green, where Mr. Keynes was imprisoned!

Good God! What was the minx up to now? Had he misjudged her *tête-á-tête* with Fieldstone? Apparently so. Yet, why, then had they been speaking of Broomhill which he knew to be near Rye on the coast? And what the devil did she think she could accomplish at Glynde Green?

There could be only one answer, and from her independent manners and airs, he could only presume the worst. How on earth did she think she could manage to release Mr. Keynes?

He followed her into the village, therefore, with a mounting apprehension and was not in the least surprised when she headed directly for the jail.

The street was cobbled and poorly lit. Only one street lamp, some thirty yards away, was maintained for public safety, and nary a lantern was lit in any of the shop windows or the small domiciles above. Moonlight was the primary source of illumination which shone in odd streaks on the sweaty flanks of Eleanor's horse.

He tied up his horse down the street a quarter of a mile away and quietly made his way to the jail. Once there, he listened at the heavy wood door and heard murmurings beyond—the laughter of a man and the joyous highs and lows of Eleanor's tremolo. Mr. Keynes sounded altogether astonished. Bucksted didn't wait a moment longer, but gave the door a shove and saw in a trice what was going forward.

The jailer, his fist clutching fifty pounds, colored up and stuffed the money into the pocket of his box coat. Miss Marigate grew devilishly pale, and the poacher, who had been rising from a chair near an old, scarred table, sank back down, his expression slack.

"Wh-what are *you* doing here?" Eleanor cried, aghast. "H-how could you have known I would be here! I—I don't understand!"

Bucksted did not speak , but advanced quickly to the table and beyond. "Is that weapon properly loaded and primed?" he barked.

The jailer turned around, and the high color on his cheeks faded abruptly.

"I see," Bucksted muttered angrily. The jailer made a move to grab for the pistol, but Bucksted was before him and pointed the finely carved wood and brass gun at the man's chest. "Put Mr. Keynes back in his cell. He's going nowhere, at least not tonight."

The jingle of traces and the clopping of horses hooves was heard in the distance.

Eleanor watched her betrothed carefully. His cheeks were flushed, and there was a hot, ireful expression in his eyes that did not seem wholly appropriate even given these tense and unlawful circumstances. She still couldn't comprehend in the least how he had discovered her scheme to break Mr. Keynes out of prison—unless . . . unless he had been following her! But how, when, why?

As she heard the gig looming closer still, she set her astonishment aside as several courses of action tripped through her head in rapid succession. The wrong one, given Bucksted's obvious anger about the situation, would undoubtedly bring about a firing of the pistol, in all likelihood awakening the entire village, or worse bringing about the demise of either the jailer or the poacher, or perhaps even herself. Whatever she decided to do, she would have to proceed with great care.

"Take him back to his cell, now!" Bucksted cried.

She swallowed hard and lifted her chin. With some effort, she drew her gaze away from Bucksted's blazing eyes and took a step toward Mr. Keynes. "Come," she said quietly. "It's time to go."

The poacher blinked up at her as though she'd gone mad.

Bucksted moved to step between them, but she was before him, placing herself in front of the poacher. The pistol rested against her neck. She met Bucksted's gaze firmly and found herself startled all over again by the rage that dominated his eyes and his face. In that moment, the most handsome man she had ever known looked positively beastly.

She drew in a deep, steadying breath. "You must let me finish this Bucksted. You must. I've made all the arrangements, including booking two successive mail coaches to Bristol for his family, all of whom are presently awaiting him in Headcorn. They will be fleeing to the Colonies where they will have a chance to begin again. Surely you would not deny Mr. Keynes a chance? Surely."

Tears filled her eyes. With his mere presence, he commanded the situation, but with the pistol in hand he was a demon with which she sincerely doubted she could reckon. Her legs began to tremble. The day had been long, the hour was nearing one in the morning, and the long ride to the town was taking its toll. Tears trickled down her cheeks. "Please!" she cried. "I beg this mercy of you. Please!"

At that moment, the poacher rose and gently set her aside. "I'll not 'ave yer life on me 'ands," he murmured. He headed back to his cell, yet at the same time she could hear the carriage draw up next to the round brick edifice.

"No, Mr. Keynes," she pleaded. "Your family is waiting for

you, and your wife is just now arrived. Bucksted will let you go, he will, I know he will!"

"I will not," Bucksted cried. "The law must be served, else we are all lost. What you are doing here is wrong, unlawful, I tell you."

A clattering outside of an undistinguishable nature drew his attention away from Eleanor. He walked swiftly to the door, then passed through it.

Eleanor thought quickly. She turned toward Mr. Keynes, who hesitated. She addressed him. "Go outside and place yourself, if possible, between Bucksted and the carriage," she whispered hoarsely. "He will not fire at you, I promise you. Go, at once!"

When Keynes didn't move, she ran forward, grabbed him by his coatsleeve and drew him toward the door. "Do as you are bid!" she cried. "As much for your own sake as for your family's. Don't worry, I shall deal with Bucksted!"

Still he refused until he heard his wife pleading with Bucksted.

She had never seen Mr. Keynes's feet move faster.

Eleanor followed behind on a run, with the jailer behind her. Everything happened so quickly. The poacher leaped into the gig and took the reins. The jailer held Bucksted back. The earl's elbow flew into the man's nose knocking him backward, blood flowing down his face. Bucksted leveled the pistol at the fleeing gig.

Eleanor screamed, he held his stance, squeezed the trigger but at the last moment deloped.

The shot sounded like a muffled pop.

Eleanor was breathing hard as she stared at Bucksted's arm which was raised high in the air.

He had deloped! He had chosen at the very last moment to forgo killing the poacher which, because of his unerring skill, he could surely have done.

A few seconds more and nightcapped heads peeked from between shutters and out of doorways. Bucksted stood slump-shouldered, on the cobbles, his arm lowering slowly and his gaze fixed to the place where the gig was seen topping a rise and disappearing beyond.

The breadmaker and the cobbler both came toward the jail on a run, one wearing boots, a nightshirt, and a shawl, the other, his nightcap, a robe, and unbuckled shoes.

"What's amiss!" the cobbler cried.

"By Jove is that Bramling with his cork drawn?"

Eleanor glanced at the jailer who had a thick kerchief wadded against his nose and blood all over his cheeks, chin, and neckcloth. "Are you hurt, Mr. Bramling?" she asked.

" 'Tis nought but a trifling nosebleed, miss. Doan fret yerself over the likes o' it." He then turned to stare at Bucksted. "Me lord, ye've been a gentleman tonight, and I do thank ee on be'alf o' Mr. Keynes and his little ones." He then took the fifty pounds he had stuffed into his coat pocket and handed it back to Eleanor. "I've no use fer this. Give it to the poor, someone like Mr. Keynes, who 'asn't a chance in 'ell of earning a decent wage in this land." He then left an astonished audience staring at him.

" 'As Keynes escaped then?" the cobbler asked. "And you've done this thing, 'ave you, Miss Marigate?"

"Yes," she murmured. They thanked her profusely, an act which finally turned Bucksted's attention away from the empty street. He stared at them in mute horror as they made their own opinions of the situation clear to her.

"You would dignify this," he cried, "by congratulating Miss Marigate?"

The baker was a man nearly seventy years old. The shawl he wore was tattered, and his boots had seen better days. His eyes, even in the moonlight, held the wisdom of the ages. "He were given a chance at a new life. These be terribool times, m'lord, fer the poor."

Bucksted looked him over. The impoverished nature of his own clothing spoke for him as well. "You give away as much as you sell, don't you?" he observed.

"With the price of grain as high as it is, how could I do ought else?" With that, he bid them all good night. The cobbler accompanied him.

Eleanor was grateful that the village folk had supported her so completely, but she felt sorry for Bucksted. He was clearly bemused by all that had happened.

Silence sat heavily between them for a long, long time. Finally, she said, "Thank you for not harming Mr. Keynes. You could have done so quite easily, as I know very well."

She turned away from him and with some difficulty attempted to mount her horse. Ordinarily she could have done so, even with a cumbersome train in tow, but her limbs had grown heavy with fatigue.

He came to her and gave her a hand up, setting her neatly in the saddle. "I'll see you home."

"You needn't do so."

"Pray don't argue with me. I haven't the patience for it right now."

"Very well."

He returned the pistol to the jailer and, taking the reins from her, walked her horse to the place where he had left his own. He mounted, still holding her reins. Gratefully, she permitted him to lead her home, dozing now and then in the saddle.

When she arrived at Hartslip, she directed him to the edge of the oak grove, where she turned her horse over to the stableboy. She bid Bucksted good night, but was surprised when he dismounted and approached her, taking her shoulders in a strong grip. Fear flooded her, for she knew he was still quite angry. She glanced toward the stableboy, but Bucksted's presence had sent him scurrying off to the stables.

Bucksted cried, "How could you choose that sapling over me?"

She blinked at him, for his question made no sense. "I don't understand. Are you referring to Mr. Keynes?" she asked, utterly confused.

But these were the only words he allowed her to utter before he placed a crushing kiss on her lips. In astonishment, she mouthed a silent oh, her lips parting. He took possession of her mouth quite roughly for nearly a minute, during which time her body became a very weak, liquid thing. She was astonished by his assault. She had not expected a kiss. If she had expected anything of Bucksted, it would have been a severe dressing-down or a sound thrashing. Not *this!* Yet how heavenly!

She leaned against him and her weary arms somehow reasserted themselves and slipped up about his neck.

How easily, how quickly he could arouse such inexplicable passion in her!

Just as abruptly as the assault had begun, however, it ended. He pulled her arms off him and stepped away from her. "I'll see you tomorrow night for the final ball—then we will have an end to all this nonsense!"

All she could do was nod dumbly. As he mounted his horse and turned up the lane, she tried to recall what it was he had said to her, about choosing something or somebody over him, but fatigue swept through her in a wave so intense, it was all she could do not to drop to the grassy sward beneath her feet and sleep the rest of the night away in the grove.

Instead, however, she forced herself to turn toward the house and make the quarter-mile trek to her bedchamber on feet she could not feel.

Eleanor did not awaken until past noon. Lady Marigate expressed her deep concern for her daughter's health and inquired gently if the sennight's activities had perhaps taken an unexpected toll on her.

"Only a little," Eleanor replied, lowering her gaze from her mother's questioning eyes. "But I am greatly recovered from what I can only describe as a delightful night's sleep. I have not slept so well in ages."

"Well, I should think not. You retired at eleven and slept 'til half past noon—thirteen hours."

Eleanor shrugged and adopted her most innocent expression.

Lady Marigate touched her forehead and then her cheeks. "You certainly don't feel feverish, so I suppose I have no cause for concern." She smiled wistfully, "Tonight is the final ball and in another week you shall be Lady Bucksted and living apart from me. Oh, I shall miss you dreadfully." She sniffled and tears sprang readily to her beautiful blue eyes. "I had not considered as much before, but now I can think of little else—however shall I bear not having my dear Nellie beside me?"

Eleanor was a little surprised by these words since she knew very well she was her mother's least favorite daughter, and rarely were they in a room together that a bout of brangling did not ensue. However, a worse truth asserted itself. How would she ever find the courage to tell her mother that she was not to become Lady Bucksted after all? She quailed at the very thought of it.

She, therefore, merely leaned forward and embraced her mother, shedding a few surprising tears of her own as she did so.

When her mother left, she had ample opportunity to scrutinize the precise nature of her tears. The truth was she didn't understand them at all! She should be grateful she was not marrying a man who had fully intended to kill Mr. Keynes and probably didn't do so only because she was there. She should be very grateful, indeed!

Only, he had led her horse home and . . . and kissed her, and his kisses always made her think of the future, and the future was disturbing her more and more, especially when she thought of a future without this wretched man!

Bucksted stood stiffly beside his betrothed in Lady Tiverton's ballroom, greeting the parade of well-wishers with all the ease of one who had been in the saddle all day and could not bend a single joint without a mild degree of pain.

Since the events of the night before, he had been caught up in a vortex of the worst sort of ruminations, of Eleanor freeing the poacher without so much as a mite of conscience, of the kiss she bestowed so freely upon Fieldstone in the middle of the night, of her obvious disdain for his own principles. Worse had followed when even his own father had unnerved him earlier by confessing that he was deuced glad the chit had freed Keynes, for though he knew the man had to be hanged because the law was the law, he truly would have regretted the incident the rest of his life.

Even his father had proved a turncoat it would seem!

Worse still was hearing several persons tease him about needing to practice his shooting skills! Did no one comprehend how painfully he had wrestled with his own conscience about that? He had let a poacher go free! If the law was not to be upheld then what was the true state of the country? Was England on the verge of anarchy of a sort that had so recently ruined France?

But what rankled most was all the hints Eleanor received concerning her misadventure. Apparently, word of it had spread throughout the wilds of Kent as rapidly as a summer thunderstorm. He had hoped, oh-so-foolishly, that the entire incident would remain buried within the quiet dignity of the town of Glynde Green, where the poacher had made his escape. However, since he had received many congratulations from personages residing at far ends of the county, he could only construe that both he and his bride-to-be had become absolutely notorious.

The very thought of it caused his jaw to tighten, and only with a mumbled sort of dignity was he able to respond to those who yet again marveled at his unfortunate marksmanship!

Never in his life did he think he would regret having perfected his skills at Manton's shooting range.

He had barely exchanged a handful of words with Eleanor. He was still too angry with her to be much more than coldly civil. The moment his hostess, Lady Tiverton, released them both from the receiving line, and after he had endured the traditional opening dance with his bride-to-be who was *not* his bride-to-be, he sought the comfort of Daphne's company and poured out his troubles into her waiting ear.

Daphne clucked and grimaced and shook her head at every complaint he had about Eleanor. He even told her of the kiss she had shared with Martin.

She overlaid his hand with hers, and he did the same so that they were stacked three sets of fingers deep. He was secure in such an intimacy because they were quite alone in the chamber, and besides, Daphne had always thought the world of him. He felt strangely weak in the vicinity of his heart and leaned down to her. He kissed her lightly on the lips.

She blushed prettily in response and whispered in her seductive contralto, "Are you flirting with me, Bucksted?"

"Why, yes," he murmured with more confidence than he had felt in *days!* "I suppose I am!"

She met his gaze, her eyes dripping with affection. "I've always loved you, Bucksted, you know that. Pray, don't trifle with my affections. My heart will break otherwise."

"I am not trifling," he said. He felt determined now, more determined than he had ever been in his life. He understood that he could never wed Eleanor Marigate, even if she held some strange exotic allure for him which he could not comprehend.

No, Nellie was not for him. Daphne was the wife he should have taken years ago. She had waited for him, too, a certain proof of her love and devotion. She would make an exemplary countess and, one day, marchioness. Everything about their lives would be even, placid, controlled.

A snapping of the door jerked his attention from Daphne's large, luminous, love-drenched eyes. "Who was that? Did you notice?" he asked.

She shook her head and smiled tremulously. "Undoubtedly a servant who will keep his tongue. For myself, I was far too preoccupied to even notice that the door had opened."

Eleanor walked away from the *tête-á-tête* with every nerve trembling and straining. Tears rolled down her cheeks, rage roiled in her stomach, and her legs would hardly support her.

So this was to be the end of it all, she thought. Bucksted, making pretty love to Daphne Westwell during their final betrothal ball. How humiliated she felt and how utterly confused. Why, then, had he bothered to kiss her in the oak grove?

From the moment she had greeted Bucksted earlier that evening, and seen the haughty disdain on his face, she had been seething. How dare he condemn her for a heart dedicated to relieving the sufferings of the poor. She would do anything to help those in need, while he lived in his luxury and comfort and spouted his strict, unyielding philosophies. And his philosophies! Why, not a one had ever supported the poor, but rather kept them imprisoned in codes of poverty so deeply ingrained in society that very few would ever have a true opportunity to escape the wretched binds of a low, pitiful rank.

How dare he!

How dare he kiss Daphne!

She found an empty chamber which housed several musical instruments and let a number of tears dapple the carpet at her feet. She stamped a foot, she ground her teeth, she tossed her head. She let a dozen more tears squeeze from her angry eyes.

And Daphne! Didn't Bucksted see what she was, a soulless female who only wanted his rank and fortune? What had Daphne's life ever been but a single-minded pursuit of one man? What was her heart but an endless craving for all manner of frippery and trumpery? Why couldn't he see who she was?

Yet, why did she care whether or not he was seduced by a gazetted fortune hunter? Bucksted meant nothing to her. Nothing. How could he ever, when he nearly shot poor Mr. Keynes in the back. In the back!

Oh, she despised him, everything about the dull-witted, self-absorbed, vain creature that he was!

There, the tears had finally dried, and her legs had stopped trembling. The truth, then, was that Bucksted deserved to have a wife such as Daphne who would no doubt provide him with an adequate number of offspring, then never kiss him again! Did Bucksted deserve more? No, definitely not!

With that, she emerged from the chamber more confident than she had felt *in days*. She admitted to herself that, for a time, Bucksted had actually forced her to question herself and her somewhat reckless manner of approaching the terrible conditions of the poor along the Medway Valley.

Not anymore. She would continue as she always had, perhaps she would even convince Martin that they could proceed with their smuggling operation indefinitely, once the excisemen had left the area.

She returned to the ballroom and began to dance.

A half-hour later, Bucksted returned, without Daphne, and asked Margaret to go down the next set with him. How very discreet!

She was disgusted all over again, and the next time she caught his eye, she snubbed him. Fifteen minutes later, he returned the favor after which he sought out Daphne quite purposely and began to pay her every manner of marked attention.

So, that was how it would be, she thought. Though her heart ached quite strangely and inexplicably, she realized tonight was the perfect opportunity to break with Bucksted permanently, to finally end the sham of their betrothal.

She had had enough of the ridiculous charade, though her determination to end things was ultimately spurred forward by the sight of Bucksted dancing the waltz with Daphne and gazing maddeningly into her eyes. She stood near the orchestra in plain view, and watched them with an increasingly haughty countenance. She did not attempt in any manner to conceal her displeasure and found that her posture soon aggravated her betrothed.

When he made a third turn about the ballroom, passing near her, he glared ferociously upon her for a long moment which so stunned his partner that Daphne missed her steps.

Eleanor wanted to laugh at the clumsy young woman, but not for the world did she intend to give up her position as the wounded bride-to-be. She found she was enjoying herself immensely, a sensation which dimmed only when Lord Chalvington approached her.

"My dear, is anything amiss? You seem a trifle overset. Would you take my arm and accompany me from the ballroom?"

She turned startled eyes upon him. "N-no, I cannot! I mean, it is very kind of you, but I wish to speak with your son as soon as the set ends."

A warmth crept into his eyes. "To give him a severe dressing-down for disgracing you in public?"

"Yes, no! That is—" She chewed on the inside of her cheek. She had been so caught up in what she intended to do that she had nearly forgotten all the kind people who would be harmed by such ballroom antics.

At that moment, the music drew to close. She laid her hand upon his arm and said, "You were very right to address me," she said. "I will go with you."

He was about to overlay his hand on hers when Bucksted's voice stopped them both. "What the devil do you think you're doing, standing there in that theatrical manner, exposing yourself in the most vulgar fashion as though you were raised in the wilds of the Continent instead of Kent!" His face was aflame and for a moment, Eleanor quaked in her pretty, silk dancing slippers.

But only for a moment. Lord Chalvington, and his attempt to defray a terrible scandal, was entirely forgotten. The hair on the back of her neck bristled as she jerked her arm from the marquess's gentle hold on her and joined battle. "How dare you speak to me in that insufferable tone, which I know you use exclusively to demean those you deem inferior to your oh-so-worthy self! How dare you, when for the past several hours, nay, days, you've been flirting with Miss Westwell and making the worst sort of cake of yourself and fool of me. I won't have it, Bucksted!"

"You won't have it!" he thundered, completely forgetting his heretofore self-appointed role as society's arbiter of fashion, manners, and superior conduct in all things. "By God, I should have laid a whip to you the first day I found you on the side of the road, waylaying my coach like a common highwayman!"

Only vaguely did Eleanor realize the crowded ballroom was attending to every word spoken between herself and Bucksted. She took a step toward him, her hands on her hips and her vision a rosy hue, to engage him more fully. "You wouldn't have dared!" she cried. "You haven't the bottom for it. All you can do is send impoverished men, like Mr. Keynes, to Tyburn Tree and for what? For trying to feed his family!"

"And what of you and your proclamations of virtue and perfection—kissing Martin Fieldstone with great abandon, as though you didn't give a fig about me?"

She was utterly stunned, utterly undone. "Wh-what are you talking about?" she responded.

"Don't even think to play the innocent with me! I saw you, the pair of you—last night!"

Her voice dropped to nearly a whisper. "Then you were there, in the oak grove! What were you doing? Spying on me? Dear

God, then that's how you knew to be at the jail." Her voice caught on a sob.

All the thunder left him. He reached out for her. "Eleanor, I—" But she jerked her arm away.

"It was innocent, at least on my part," she cried. "But I suppose that hardly matters. You have shown your true colors these many days. I am sorry to have done so in the midst of our *fête,* but I beg to inform you that I cannot marry you after all, Lord Bucksted. I don't esteem you, and I never shall."

With tears brimming in her eyes, she turned from him, still only vaguely aware that, except for the creaking of the instruments in the hands of the musicians, the ballroom was as silent as a tomb. She walked in as stately a manner as she could summon, passing hundreds of Lady Tiverton's guests all of whom appeared utterly stunned. She was joined by a white-faced Lady Marigate and her sisters, who were equally pale complexioned. Together, they moved into the long hall and toward the front entrance hall of the mansion.

Bucksted was still standing where Eleanor had left him. The ballroom was yet as silent as when she had made her dignified exit.

"Son," Lord Chalvington said into the silence.

Bucksted turned toward him. His mind felt numb to excess. He couldn't think or even move. He stared at his father.

Lord Chalvington's lips twitched. "Quite a baggage, isn't she?"

"What?" he snapped. "Father, I don't like to contradict you, for you are my parent, but how dare you criticize Eleanor! She is merely a trifle headstrong and dramatical. Good God, did she say she has jilted me?"

He glanced toward Daphne, who was standing beside her mother. Daphne was clearly in shock.

As he continued to watch Daphne, he recalled the last half-hour he had spent with her, kissing her and expressing his affection for her, his interest in having her become his wife. She had hugged him and then laid out a most precise future for them both, which gave him the strongest impression she had been considering such a scheme for a *very* long time. They would travel to the Lake District since Napoleon was still rampaging over the Continent. They would have two children, but no more since the squalling of babies was inclined to give her the headache. They would be the most fashionable couple in all of London and would teach everyone just how a marriage ought to be conducted to perfection. She would become a great hostess, and he would sit in the House of Lords and perhaps one day become Prime Minister. She would keep his various estates in excellent order. During the summer they would make a round of country visits, and in the fall she would permit him—here she laughed teasingly—to visit his hunting lodge for a full fortnight, but no longer.

Bucksted drew back to the present. He had never known before how fully bored he could become in the space of only thirty minutes. He was even now astonished by it.

"What do I do, Father?" he asked quietly, finally coming to his senses. "For as God is my witness, I believe I love the chit to distraction!"

Lord Chalvington threw back his head and laughed. "Well," he said. "Then I wish you every happiness, but first let us see to our guests. That done, I would suggest you go after her."

Bucksted made a short speech apologizing to his friends and to his family for making such a cake of himself that he had completely misconstrued an event of last night. Yes, Miss Marigate had kissed Mr. Fieldstone, but he now realized that he had viewed the quite harmless event through the eyes of a jealous lover. "Pray forgive me for having brought this evening down about your ears. I beg you will remain and enjoy Lady Tiverton's *fête,* which, as you all know, will certainly be accounted the finest of the summer—save, of course, my own mother's. In a little while, I intend to pursue my betrothed and do what I can to make amends for my truly horrendous conduct this evening; in other words, I shall throw myself at her feet and beg for forgiveness." This brought a round of sympathetic chuckles from every married male in the room and the hasty withdrawal of at least three score of kerchiefs from the inside of elbow-length gloves.

Between all the feminine sniffles and the masculine chuckles,

Lady Chalvington moved forward and embraced her son. "Dear, dear Aubrey. Now you have made me happy. Now I know you will enjoy a truly wonderful marriage—if she will still have you, of course."

Later that evening, he approached Daphne with a contrite heart. "I'm sorry for having said the things to you that I did. I was a complete gudgeon to have—"

"Please, Bucksted," she whispered, her eyes filling with tears. "Even at the time I felt it was too good to be true, and so it was. I always knew you didn't love me, but until I saw you quarrel so passionately with Miss Marigate, I never gave up hope." She extended her hand to him, "Good-bye, and may I wish you every happiness."

"And you," he returned gently.

She nodded and quickly walked away. He was not surprised when she sought out her mother, both of whom took leave of their hostess and then left the ball.

Bucksted remained until most of the guests had departed. Lady Tiverton kindly loaned him a horse with which to make his much-needed journey, and so it was he did not leave his final betrothal ball until after midnight. When he arrived at Hartslip, he found the ladies had been abed for over an hour. He insisted that Miss Marigate be roused from her sleep that he might speak with her. The butler was entirely unconvinced until Bucksted laid a hand on his shoulder. "My good man," he said quietly, "I will be forever in your debt. We had a dreadful row at the ball, and I'm certain unless I speak with her tonight, I shall lose her forever."

These words were not without a proper effect. The butler frowned and scowled and shook his head. He muttered savage words about the manners and mores of the modern generation. In the end, however, he mounted the stairs slowly in search of the eldest daughter of the house.

When he returned, both sisters and mother were in tow.

Lady Marigate spoke while descending the stairs, a long dark brown braid dangling from beneath her mobcap and hanging over her shoulder. "Oh, my dear Bucksted. 'Tis the most dreadful occurrence, but it would seem Nellie is gone!"

Thirteen

The household was turned out of their beds, and within a scant few minutes, every chamber, every alcove, and recess of the manor, even the stables and the gardens, were searched by rush-light, oil lamp, and flickering candle.

Eleanor was nowhere to be found.

Bucksted, unfamiliar with Hartslip, remained in the drawing room to await his betrothed's discovery. His mind was full of the evening's wretched events as well as the vision from last night of Eleanor held captive in Martin Fieldstone's arms.

When at last footsteps were heard in the hall beyond the drawing room, he rose to his feet, his hat in hand, and stared in stunned disbelief at Lady Marigate's crumpled face and tear-stained eyes.

"She cannot be found!" the poor widow cried. "I have the greatest fear that thieves have entered my home and stolen her away. A band of Gypsies perhaps, or . . . or some wayward nuns looking for converts among the Catholic faith."

This thought was too ludicrous to be met with anything but a shocked protest. Lady Marigate fell to sobbing. "Then where is she, pray! Where could she have gone?"

Bucksted of course had been considering the very same question for the past half-hour and thought he knew where she might be. If the word "elopement" jumped into his mind, he quickly shunted it away. Eleanor was *not* in love with Martin; she simply couldn't be, not when, well, not when he loved her as much as he did.

He felt the blood leave his face at the very thought of it. He knew where to look next, but what would he do if he discovered that she had decided to wed Martin after all? Mr. Fieldstone was heir to a tidy property and because of their obvious affection for one another, he had little doubt Fieldstone would be more than content to help her in her philanthropic efforts.

But, damme, so would he! He would, in a trice! That is what he must tell her, what she didn't understand about him. He was not the heartless beast she thought him to be, he only wanted a little order, lawfulness, and decency about *how* his fortune was to be distributed.

He handed Lady Marigate his kerchief and said, "I believe I know where your daughter is, at least, where I think she might be found—with Mr. Fieldstone."

Lady Marigate, in the process of blowing her nose, looked up at him over the top of the rumpled kerchief. "What?" she mumbled, aghast, through the white cambric. "Whyever would she be with him?"

He told her of the meeting he'd observed on the night before, omitting the fact that Fieldstone had kissed Eleanor.

Her mouth turned down in a silly manner, and her eyes filled with tears again. "She was always the most headstrong, incorrigible child. Henry could manage her, but I"—she sniffed several times—"I could do little more than brangle with her and threaten her. She ignored me every time. I had thought, when her father died, some of her spirit would have settled down, but now it is obvious to me that it did no such thing. Oh, Bucksted, I am so ashamed. What manner of daughter have I raised! And to think how she spoke to you this evening, the spectacle she made of herself, the scandal into which she has plunged us all! We are ruined, every last one of us, but worst of all, what is to become of my poor Nellie?"

He sat down beside her and slipped an arm about her shoulders. "I'll tell you what: if I have not lost all my ability to persuade her on a proper path, then I will make her my wife and spend the remainder of my existence keeping her out of scrapes. Would that suit you, dear lady?"

Lady Marigate leaned backward and stared at him. "You've gone utterly mad if you still wish to marry my daughter," she stated, horrified.

"I believe I have," he responded, chuckling.

Lady Marigate began to wail. "And I thought you was too stiff rumped to make any lady a proper husband?" She threw herself into the hollow of his shoulder. "I was utterly and completely mistaken!"

He held her close, marveling at this final revelation. He could only chuckle a little more before finally settling the weeping lady into her second daughter's open arms.

"I shall send you word or return to you myself as soon as I learn where your daughter has gone."

"Bless you," she murmured into Margaret's mobcap.

Bucksted pounded on the front door of Chidding Moot for some five minutes before finally rousing a servant. The hour was easily two o'clock as a blear-eyed butler squinted his eyes at him. "Lord Bucksted?" he queried in amazement, lifting the oil lamp high overhead.

"Yes. I'm only grateful you remember me. Something terrible has transpired, and I must speak with Mr. Fieldstone immediately."

"Nay, but ye cannot. The master is gone from home at present. He'll not return 'til a sennight Saturday."

Bucksted lifted a hand, "Martin. It is Martin I must speak with."

"Ah! Yes! Do come in. I beg yer pardon. The sleep still has my brain."

Bucksted crossed the threshold and bade the butler to retrieve the *young* master at once. Waiting for Martin's appearance, he began to pace the entrance hall, several of the planked boards creaking beneath his feet.

Somehow he was not surprised when the butler returned with the news that Martin was not abed. Before the harassed man could suggest a course of action, Bucksted stated, "Fetch only his valet."

Five minutes later the valet, also sleepy-eyed, shook his head. "I haven't the faintest idea where the young master might be. He occasionally leaves the house for a day or two, during which time he does not take me with him. I believe he goes to one of the seaside watering holes."

"What makes you think that?"

"Sand in the folds of his pants and in his shoes, the damp smell of salty air in everything when he returns. Would not take a genius to comprehend what the lad's been up to."

"The sea," Bucksted murmured. "Do you think that's where he's gone? Did he tell you he was leaving? Did he ever mention Broomhill?"

"He's never mentioned Broomhill. As to where he's gone, though, I would lay stakes on the sea."

"Is there anyone else among the staff who might know more about his, er, adventures?" He certainly had no intention of bringing Martin's mother downstairs to account for her son's absence.

The valet nodded. "He's quite good friends with one of the stableboys—John Selsted. Grew up with him, that sort of thing. More like brothers."

"Thank you," he said. He turned to the butler, "If you would fetch him, I would be deeply appreciative."

"O' course, m'lord. At once."

The stableboy's complexion was beet red by the time he arrived in the entrance hall, appearing as though he was meeting with the Inquisition rather than with a concerned acquaintance.

Bucksted took a deep breath. "Where is he, what is he about, and was Miss Marigate with him?"

John nodded, his eyes wide with fright. "To the coast, a place near Broomhill. Miss Marigate insisted, otherwise he would not a done it again."

"Done what?" Bucksted asked, thoroughly bemused. By now, he began to understand that there was no threat of an elopement, but rather that the rascally pair were up to some sort of mischief.

Somehow, he was not surprised, though a certain dread had begun to fill his heart.

"To the coast. Smuggling. Brandy and silks mostly." He rushed on. "But 'tis not wat you might think. 'Twere only fer the poor! Miss Marigate 'as a big heart, and she never kept a tuppence fer herself, neither did Martin—I swear it!"

Bucksted blinked. "What did you say?"

"Smuggling—brandy and silks—because o' Boney's embargo."

Eleanor and Martin were smugglers? He shook his head. He was so stunned he could not speak. He tried to make sense of what he had just heard. His bride-to-be was a smuggler? The woman he loved trafficked in alcohol and fine cloths?

"Ye didna know, nor even 'ave a clue?" John asked.

"No, I did not," he stated.

"Then you need to know the worst of it. The last time they ventured out—two nights past—they were nearly caught by the excisemen. I fear fer them both tonight. Their plan was to go very late, just afore dawn, hoping that the patrols would tire and find an alehouse and a warm fire when the fogs rolled in."

"Good God," he murmured, still feeling numb with shock. "Well, at least I have time to find them, only, do you know where, exactly, they collect the merchandise?"

"Aye. I went with Martin once when Miss Marigate were feeling poorly. I can take you there. 'Twould be a relief for me, as worried as I am. I tried to talk him out of it, but 'e said Miss Marigate 'ad to 'ave funds since she gave the last to that poor poacher wat was to be 'anged."

"Dear God," Bucksted muttered. He then addressed the butler. "Will you be so good as to inform Mrs. Fieldstone of what is going forward and for what reason I have commandeered her traveling chariot?"

The butler nodded. " 'Twould be best. Go now. Ye've not much time. Broomhill is at least an hour and a half away, longer if the toll booths are not properly manned as they sometimes aren't in the early morning hours."

* * *

John led him directly to the place where Martin's wagon was cleverly concealed. He doubted even in the light of day that the exact spot could have been located, certainly not at night.

The traveling chariot also fit neatly into the hidden space. John told him the nature of the cove into which the goods were delivered from rowboats, then carted by canvas stretchers up the shallow, grassy hill. By agreement, John remained with the horses, caring for them and immediately wiping them down with handfuls of grass.

Bucksted began easing his way past the wagon, speaking in low tones to the horses and avoiding any errant hooves. A spidery fog clung to the trees and shrubs. The moisture quickly collected in a thin sheen on his forehead, nose, and cheeks. He still could not believe he was here, that Eleanor was but a few yards away, that she had been smuggling as it turned out for the past twelvemonth.

And he had once thought her a quiet, demure, conformable female!

He was about to step into the clearing which separated the wood from the beach cliff when a muffled shot rent the air a considerable distance down the beach. His heart began to thump wildly in his chest.

He listened intently, unwilling to move forward and give away his position until he knew more of what was happening. He heard an indistinguishable sound, very faint, coming from down the slope directly in front of him. He keyed his ears to the spot and concentrated very hard.

There it was again, a low, plaintive sound.

As though his feet understood the message first, he shot across the clearing and began a quick descent. A dark figure, strewn across the path, lay not more than fifteen feet away.

He felt sick with dread. He crossed the distance in less than two seconds and found a young man—no! it was Eleanor, dressed as a man, moaning in pain. He picked her up and retraced his steps, fairly running up the hill.

Eleanor moaned again but he hushed her. "Not a sound, m' dear. We're not out of the woods yet."

He heard her sigh, quite deeply, and as though certain of safety, she fainted in a slump against him. He felt the wetness of her wound against his wrist. Quickly, he moved back into the woods, nearly toppling over John as he rushed Eleanor to the carriage. At the same moment, Martin arrived, breathing hard.

"She's been shot," Bucksted stated in a harsh whisper.

"We must leave immediately!" Martin cried, not pausing to give an explanation. "I led them in the other direction, then circled back. There were only two and they're on foot."

John began easing the horses backward, while Martin unharnessed those hitched to the wagon. He quickly roped them together and scrambled up on top of the lead horse.

When the coach was in position and John had mounted the leader, Martin drew up to the window. "I'll call later today at Hartslip. In the meantime, I have to return these horses to their owner."

Bucksted nodded. Martin gave his horse a kick and was off.

To John, Bucksted called out, "Spring 'em!"

Eleanor awoke fully only once during the journey. A terrible pain ripped through her shoulder when the carriage hit a rut. She struggled to sit up, but a strong arm encircled her, holding her back.

"Do not move. You've been injured, and you'll break open the wound again."

The voice was faintly familiar to her, but she couldn't quite place it. One of the excisemen, perhaps? No. Where was Martin? Oh, God, Martin!

She wanted to cry, for she was certain her dearest friend from childhood was dead, but she was in too much pain to do more than heave a terrific sigh and then fall into a stupor. The rest of the journey was a mixture of tangled nightmares, pain, and sadness. Every jolt and sway of the carriage hurt her anew.

In moments of lucidity, she cringed with thoughts of the terrible things she had done. She had gotten herself wounded and her friend killed. She must tell the man who was holding her to go back and find Martin, yet she couldn't open her mouth to speak.

She dreamed she was being chased again and awoke with a start. She felt very hot but every time she tried to move, the man hushed her. Every time she groaned, he tried to assure her that all was well and that she would be home very soon. The carriage drew to a halt, and she could hear voices outside. A moment later, the man holding her forced her head back. "Drink this," he commanded her.

She sputtered on a long draught of brandy and would have protested, but the man was insistent. Again, she wanted to cry, yet she hurt far too badly.

Finally, as the wheels rolled on and on, she fell into another fitful sleep, which at least had the advantage of making time pass. The next thing she knew, she was being settled on her bed and undressed by several capable hands. Her wound was washed and dressed, oh-so-painfully. A fresh nightgown was somehow bundled over her head, a slit cut for her shoulder and arm, neither of which could be moved.

Again she slept, though she grew hot and uncomfortable in the stifling chamber. A surgeon forced a large dose of laudanum down her, and only through the stupor of the drug did she feel the removal of a pistol ball from deep within her shoulder. She wanted to push his hands away, but her own limbs seemed weighted by heavy stones.

The man who had brought her home seemed to hover nearby the entire time. He frequently bathed her face and her arms, he held her hand, he read to her, which somehow made the heat enveloping her body and the pain of her shoulder more bearable.

She awoke but didn't know where she was; she recognized no one. She clung to the man who read to her. Only he could comfort her, caught up as she was in a vicious nightmare that refused to let her go.

She was constantly being chased up and down a cliff, along a beach, and into a thick wood. Martin would race along behind her. He kept telling her to hurry up, hurry up. She would hear a shot and then another. She would fall and couldn't run any longer. Martin shouted at her, over and over. Then the stranger would pick her up and carry her away to safety. She would be peaceful for a time, until the chasing started again, and again, and again.

Bucksted could not remember having been more weary in his entire existence. Once he had seen Eleanor safely in the surgeon's hands, he had left her side only for those moments of required modesty when her maid and her former nurse would change her sleeping garments. Otherwise, he was at her bedside, pressing cool damp cloths to her head, holding her hand or reading to her.

She had been five days caught in the grip of a terrible fever. Each day saw her face grow thinner and the dark shadows deepen beneath her eyes. He had never watched anyone die before, and he couldn't help but wonder if he was doing so now.

He felt a hand on his shoulder. He looked up and saw Martin Fieldstone. His heart hardened instantly into a ball of flint. He doubted he would ever be able to forgive him for having jeopardized Eleanor so foolishly.

Carefully returning Eleanor's hand to the bedcovers, he rose from his chair and with only the barest nod of his head acknowledged Martin's presence. "She has been sleeping for only a brief time. I expect her sufferings to return shortly."

"I shan't stay with her long," Martin said abjectly.

Bucksted left the room, but waited in the hall outside the door. At the far end of the hall, he saw Nurse marching toward him bearing a tray which, given that the hour was ten, would include a fresh bowl of cool water, a glass of the same, and a vial of laudanum. Her expression was grim. Eleanor's maid tagged along.

He held the door wide for her and caught Martin's expression of anguish. Tears were on his cheeks. In spite of himself, he was moved, but he could not pity Mr. Fieldstone, not by half.

Nurse spoke gently to Martin and patted him on the shoulder several times. Martin rose to leave. Already, Eleanor was beginning to toss on her pillows. He would need to return to her soon, but there was nothing he could do until Nurse had completed her ministrations. The bed was kept cool and dry at all times. Nurse had not seen all three girls through a round of childhood diseases not to know how a sickroom should be conducted. Bucksted was allowed to remain solely because it was obvious to her discerning eye that as long as he was present, poor Miss Marigate was not half as distraught.

When Martin passed through the doorway, Bucksted closed the door. He would only reenter when Nurse gave him permission to do so.

He expected Martin to leave; instead Fieldstone remained, leaning against the wall, a hand over his eyes and tears rushing down his face.

Bucksted could no longer contain his anger. "Well, what the devil did you expcct would happen when you engaged in this unlawful trade? Did you think you and Eleanor were special in some manner, that the excisemen would fail to discover your activities, or that once found, their guns would not hit a target? I have no sympathy for you, so if you please, take your distress elsewhere."

Martin leaned his hands on his knees. "I am a paltry fellow, you may say it a thousand times."

"Saying anything does little to make her well or to undo what has been done."

"I—I just couldn't resist her. She was made of sterner stuff than I, always setting others before herself and being a madwoman in the process. She—she had a dozen families to provide for. Her father's annuity could not care for them. Two months after her father died, they began coming round and begging for the relief they had once enjoyed under his administration. She came up with the scheme because of some article she'd read in *The Times* about smuggling and how many were gaining fortunes at the nefarious trade, what with the embargoes and taxes. She hounded me for two weeks until I acquiesced. She took me to every hovel about Hartslip and forced me inside to see what wretched work the war with France and the beleaguered economy had made of these people. She told me that a few months of hard work would see a sufficient amount invested on the Exchange to care for all these families for decades to come.

"Maybe I was a fool, but her zeal swept me away, that and the simple fact I loved her." He looked up at that and added, "And don't tell me you haven't been lured as well, for I won't hear such lies." Bucksted thought he knew what Martin meant, but wanted to hear him out.

"I don't know what you're talking about."

"Everyone saw you flirting with Daphne, dear, poor, mealy-mouthed female that she is. You could have had her and a thousand like her, but instead you chose Eleanor. Your devotion to her since she was wounded tells me it isn't just a matter of friendship or even common decency. You love her as . . . as I do."

"Yes, but I would never have jeopardized her life."

"You think not?" he asked. "Then, what did you suppose she would do once the poacher had been caught on your lands, or once Hartslip and its fine income fell into your hands? She is not a young woman to sit idly by!"

"She was smuggling!" he cried. "Good God, have neither of you a tuppence worth of sense? There must be a dozen ways to have provided the funds necessary to help the indigent. Did she not think to request donations from her more fortunate neighbors?"

Martin's expression grew hard. "Even your father refused to help her."

"What?" Bucksted cried, astonished.

Martin then outlined very quickly all the ways in which Eleanor worked for several weeks to raise support for the poor of her parish, the scores of visits to beg for charitable contributions. "She was able to raise two hundred pounds, a goodly sum but hardly sufficient to care for everyone in need. She held a fair, the proceeds of which went to the needy, but after all the vendors had donated the agreed-upon twenty percent of the day's earnings, she was only able to add another hundred and fifty pounds to her fund.

"I did what I could. I entered into every scheme with as much enthusiasm, time, and energy as I could muster, but it was never enough. That was when she decided we should take up the art of smuggling. We cleared over a thousand pounds the first three weeks."

"Good God," he whispered. "How many runs did you execute?"

"At least one per week, with varying success. This was to be our last. The one two nights ago should have been our final run, but she gave nearly eight hundred pounds to the Keyneses and subsequently persuaded me to return to Broomhill one last time. She was completing her father's work, you see. She loved him very much."

Bucksted turned all this over in his mind. "Did she ever tell you why my father refused her request?"

He nodded. "She felt nothing but kindness toward him. He told her that, though he wished he could help continue her father's work, his own private commitments forbade a single farthing to be extended elsewhere."

Bucksted could very well believe this. Lord Chalvington was a man of stern convictions about the allocation of his fortune. He was not so great a philanthropist as Sir Henry Marigate, but he supported several institutions, including three orphanages in Kent alone. "I wish she'd spoken to me about her needs," he murmured.

"Would it have made a difference?" Martin shot back.

Bucksted felt as though he'd been planted a facer. He met the young man's gaze and wanted to blame him yet again for the precarious state of Eleanor's present health, but something in the blaze of Martin's eyes stopped him.

Herein lay the truth, he thought, about himself and his pomposity and arrogance. What would he have said to her, had she asked him to complete her father's work? He would have denied her.

Would he deny her still? No.

Martin frowned him down. "I've always despised you," he stated harshly. "I still don't believe you've even the smallest understanding of Nellie's worth."

"You're out there. I do have some understanding, but you're right, not enough to value her completely, though I must say I am quickly coming to comprehend a great deal more than I ever expected to. I do know this much: she was right to have jilted me. I don't deserve her."

"No, you don't," Martin agreed. He heaved a sigh. "And neither do I, for having known the dangers rampant in our effort last night, I did not have the strength of will to thwart her as I should have. For that, you may despise me."

"I do," Bucksted agreed.

Martin met his gaze, and a strange understanding passed between the two men. Somehow the anger and intolerance each shared became a source of agreement. "Make her live," he said quietly.

Bucksted thrust out his hand to Martin. "As God is my witness, I shall do everything in my power to make it so."

Martin looked at the proffered olive branch and took it firmly in his own grasp.

Bucksted shook his hand tightly almost fearing to let go. A moment later, Martin withdrew his hand, turned abruptly on his heel, and marched down the hall.

Bucksted watched him go, understanding the depth of his love for Eleanor. That was one thing they shared.

He heard Nurse call to him and immediately jerked his attention back to present needs. He returned to the sickroom and to the sight of tears flowing from Nurse's eyes.

"She needs yer voice, m'lord," Nurse cried. "I fear . . ."

Fourteen

A sickening dread swept over Bucksted. Had Martin paid his dearest friend a final visit? He moved toward the bed slowly, a ringing in his ears.

He glanced at Eleanor's white face and the pale color of her lips. She wasn't moving as she normally would be.

"Summon the doctor at once!" he cried.

Nurse swept from the chamber, and Eleanor's maid began to cry. "Oh, miss! Oh, miss! Pray don't leave us!"

Bucksted leaned over Eleanor's chest and listened for a sound coming from her mouth, even for the feel of her warm breath on his cheek.

There! He felt a faint flutter over his face.

He turned toward her. How wet her brow was. He thumbed a thick sheen of perspiration from her forehead. A smile began in his chest that rose into a hearty laugh. "She lives!" he cried. The words rang about the room and bounced off him several times. *She lives! She lives! She lives!*

"I've sent fer the doctor!" Nurse cried bounding back into the room. "Wat's happened?"

The maid was by then leaping up and down, and Bucksted grabbed poor Nurse tightly about her waist and danced her twice in a circle.

"She lives!" he cried again.

"What? Then it is not—! Dear me, let me look at her."

Bucksted released her as together they bent over Eleanor, whose sleep had suddenly become quite peaceful.

"She's sweating buckets!" Nurse cried. "Glory be to God!" She took a soft, dry cotton cloth and began gently wiping Eleanor's face, arms, and as much of her chest as was seemly.

Bucksted addressed the maid. "You must fetch Lady Marigate and her daughters—at once!"

"Oh, yes, indeed. At once! At once!" Alice scurried from the room.

Bucksted again took up his place, possessing himself of Eleanor's hand while Nurse continued to dab at Eleanor's forehead and neck. A soft moan escaped her lips and twice her eyelids nearly fluttered open. She pushed back the covers, quite slowly, for there could not have been much strength in her thin arms.

Nurse clucked at her, cooling her with the cloth, then covering her again.

"No," Eleanor murmured, the first comprehensible sound she had made in days. "I'm too hot."

"She spoke!" Nurse cried, turning wet eyes upon Bucksted.

His were none too dry either as together they laughed.

Lady Marigate, Margaret, and Kitty were heard running down the hall toward the bedchamber. A moment later, they burst over the threshold.

"Is it true?" Lady Marigate called out.

"Yes, is it true?" Kitty intoned.

"Will she live?" Margaret asked.

"See for yourself," Bucksted murmured beckoning them to come round the screen and witness Eleanor's improvement for themselves.

The chase has finally ended, Eleanor thought. She stretched, aware that she was in her own bed at last, safe and warm. Well, perhaps a bit too warm, and why did her nightclothes cling to her so stubbornly?

She shifted and turned.

Yes, much too hot.

She tried to push the covers away. She could succeed for a time, but then some magical force kept dragging them back up to her chin.

Something drifted over her face. She heard much laughter and what seemed like shouting, only at a great distance. Was there a party somewhere?

Her betrothal ball? No, of course not. She was home. Her betrothal ball had been at Lady Tiverton's. Why was her night-dress so damp and uncomfortable?

She blinked and opened her eyes. The room smelled odd, like a sickroom cloaked with perfume. Ugh! Ambergris!

"Hello, dearest?"

She squinted and peered at the figure rounding her bed on the right. "Hallo, Mama. I'm very thirsty, and my shoulder hurts abominably."

Her mother nodded. Were there tears on her cheeks? Why? "Yes, my love, very understandable. You've been quite ill. But now you will be fine. Try to rest."

She closed her eyes, too fatigued to ask the questions which came to mind. Why, for instance, was she so pitifully weak, why was she so wretchedly damp all over, and why the deuce did her shoulder hurt? She fell into a profound sleep.

She was awakened much later by a man's voice.

"Yes, yes, 'tis very true, Lady Marigate. Your daughter's fever is broken, her wound is healing quite well. She'll be as right as rain in a week, perhaps a little more."

Eleanor laughed to herself. What absurdity was this? A week or more. She had only to sleep until the morning and then she would go riding perhaps. She hadn't been riding in ages.

Late the next day, a full sennight since Eleanor was shot, Buck-sted looked up from his copy of the *Morning Post.* Both Margaret and Kitty had entered the morning room together, quite solemnly.

"Has she asked for me?" he inquired, by ritual.

Together, they shook their heads, looking so sad that he could only smile. "Don't fret on my behalf."

Kitty moved forward quickly, taking up a seat opposite him. "But it isn't fair, Bucksted, not when you were by her side day and night! You were the only one who could comfort her. It truly was the most amazing thing!"

He reached out and covered her hand with his own. Her lip trembled.

Margaret approached him and patted his shoulder. "Let me tell her, talk to her! I'm sure she'll remember, and then she'll beg to see you."

He shook his head. "It's as I told you, my sweet, we were badly matched from the beginning. I daresay she would despise me even if she remembered that I had stayed by her bed during her illness. I was unutterably cruel to her during our betrothal."

He had made a complete confession to Lady Marigate and to Eleanor's sisters about the sham of their week together, even going so far as to confess that he had bribed Eleanor to remain betrothed to him. The ladies had all been shocked, yet not a one had chastised him.

"The night of Lady Tiverton's ball," Lady Marigate had said quietly, "Eleanor cried all the way home. We couldn't get the truth from her, about why the pair of you quarreled as you did. Did she really kiss Mr. Fieldstone as you insist she did?"

"Yes, but Fieldstone has since told me he forced the kiss on her. You see, he has been in love with her since time out of mind."

"Of course he has," Kitty stated. "Who wouldn't love Eleanor? She's so beautiful and adventuresome, and her heart is as big as the ocean."

He had agreed. He also confessed these were the very reasons he himself had tumbled so violently in love with her. All the ladies had stared at him.

Margaret said, "But you were not in love with her when you offered for her, were you?"

"I was drawn to her even then for reasons I didn't understand. However, the more I came to know her during our betrothal week, the more those reasons became clear. Later, when I saw her kissing Fieldstone, I nearly went mad with jealousy even though we had both agreed to end the engagement."

Kitty had held his hand sympathetically and Margaret had offered him a second glass of sherry.

Now, as he glanced from one pretty visage to the next and back again, he realized once he left Hartslip for good, he would be taking with him yet one more regret for his misfired betrothal.

Over the next sennight, Eleanor began piecing events together in her mind in much the way she had once helped sew a quilt with her grandmother. Images would come to her, appearing for a moment only to vanish before she could grasp them fully. A kindly shadow hovered at the fringes of every errant thought and vision, a large figure in a dark cloak. How selective her mind was during these days of recovery!

Martin visited her and wept openly about the stupidity of their having attempted one last smuggling adventure.

"Oh, Martin," she breathed, grasping his hand strongly. "What if you had been shot and killed? How could I have borne that, my dearest friend, through the years to come? I should have perished as well, I'm certain of it, even had I escaped unharmed from the night's hapless adventure. I could never bear the knowledge that, in my willfulness, I had got you killed!"

He smiled tremulously. "Then you know in part the scope of my sentiments."

"Will you ever forgive me for this being all of my doing?"

He nodded and clasped her hands more tightly still. "So long as you do the same for me."

She smiled, then chuckled. "Aren't we a frightful pair?"

"Terribly."

He came to visit daily, and with each day, more of her memory returned. "Was it you then," she asked nearing her seventh day of wakefulness, "who held me all the way home and who read to me during my illness, for I can now recall that a man was with me throughout the ordeal."

He shook his head, appearing quite flustered. "No, it wasn't I."

"But there was a man here? The doctor, perchance?"

"No. It was Bucksted."

"What?" she cried. Memories began flooding her, and the quilt of her mind began to fill in quite abruptly. "Merciful heavens, it was, wasn't it? I thought I had only dreamed of him. Do you mean to tell me he visited me while I was ill?"

Martin shook his head. "No. He remained by your bed. Apparently, he was the only one who could calm you when your sufferings grew heightened and torturous."

She stared at Martin in wonder and disbelief. "I can hardly credit that it's true. Imagine, Bucksted holding court in a sickroom."

"He hardly held court, Nellie. Except for changing your linens which Nurse did, he fed you and gave you water; bathed your forehead, hands, and arms; and poured medicine down your throat, even though you fought him violently every time."

She felt herself shrinking back into the pillows, unwilling to accept as true what he was telling her. She struggled to make sense of it—Bucksted in a sickroom! Was it possible she had never truly understood him?

She felt her cheeks warm with misery. How could she have ever sat in judgment upon him when here she was nearly dead from having been shot in the act of smuggling. Her conscience smote her sorely. She felt as though she wasn't just awakening from a sickness, but from a wildness of temper that had transfixed her from the time of her father's death.

"What have I done?" she murmured. "Is he yet here?"

"Yes."

She winced. He had not come to see her since she had awakened from her fevers. He might have shown a great deal of compassion in keeping her calm during her illness, but clearly, once the danger had past, he wanted nothing to do with her. "Has—has he asked after me?"

"Constantly. He is determined not to leave until he is convinced you are well."

"Oh." She felt humbled and miserable. She wanted to speak with him, at the very least to thank him for saving her life, but she didn't know how to do so. His opinion of her had always been less than pleasing, but what must he think of her now?

She decided to wait, to bathe, to dress herself properly, to begin moving about her chamber and regaining her strength. Then, perhaps, she would find the courage to see him. Besides, the smell of the sickroom was making her feel nauseous. The odor of burning pastilles, which Nurse had insisted upon from the beginning, now clung to every fabric in the room as well as to her hair and bedclothes.

She demanded first that the pastilles be taken away and shortly afterward that a bath be brought to her chamber. Nurse was horrified, and a compromise was reached only when she allowed the servants to build up a large fire in the hearth even though the day was warm and she promised to bathe wearing her nightgown. She agreed readily, though she insisted her hair be washed as well, a circumstance which nearly threw Nurse into a pelter of no mean order.

The bed was stripped along with the draperies which hung from the bedposts and the windows. The feather mattress was properly aired, and so it was that two hours later Eleanor found herself exhausted but clean and stretched out in a bed that smelled of sweet peas and roses. The undermaids had slipped a muslin bag of potpourri beneath her pillows.

She fell asleep immediately, her last thoughts of Bucksted.

The next morning she walked about her bedchamber several times by herself, her weak, trembling legs gaining strength with each turn.

Two days later, her strength was so far improved and her appetite increasing so rapidly that the doctor pronounced her completely out of danger and said that as soon as possible she should be carried out of doors to take a little sun and fresh air.

His words created the strongest excitement in her heart. She knew that Bucksted was still residing beneath her mother's roof, asking daily after her, yet never once had he come to see her. She knew his heart: he was thoroughly disgusted with her conduct and could not forgive her terrible deeds. However, if she could descend the stairs and catch him unawares, she could force him to hear her repentant heart.

Bucksted listened to the doctor's glowing report of Eleanor's health and was finally and completely satisfied that not only would she live but that she would thrive. Apparently, she was still quite thin, yet there was a glow on her cheeks, or so the doctor said. Bucksted would have liked to have seen her himself, but he steadfastly resisted the temptation to do so. She had not asked for him to come to her, a circumstance which bespoke the entirety of her heart, of that he was convinced. Surely, she blamed him, in his lack of generosity, for having to turn to so desperate a measure as smuggling in order to complete her father's work.

He recalled the day she had taken him about the parish and shown him every wretched hovel to which her father and she had ministered. He had been distantly compassionate, expressing his concern for their unfortunate circumstances, yet not once had his heart truly been touched, not in the way Eleanor's was, at least not until now. Having witnessed for himself the zeal a true devotee would endure to help those in need, his heart had become a changed thing.

During her recovery, he had himself retraced the route in its entirety in the company of several of the vicars who served in that area of the county. He learned the inmates of each hovel by name, he met with every donor of clothing or money in the same district, he examined the extent of her father's daily labors and contributions down to the penny.

He was overwhelmed with what he had found, especially after taking the opportunity of visiting a parish in Kent some fifteen miles distant and quite out of the reach of Marigate hands. The difference was distressing and abominable. He saw poverty as he had never witnessed it before, except in London's East End, and realized how much one, nay, two people had been able to accomplish with a great deal of industry and, yes, a little smuggling.

Eleanor's zeal had changed him. He had worked through the

documents of the Hartslip Estate, which by law belonged to him. With his solicitor, he had created a foundation on which the Marigate ladies could live at Hartslip so long as any remained in either widowhood or spinsterhood, and had endowed a board of three trustees with the sum of thirty thousand pounds to be administered by Eleanor, or, upon her resignation of that office, by any person deemed suitable by the board for the relief of the poor in her neighborhood.

To Lady Marigate he designated an annuity of five hundred pounds per annum which, though he was certain she would exceed that figure, he felt confident, with her daughters' guidance, would keep that lady in the style to which she had become accustomed during her husband's lifetime.

When he presented these documents to Lady Marigate, she only blinked and frowned. Instead of thanking him, after a moment, she said, "Are you no longer in love with Nellie, then?" she inquired, a tear seeping from her left eye.

He sighed and repressed an impulse to proclaim just how much he had grown to love and esteem her. Instead, he overlaid her trembling hand with his own and said, "Madame, I love her beyond words, but it is not sufficient for a proper marriage. Such sentiments must be returned, and unfortunately, I don't believe your daughter can ever esteem me sufficiently to return such a regard."

A tear from her right eye joined its counterpart and rolled down her cheek, splashing onto the violet silk of her bodice just below a lovely trim of Brussels lace. "Very well," she murmured. "Do you mean to take your leave of her?"

He shook his head. "In all these days she did not send for me once. Knowing her sentiments, I wouldn't dream of hindering her most excellent progress by invading her sickroom now."

"She will be joining us presently. The doctor is permitting her to take the air this afternoon so long as a strong wind does not blow through the gardens."

He rose. "Then it is time that I left. Please, tell her that I—that is, I beg you will give her my kindest regards and express my great relief that she has recovered. No, no. Don't trouble yourself to ring for the butler. I would feel happiest could I merely make my way to the stables and see my carriage harnessed by my own instructions."

"As you wish," she replied solemnly. She watched him go, frowning after him.

She wondered . . .

Eleanor had just reached the bottom step when her mother emerged from the drawing room. She glanced beyond her parent, peering into the receiving room, hoping to catch a glimpse of Bucksted. Her heart was beating furiously in her chest. However, she did not see him.

"Is . . . is Lord Bucksted within?" she queried.

Lady Marigate shook her head. "No. He is gone. Five minutes past. He went directly to the stables to see to his carriage himself."

Eleanor felt as though her world had crumbled once more. Her eyes filled with quick tears. "Oh," she mumbled.

Lady Marigate said, "Where are Kitty and Margaret? They were supposed to help you descend the stairs?"

"I knew I could manage by myself. I sent them to fetch my shawl and my watercolors. Only, Mama, did Bucksted not wish to speak to me, is that why he left without waiting to greet me?"

Lady Marigate frowned. "Nellie, my darling, come with me. I want to show you something."

She accompanied her mother back into the drawing room. There, her mother handed her a set of unfamiliar documents. Puzzled, Eleanor untied the maroon silk ribbon which bound them and let the papers fall akimbo. They appeared to be legal in nature. "What is this?" she asked.

Lady Marigate told her all that Bucksted had revealed to her not a half-hour past.

"I misjudged him, Mama, so completely," she moaned. "I—I think I love him, and I can't bear to think he regards me so badly, which of course he has every right to—"

"Oh, but he doesn't," Lady Marigate said. "Not by half. In

fact, though I didn't quite follow all that he said, I could only determine that he believes himself unworthy of you."

Eleanor swiped at the tears that rolled down her cheeks with her right hand. Her left arm and hand were held immobile by a sling designed to protect her left shoulder from further injury. "How do you know? What did he say?"

"He said he loved you beyond words, that is what he said exactly."

Eleanor stood up abruptly. She gasped in wonder. She was shocked. She could hardly breathe.

"Nellie!" Lady Marigate cried. "You've grown very pale. Pray sit down. Let me cover you with my shawl! Dear, dear, I shouldn't have overset you. You will suffer a relapse and likely fall into a decline. Oh, my poor Nellie!"

"Nonsense, Mama!" Eleanor returned gaily. "I am perfectly well, only a trifle weak, but I do believe there is time! You say Bucksted refused to order his carriage brought round, but instead went directly to the stables himself?"

"Yes."

She left her mother quite abruptly without a word of explanation, which undoubtedly left Lady Marigate in a completely bewildered state. She crossed the hall and passed the nearest tower and headed toward the doors leading to the garden. She could not run, but she could walk well enough, even if her muscles tended to twitch here and there.

After a few minutes, she finally passed through the yew hedge and reached the turnstile. She had arrived just in time, for Bucksted's traveling chariot was pulling out from between the heavy wrought-iron gates of the manor drive. She moved to the edge of the grassy pathway which flanked the macadamized road. A breeze caught up her blue silk skirts and wrapped and unwrapped them about her legs.

She was trembling now, all over, partly from her horrible weakness, but also because of her hope that Bucksted might yet find it in his heart to forgive her. Her eyes had been opened, so swiftly, to the true state of her feelings that a powerful wave of love flooded her.

The postillion, having caught sight of her, approached at a gentle pace and slowly drew close.

The door opened. Oh, how her heart lurched at the sight of the aperture widening. A gloved hand appeared, then a booted foot, finally a black hat beneath which a rather stunned Bucksted stared back at her.

He leaped to the ground before the coach had even drawn to a complete stop. He walked quickly toward her. She wore no bonnet, and he abruptly pulled his hat from his head and let it drop and roll on the grass at his feet. He caught her up with his left hand in a hard embrace, carefully avoiding her wounded shoulder. "Tell me, my lady mischief, that you did not come out here to upbraid me! Tell me, my love, that you came to prevent me from leaving"

"Oh, Bucksted, pray don't go!" she cried. "I have not yet thanked you for saving my life!" She was being a silly female, for she was weeping and grabbing at the hair at the back of his neck as though to hold on to him.

He kissed her fully on the mouth, bruising her lips in the sweetest way imaginable. After a moment, he said, "I didn't think you wanted to see me again, not after—"

"Don't speak of it, any of it!" she cried. "I forbid you, else I will remember my own shameful conduct and be unable to keep letting you kiss me."

"Then I shan't speak of it—because I wish to kiss you more than anything else in the world."

"You are not completely vexed with me, then?"

He gave a crack of laughter. "I am utterly vexed and bewitched and sunk in my love for you."

She smiled between the tears that plagued her cheeks and chin. He wiped at her face, and he kissed her a little more.

After a time, when the postboy had coughed discreetly more than once, Bucksted finally released her, at least in part, and began drawing her toward the coach. "You shouldn't have come out here," he reprimanded.

She climbed aboard. "Nothing could have stopped me once my mother revealed all that you told her."

She took up her seat as Bucksted directed the postboy to find an outlet by which he could turn the coach around and return to Hartslip. Once he was settled beside her, he supported her with an arm about her shoulder on her uninjured side. "I'm glad you came to waylay my coach, but I can feel that you are trembling. I shudder at the thought that you might suffer a relapse."

"How could I do any such thing when I have just come to understand your feelings for me?"

"What a strange ending this is for us after so much has happened? I feel I've known you an eternity, yet I am just coming to know you."

"It is quite magical, isn't it? But there is one thing I must say to you, I was very wrong to have taken up smuggling, even if my motives were of a tender nature. I shan't do so again."

He touched her cheek. "My dearest Eleanor, I only ask that should you take such a notion into your head again, you include me. Mayhap, I will want to assist you." He smiled crookedly.

She chuckled and her eyes became watery all over again. "The deuce you would!" she cried.

He laughed and kissed her, then grew very solemn. "Eleanor Marigate, will you do me the honor of becoming my wife, my true wife this time? Now and for always?"

"I will," she breathed against his lips as he kissed her once more.

ABOUT THE AUTHOR

Valerie King lives with her family in Glendale, Arizona, and is the author of twenty Zebra regency romances. She is currently working on her twenty-first, *A Christmas Masquerade,* which will be published in December, 1999. Valerie loves to hear from her readers and you may write her c/o Zebra Books. Please include a self-addressed stamped envelope if you wish a response.